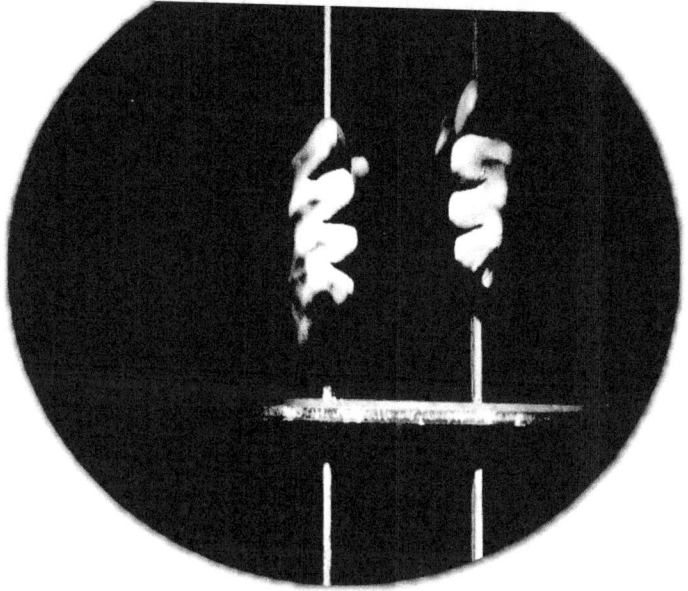

THE

TERRORIST

a novel

by Anastasia Goodman

The Terrorist

By Anastasia Goodman

A Sasha Perlov Novel

Copyright 2018

ISBN -13:978-1719408943

ISBN-10:171940847

Published by Ocean Breeze Press

THE TERRORIST

By Anastasia Goodman

a Sasha Perlov novel

CHAPTER 1

"Pig, fascist pig," she screams at me in a wailing shrill. Her voice shatters the dull drone of nearby sounds.

"Hey pig cops."

Will they need me in the wee hours as dawn approaches? When three thugs follow them to their cars after hours? At that moment as I fend off the intruders, will they be thankful for the presence of men and women in blue on the streets?

"Nazi Stormtroopers, pigs," I hear the screams at several decibels higher than normal human speech. I am older than some and younger than many here. Their power derives from their sheer numbers, thousands perhaps. Bodies of all types, big and fat with blubber protruding from too tight tee shirts, skinny and pale people who spend all their waking moments indoors, and us, their enemies in blue uniforms.

"Oink, oink," the woman in front of me threatens me with her childish taunt, clapping hands and stomping feet encouraging her. Wild in the exuberance of youth, she owns nothing yet worth protecting.

Then I feel her slimy spit oozing down the side of my face. A wide smirk covers her pale face; the blue-green eyes invite a confrontation.

My first impulse is to pulverize her, starting with that

smug smile. But I can't do that. I'm a veteran of the NYPD on crowd control duty. Besides, my European manners don't permit me to wallop a woman not too much older than a teenager, her face erupting with acne, clearly indifferent to Miss Manners' rules of basic etiquette.

I don't even flinch, letting the disgusting scum make its way down my chin, landing on my crisp, neatly pressed uniform. I won't even give her the tiniest bit of satisfaction by wiping away the repulsive goo. The government reimburses me for my cleaning bills.

"Bush's war, no war," they scream in defiance. The gray-haired, wrinkled ones must be reliving those glorified bygone days of the 1960's when demonstrating was quite the thing to do. Most citizen expressions of rebellion don't stop determined governments; deaths viewed by the public on television create transformational images: blood-soaked infants, carnage so vivid eyes cannot linger, pieces of body parts hanging from tree limbs, whimpering orphan children. War veterans in wheel chairs assembled at rallies can't stop a war machine on its dogged path. But those graphic images from a war, thousands of miles away can effectively turn the populace against a government's war. Control the press and the war goes unchallenged.

The human cost of demonstrating is something I

witnessed as the son of a Russian Jewish dissident. There were scary moments when my mother engaged in hand-to-hand confrontations with the Soviet police and KGB. Eventually, the Soviet government reached its limit and patience with her noisy protests, and exiled her, as they did most of the other enemies of the state. Many died in their vast, secret, labyrinth prison system, and none escaped without both visible and concealed scars. Ultimately, most were simply sent away like naughty children. When the Evil Empire collapsed of its own dead weight, a new movement grew up in response to the failed promises. They called it democracy, but hardly the one of life and liberty and the pursuit of happiness we enjoy in this country. The Czarist and Soviet, and now Putin's government maintains the strategy of controlling the press. But do these demonstrators understand the liberties they enjoy?

As an immigrant, I respect this most precious gift of political freedom. I could tell these malcontents stories about what strong-arm political repression really looks like. It's very difficult to refrain from smacking some of them across the face. Unfortunately, that's a violation of their civil rights and as a law enforcement officer I obey the law. I am certainly not an enemy of the state.

We are few compared to the demonstrators, but we are the instruments of officialdom with our guns, nightsticks, dogs and horses on patrol. They stand inside the cordoned off area and we guard them. Their dissent cannot move beyond this designated spot. Those are the orders. The permit restricts the demonstration to this specific location, this piece of concrete and no other.

They know, and we certainly realize that the designated spot is too small to contain them. The police have a policy of never announcing the number of protestors at any event, but the number today is more than this area can safely sustain.

My fellow officers on both sides inch closer to me, ready to assist if I decide to grab and arrest her. I react by stepping back out of spitting range.

Her face focuses on me. Someone next to her yawns, arms extended, his hand accidentally striking a nearby fellow protester. My anxiety grows because it's obvious that the crowd needs to expand; the seams are beginning to bulge. Somehow people are mysteriously adding to their ranks, slipping through the manned barriers. A covert group of "Invisible Men."

I feel the legs of the barrier pressing against my boot. Today, I don't wear my Sears' specials, my ordinary leather shoes for detective work. This day demands my police-issued combat boots with the metal plates. I will not be deterred from my duty by them stomping on my toes. I have only to strike with my handy nightstick against their exposed fingers, at the sensitive pressure points above the knuckles, or the soft fleshy area between their shoulders and neck. Most dramatically, I could deliver a swift and shattering crack to the top of the tender head. These are the tricks a police officer assigned to crowd control learns.

Always a few pains in the ass. When they're not screaming at us and performing before the television cameras, they're strumming guitars, juggling, singing protest songs from a bygone era." The atmosphere is merry like a carnival filled with colorful hand-made banners, funny-shaped masks, tall hats, and buttons, lots of different sized and colored buttons.

Glancing at the demonstrators, I realize that at any moment the hollow juggler's prop can become a perilous weapon. My mother, an expert on demonstrations, warned me to be wary of the anarchists, a scary and most unpredictable bunch.

I hear one of the sergeants tell several officers. "The police are greatly outnumbered by the demonstrators. Remember, we are in control.,"

Gently, I poke the guy next to me, George Reilly from the Bushwick station house, still number one in unsolved murders. "We are ready," I rub my hands together.

George says in his deep baritone, "Let them break through and they will be arrested."

The sergeant overhears his comments. "No cracking heads if they behave. No one wants trouble."

Our bantering stops when a new strident sound is heard, a small group within the larger crowd explodes into a raucous growl. My favorite demonstrator gives me a sinister, nasty look.

I smile with my pearly whites showing.

Her response to my act of friendliness is to lean across the barrier and scream in my ear, "Motherfuckers," at the top of her hoarse lungs. I want to pull her long hair by its roots and possibly knock a little sense into her.

"Impeach Bush. Support the troops, bring them home now." The thousands of voices repeat the phrase over and over until a few grow weary and drop out of the sing song routine. There is a rambunctiousness as dozens of people press against the barricades and the atmosphere fills with heightened energy. The silliness and merriment seem to have reached a more ominous point. You can feel the sparks between us; the police with weaponry, and them. Through a break in the milling crowd, I observe the restless people at the center hovering together. They begin marching in formation towards the police as if they were spokes in a bicycle wheel; the barricades start slipping from their original moorings. The scraping sound of wood against cement echoes in our collective ears; the moment of confrontation is nearing fast.

The police signal is heard above the din and my hand automatically grabs my nightstick from my police belt. We are about to face off against each other. Although intellectually I support their right to resist, my mind loses out to instinctual survival. I'm ready to crack heads. I cannot look behind me, but I hear the snort of the horses, their hoofs pawing the concrete as their riders prepare for action. With the best view of the crowd, they will chase after the most aggressive agitators. The horses bray in their anxiousness. It is our duty to maintain order at any cost.

In their inconspicuous corners, the canine unit readies the dogs to quickly subdue the protesters after they topple the barriers. I cannot see any of the dogs and no barking sounds are heard, but they are present, awaiting instructions from their handlers.

Not anticipating massive rioting or substantial destruction of private property, the fire hoses are absent from the scene but can be called if necessary. The fire stations are on call and alert. The Mayor and the commissioners are ready for all possibilities as the uniform services stand together.

Our orders are to remain calm. We are not to ignite any sparks. Those of us closest to the wooden barriers were chosen by our commanders because we were known to be even-tempered. Hot-heads accused of overzealousness and the inexperienced were barred from this duty. Anyone ever charged with police brutality was forbidden to join this overtime assignment.

The girl's eyes look ahead and not at my face as her hands push against and then release her grip on the wooden barrier. I catch her glancing at me. I smile. She tries to act stone cold but there's a slight widening of her lips, just the very edges of her pearly whites show. They push, push and then back off as if in a rehearsed routine. The sound of scratching wood on concrete continues and the scene proceeds, give and take, forward then back. Each time the barriers move inches but do not break.

I am at the gates. Call me a modern Inspector Javert. My role is to follow the law without analyzing or evaluating its merits. Young, idealistic students and fearful parents are at the barricades demanding explanations about a war they do not support and against a government they think lies to them. Instead of the French Revolution of Victor Hugo's "Les Misérables," it's a war in Iraq. There better not be a dead Marius, the student leader of Hugo's novel, at this scene or my promising police career would be in jeopardy.

As a student, I fell in love with masters like Hugo. Although the Soviets tried to stomp it out, Russians have unrepentant urges of emotion, deep wells of uncontrollable feelings. We were never rigid communist robots seeking world domination; despite two generations of engineers and scientists, we are still romantics and dark cynics. It's the Russian schizophrenia, open to life's wonders and yet skittish about what can happen.

We live in an ambiguous world and even cops are capable of understanding shades of gray. Although, like Javert, I am incapable of letting go and my doggedness earns me my police reputation of demanding to know exactly what happened at a crime scene. No loose ends for Perlov the Protector. Still, my dark Russian soul knows that not all crimes are deserving of punishment, despite what the law dictates. I am more interested in the motivations of criminals rather than their DNA. The fast confession will never satisfy me. I live each day still more Russian than American, but I am trying to become assimilated.

A bellowing shout is heard through a bullhorn as the civilian troops gather. Peeking between shoulder blades, I notice that a small cadre of leaders begins breaking out of their center huddle. The action begins. The clock is ready, legs move; hands grip one another, hearts race. The end is unknown -- we are at the beginning. The spokes of the bicycle are in position; the voices of the leaders shout out signals. The dogs bark and the horses' hooves strike the ground. The animals feel the tension. It's almost as if a bullwhip is set loose-- the air is crackling with exhilaration. The crowd is on the move. It's time to bring down the wooden barricades. A chain-link fence of humans is about to test the strength and restraint of the police as they force themselves out of their enclosed pen.

"Impeach Bush," the sound goes out and the feet start marching towards the front line. On cue, a few dozen trudge forward, pushing harder against the barriers, the sacrificial lambs to be arrested. Another several dozen create a human buffer standing shoulder to shoulder. The bodies are in motion.

My antagonist gets caught up in the flurry of activity. Standing erect, her feet solidly anchored to the concrete, her wrist is pressed against the unyielding barriers, which continue to hold. She must have forgotten her orders. Suddenly, I see her lose her footing, slipping off balance, her thin torso disappearing under the barricade. Her fingers cling to the wooden restraint. Involuntarily, she is pushed by the crushing crowd behind her. Her foot presses against my boot, her body sliding uncontrollably towards the hard concrete. I grab her under the armpits, catching her fall, freeing her from the ensuing throng of her fellow protesters.

Her face is pressed against my uniform. Out of immediate danger, I swing her to her feet.

"Wow. Thanks, I could have been pounded to the

ground," she smiles at me. It's a shy, defensive look but it is genuine gratitude.

"Just doing my job," I return the smile; behind that bombastic screaming is a soft-looking, young woman. Dissent and political beliefs are a demanding mistress; I know because they are in my blood.

The young protestor allows herself to be quietly arrested with hundreds of others. Our eyes follow each other as she is walked to the police wagon and voluntarily steps up as the doors are shut closed. My eyes track the van, its sirens earsplitting, its lights hallucinatory as it slowly weaves towards the processing point where pro bono lawyers await its arrival.

Then there is a sudden stillness as if all of us are breathlessly awaiting the next act. We stand guard, our nightsticks in position during this intermission. The crowd reassembles, having taken enough time to inhale, the chanting beginning again but more restrained. There is no need to topple the barriers; they have fallen. The mission is accomplished. The TV cameras have fled after the racing sirens. The circus is over.

As dusk approaches, the remaining protestors start to disperse through a pre-determined escape hatch. Before the sun sets the public square is quite empty. My job as government protector of the establishment is finished. It's now the job of the sanitation guys to clean up the mess.

I turn around in a complete circle. What's left are lovers hand in hand, torn signs and banners, small clusters of cigarette butts, hundreds of shiny food wrappers. The pigeons have returned to gobble up whatever scraps remain before the sanitation men remove the crowd's trail of treats. It's over except for the evening news and tomorrow's papers.

My duty is finished so I catch the subway and head back to my desk at the 60th Precinct. The Precinct includes some of the best beach property in the world, Coney Island and Brighton Beach; South Brooklyn's most famous communities.

CHAPTER 2

"Sarge," I call out. Usually he's not on duty, a day shift guy, but everyone seeks overtime. I guess someone must be sick. His broad frame sits in front of a desk, perched above the floor in the lobby of this old, crumbling station house. He is our eyes and ears to the sometimes hostile community we are sworn to protect. People enter his territory without appointments and often leave their good manners behind. Gazing at him on high, they make demands about finding bad guys or reporting some misbehavior by cops.

"Perlov the Protector, no personal damage from the demonstration?" He smiles looking at the spit marks. "The Lieutenant is looking for you," as usual his eyes return to his newspaper in front of him.

I have no partner to meet as I begin my regular shift. I am a cop on the loose, running alone in an organization that values duos and looks askance on solo acts. My former police partner and best buddy, Jimmy Sutton, is on sabbatical to pursue his dream of becoming the world's next middleweight boxing champion. He is on a path to happiness as a second generation American. But his pursuit of happiness has left me in a void. A cop without a partner is a man without a rudder; no sounding board, no advice, no grounding. I am managing this period of turmoil as best as I can, reverting to my natural inclination of brooding and introspection.

Luckily, I have an understanding commanding officer and a unique new position as liaison between the NYPD and the US Attorney's Office, a member of the new Terrorist Task Force. Our goal is to track down the evil-doers, those terrorists out there threatening my beloved adopted city, catch them before they crash into any more buildings. I was there. I didn't see it happen except hundreds of times on the television. I went without an assignment, without an official word, I just went. I had to be there to save my adopted city. My mother saw the TV and screamed that we were at war. She lived through the Battle of Stalingrad, so she knew what it was like to breathe in human remains. What it is like to smell gaseous odors so debilitating that you stumble and fall, grow dizzy and disoriented. But I had a duty to serve and protect.

We here on the home front must do the saving. I sit at the 60th precinct but my work is global. Typical of all bureaucracies, our first enemy is mistrust among agencies. I am a soldier spy, although it's not entirely clear to me who am I spying on. The NYPD brass encourages me to find out all the little secrets that the federal agencies are concealing. Meanwhile, my other 'sorta boss,' US Attorney Gary Cohen, a federal officer of the court, isn't interested in the NYPD but the activities of the FBI and the CIA in New York City. Days and weeks are wasted in immature and mundane fights over jurisdiction and political territory.

So far in the first year of my new assignment nothing important has occurred. I have done the usual eavesdropping and videotaping potential persons of interest. I have participated in the customary and excruciatingly boring, late night surveillance stints, boosted by endless cups of the blackest coffee; sitting in an unmarked police car that everyone being watched recognizes. At 3:00 a.m., the differences in people are tricky to detect through the murky shadows of semi-lit overhead streetlights and my own half-slit eyes.

I walk towards the Lieutenant's corner office, knock loudly and hear his booming voice, "Enter." The word just got out about his promotion to Captain. We all revel in the Lieutenant's good fortune. He is my mentor, my champion, my 'go to' guy, and I am his loyal minion. My career would be a big zero without his active intervention in my professional life. We share secrets due to my reputation as a man of discretion.

I noisily and forcefully open his door. I am about to yell out in one of my high- pitched hockey spectator roars, "Congratulations," when I see that he is on the phone talking with enthusiasm, his arms gesturing in the air.

He beckons for me to approach, flicking his wrist as if

throwing a dagger. I sit and try not to eavesdrop on his private conversation. This conversation is quiet and soft. In his official capacity as boss, his voice is thunderous; there are not sentences, just quick phrases, and he's always interrupting the other party. This is a different conversation. I try and look indifferent, my eyes observing all the tiny cracks in the walls, zeroing in on one rather large gash.

When the boss speaks people listen. Even when he addresses the brass, he never demonstrates subservience. That's one of the reasons I admire him so much, not a *tuchis lecker*, an ass kisser. He is earning his new promotion based on achievements, and my successful closing of important cases is a part of his resume. Never a greedy man or a selfish one, he rewards those who produce for him.

His hand returns the phone to its cradle. Those big Irish eyes are smiling as he faces me.

"Congratulations," I move my arms across his big desk to shake his hand. We rarely shake hands, but this time he accepts my offer with poise and a slight blush of modesty.

"I didn't earn this promotion alone. It's the good work of all of you," he winks at me.

I just smile in satisfaction knowing I have a champion in the right place.

"I've got good guys," he pauses, "and ladies on my

team," he adds. The police department is a multi-cultural melting pot. We try very hard to get along. We are more successful than the larger community because in a pinch a cop must depend upon his partner. Enough of the brass knows this reality from their own experiences to encourage each commander to create mixed partnerships—a white man and a black woman, a Hispanic woman and a black man, an immigrant with a third generation American. That doesn't mean we don't have some spats occasionally; it's not a love fest and no one considers every fellow officer as their best friend, but we avoid race riots in the precinct houses.

"For the new Captain, only the best will do. I suggest a big party in Atlantic City, the same night that Jimmy fights. The whole station house rents some buses and we go together to cheer on our former colleague and celebrate his victory and your ascendancy. Middleweight champion and who knows," I wait for his immediate response. "Deputy Inspector or Assistant Commissioner. Right?"

His blushing cheeks turn rosy red. "Na, no," he mutters but I've got him thinking big thoughts. "I'm not sure that my wife would appreciate the bus trip to see a fight, even if she is quite fond of Jimmy," he tells me.

All the women love Jimmy, with his velvety voice and baby blue eyes. The charm just oozes from his pores and he doesn't discriminate. Beautiful women, pimply-faced girls, middle-aged women with thickening thighs, and wrinkled senior citizens all receive the same attentive stares and compliments. Handsome men can be aloof and demanding but not my Jimmy. He walks the earth to enchant the ladies, to make their days more enjoyable, to give them a purpose because without his presence, even if it is only for a few minutes, their lives would be emptier.

The new Captain's attention to details returns, his eyes glancing at my blue uniform. "A bird got you?" his finger pointing to the messy spot.

"A female demonstrator," I unconsciously attempt to clean the untidy smudges.

"How many were arrested?" he asks, his tone demanding. The displeasure is not meant for me. "The news broadcast didn't mention specific numbers, only a vague announcement of police arrests."

"My guess is about a hundred, really quite peaceful although at moments it felt threatening. They were testing us for the next stage. It's their constitutional right," the immigrant speaks.

"Yeah," the apolitical, native-born American replies. "Your job is not to interpret the law, but to ensure that it is followed. When you graduate from law school, you can argue the case. Right now, you enforce the existing laws." He pauses and then smiles. "Your problem is you're always thinking. Is it right or is it wrong? What exactly happened? You've got to know all the details, mull over the facts and then make a decision."

I immediately react. "That's what you like most about me. The thinking part," I repeatedly tap the side of my temple with my index finger. "The Russian with the dark heart who can read the minds of criminals. The psychology major in college. Go to Perlov to analyze the case. Right?" How my superior views my talents is significant. A good commander understands their people, is empathetic but firm when someone steps of out of line. They recognize the individual's strengths and flaws but are never overly critical of those frailties unless the person is a total fuck-up. Then it's essential to quickly expel them from the station house because a bad apple corrupts others.

His grin is friendly and warm. His voice grows stronger. "You're right," he raises his voice. "That's your strength. Quietly prodding along until the case is solved. Thinking, always thinking, considering the consequences. It's best to have someone onboard at a demonstration that is thinking about how it's all going to look in tomorrow's tabloids if we trample our tax paying citizens in front of photographers and worse, television cameras."

"We were all well behaved, but it should have been

better planned." That's my final word on the subject.

"What's happening at Police Row and with the US Attorney? Can the FBI see up its own asses yet?" How we street cops love the feds.

"We're watching the mosques in Brooklyn. Not much happening." My initial enthusiasm for this extraordinary assignment is waning, but the bureaucracy is paying my law school expenses so not being a greedy man, I am attempting to be content. This is not yet my pursuit of happiness. This assignment, splitting my time between New York's finest and my federal colleagues at the US Attorney's office, suits me just fine for the moment. Reading all the intelligence documents that they permit me to see prepares me for studying my law school materials. This new assignment is piquing my interest in constitutional law. How to legally interpret the Patriot Act consumes my police and student activities.

"I know you'll keep me posted. They are still alright with you camping out here at the 60th?" Originally, they requested that I be assigned to Police Row in Lower Manhattan, close to the US Attorney's Office, but I preferred staying at my own precinct.

"So far no one is saying anything. I get to meetings without difficulty. It's cheaper for me to be here." I am confident that the arrangement works and is cost effective.

"OK," he loudly announces and it's clear that I am being dismissed. "Keep me informed. You're actually our spy, you know." He gives me one of his famous, anti-authority smirks.

I wink at him. "I thought we're all part of the same team," I sarcastically add.

He has another thought. "You can count on me joining the bus caravan to see Jimmy fight," his eyes return to the papers on his desk. I return to my desk and reading intelligence reports.

As I head out the station house door, my shift completed, the Sarge yells out, "Perlov, I forgot. You got a call."

I stop at his raised front desk and he hands me a 'While You Were Out' slip of paper.

"Not one of yours with a name like Diaz." He gives me the paper. I am the protector of all members of the community but, it's assumed that I have a very special relationship with my fellow immigrants, who make up a sizeable population of Brighton Beach – Little Odessa.

I study the name because it doesn't instantly make an impression.

"Hector Diaz. Said it was very important. Wouldn't speak to anyone but you, insistent, would wait for your return. You are the only one he trusts." He looks down from on high at my face.

"Your protective shield expands," he laughs with a hearty, gargantuan outburst, his body rocking, that puts an immediate smile on my face. "End of shift, go home my boy," the wizened elder announces.

Examining the tissue-thin paper with care, a light bulb goes off. "Of course, Hector Diaz, it's my tire guy." I stuff the paper in my shirt pocket. I'll drive by his shop although it's late. Very important, the message says. He may keep late hours. My Inspector Javert instincts are piqued. The 60th is not even his station house. Very important, what can be so important?

Hector provided that all-important first clue that led to a golden string of solving intricate cases. The result was my promotion to investigating terrorism, the new priority of the NYPD. The owner of a tire repair shop in Borough Park, it was his diligence that produced a fingerprint of a man wanted by Interpol. From that slender clue, my police life changed in the most positive way. I owed Hector.

Very important, only I can be trusted. These are words that cops treasure. I remember the address and easily find Hector's place. The shop is tightly closed with a heavy metal lock; barbed wire tops the sturdy metal fencing. Not a sound is heard, the lights inside the store are off but the outside work area is well lit, aglow with smaller versions of high intensity stadium lights. The location is far from dangerous, but shop owners must be cautious.

I don't want to rattle the fence because the alarms will be triggered. The last thing I need is to have a couple of uniforms converging on the location with sirens blasting into the night and pulsating strobe lights waking the entire neighborhood. Quietly, I walk around the perimeter, searching for a hidden light indicating some human presence. Nothing. The place is locked up for the evening.

Standing in front of the empty store, I call the number on the piece of paper. It's early but important, the man said it was very important.

"No one is available to take your call, at the sound of the beep, please leave your name and phone number,"

"It's Detective Perlov. I got your call. I'll call back later. You can trust me," I reply into the non-human cell phone's answering voice.

Hector Diaz is another fellow immigrant, from Central America. Now what could be so important? Where does he live? I know it's nearby, but an exact location? I could go back to the station house and get one of our computer geeks to track him down. I am tempted but my stomach starts growling. If it is urgent, I will be expecting another call. No, it can wait till daylight; my hunger pains call to me.

CHAPTER 3

It's past 2 a.m. and all the shops are closed in Brighton Beach except for the Atlantis Ocean Theatre. The theatre's lights are off, but the restaurant is open. No flashing neon lights for this place. A quiet elegance. Great detailed woodwork along the archways, brass doorknobs and a brand-new awning. It's never too late to eat and my friends here are always accommodating.

I could bang on the back door, but I enter like any customer. Only the bar area appears open and it's crowded for a week-day, mostly men, but a couple of young women laughing and drinking. The cigarette smoke is thick and enveloping. The smell is intoxicating. A reformed addict, I miss those cancer sticks. I move slowly hoping that a few fumes float through my nostrils and cracked lips. I dare not stop so powerful is the urge to indulge. Eyes follow me for a moment and then return to their private conversations. It's all in Russian.

Away from temptation, I glance towards the dining area but there are only dark shadows in the rear. I hear clinking and clanging sounds and muted voices of men moving around. The clean-up crew is at work, probably the few non-Russians here. The head man sees me searching the empty tables and directs me through a private entrance.

"Vasily, Vasily," I speak his name as we hug tightly.

"Sasha, never too late, *eppes essen.*" He pours out the vodka into a glass and before I can make myself comfortable a waiter brings in trays of food.

"We can heat something, but this is fresh," the waiter announces pointing to the cold borsht; another man suddenly appears and places the linen tablecloth on the nearby table. "The kitchen is closed but do you want something?" he asks but hopes I don't answer in the affirmative.

The platters look very good, cheeses and crusty black Russian pumpernickel on one and fresh fruit on the other. "No, this looks great," I answer, and he sighs quietly relieved that the kitchen staff can leave.

"You," Vasily pokes me on the arm. "You want something else," he gives the waiter a sharp look. "We can get you something hot." And he turns to the waiter. "What's leftover? You can zap it in the microwave. He's not too picky, but hot," he orders, and the waiter clicks his heels in an exaggerated stance. "Yes, yes, my master," he and the other man turn and leave.

"No fussing. It's been a very long day from the wee hours to just now," I want to put my head on the table and nap. Instead, I finish my glass of vodka and Vasily pours a refill.

"Insolent bastard that waiter, but I know his family from Mother Russia. You remember the clockmaker? His son," he points to the closed door. "Completely trustworthy, he sees nothing."

I continue sipping the strong vodka, Russian mother's milk, until the new dishes arrive. I soon eat as if my body has been refused nourishment for days. Cheese on black bread and slices of fresh mango, oranges and even a yellowish apricot topped with red and green grapes all gone in minutes. Then the hot food arrives and I'm gorging myself.

Vasily watches. "I don't know how you manage. You should *plotz*," he studies the trajectory of the fork in my hand as it enters my open mouth. He reaches over and slaps my stomach. "You still look good. Amazing, must be your good genes."

"The food is all wonderful and I haven't eaten all day," the act of replenishing my body with nutrients has drained all my remaining strength. The fatigue starts to show, the fork just doesn't want to travel any further, the hand's muscles refuse to work.

"You look tired," he sympathetically adds. "The terrorism business has gotten you. *Nu*, when can we expect another attack?" he smiles not anticipating a real answer.

"You don't have to hide in a bunker, not yet," I reply trying desperately to suppress the yawn that overwhelms me.

I try standing but fatigue and the vodka leave me off balance. He quickly comes to my assistance. "Sleep time," he proclaims as his arm slips under my mine, propping me up.

"Should I drive home or go to my parents' house?" I ask, my words sloppy and my tongue stumbling on the pronunciation.

"Driving not such a good idea," Vasily says and it's obvious.

"I can walk to my parents' house;" it's just a few blocks away.

"I don't think so," he answers and suddenly I see a big guy in the room with us.

"He could drive me to my house in the Rockaways," I look into his massive face and nod at Vasily.

"No, go home to your parents. Your mother will fix you up later. It's too late to stumble to your place." He authoritatively tells me, and the big guy nods his head.

"Yeah, yeah," I let my body fall into the arms of my friend and one of his body guards.

Home is really two places. There's the one I own and the one where it all started in America. Brighton Beach is congested, all the people just barely able to share the sidewalks; the other is isolated, jutting out of the large land mass called Long Island. Both are beach communities. The Rockaways are a New York City neglected gem, a vast thin strip of beach along the Atlantic

Ocean across from John F. Kennedy airport and adjacent to Brooklyn's famous Coney Island Beach.

I am one of the area's early urban pioneers, part of the vanguard, the returning middle-class homeowner. We are neighbors of those in public housing, close, visible to one another but alien. It's an edgy experience to be among the pioneers, a white guy, a foreigner, an outsider amid bleak blight aided by government abandonment. But my people have been pioneers before, when the first Soviet émigrés to Brighton Beach arrived during the 1970's.

Back then the Brighton Beach community was on a path to becoming overwhelmed by the poverty and apathy of those living in the low-income area in neighboring Coney Island. Our arrival marked a change as a massive inflow of fresh immigrants, with high hopes and good educations, transformed the decrepit homes and World War II era apartment houses into a prosperous middle-class enclave. The stores were reborn with foreign lettering on the signs; the products sold in the local marketplace bore no resemblance to the goods sold in Coney Island. Another New York City neighborhood, saved by immigrants.

The Rockaways have this panache that draws someone like me from Brighton Beach. The predictable ravages inflicted by nature onto man-made structures are visible; rusting metal and decaying wood are nature's instruments of change. For me the deepest attraction for living in the Rockaways is a spiritual one. Maybe it will be a vision in the bluest sky or a message delivered by a squawking seagull, but here in this place, Hashem will find a way to speak to me. He will show me my path to the pursuit of happiness.

The upstairs balcony is the point of my discovery as I witness the birth of the dawn, the moment of redemption as the sea and sun cross paths. Each morning, I rise to meet the temptations and unknowns of the day, and although the chances of my facing imminent danger as a cop are remote, I realize each morning that this could be my last. It is my religious faith that demands that I never squander a moment of life. As a sinner, I seek repentance and my salvation.

The Talmud speaks metaphorically of each dawn as representative of that moment of redemption, of forgiveness, or rebirth so I am drawn to that powerful point in time. From the supremacy of the sun and Hashem's majesty, I draw my strength and attempt to resist all my baser instincts.

My heroes are the great and sometimes unappreciated people found in the Bible. Hashem is a demanding deity. Poor Moses, he did so much for the Israelites, revered by the multitudes, but still he is never allowed into the Land of Milk and Honey. And why? Because on one occasion he did something to really piss off the Lord. Yet he is one of my models – always be humble because wondrous acts of leadership do not guarantee the fulfillment of one's dearest wishes. He never lived in the New Jerusalem where the pursuit of happiness is guaranteed by the US Constitution.

Then there is Yehudah, the one responsible for selling his brother Joseph, the great seer and interpreter of dreams, into slavery. A classic sinner who seeks repentance, God rewards him. It is his story that provides me solace. Despite all his many sins, and there are many, including lying to his father about selling Joseph, the old man's favorite; yet, he receives the keys to the kingdom. And there is more to his evilness - he mistakenly rapes his daughter-in-law Tamar, thinking she is a prostitute. These terrible acts are forgiven because God sees his strength of character through his public confession of his sins and his willingness to die for another brother. It is his seed that produces the mighty kings of Israel, not his more pious brother Joseph. That's a story to embrace.

Women always factor into my need to search for redemption. My failure to protect my sweet love still causes an aching that I cannot remove from my dark heart. My darling Dr. Marina, the picture of her blood-stained white doctor's coat flashes before me in my daydreaming and in my dreams. The red stains on my suit that afternoon, I keep it as a perverse souvenir. The blood, her blood, her goodness brought to an early end. Where is the justice? No punishment will ever be enough although her murderer is dead. My job is to prevent victims, but I did not shield her from danger. Our motto is to serve and protect but I failed her and her family. They hardly speak to me.

A crazy patient killed her in the Emergency Room of a Brooklyn hospital located in a nice neighborhood. I was there; we had planned to meet but my presence was too late to stop him. He was later fatally knifed in his holding pen, but no matter, the killer's death never brought me or Marina's family any consolation. Revenge was not the answer that people promised.

Then there was my obsession, Olga. I investigated the death of her fat, ugly husband. As a law enforcement agent, it is my responsibility to ascertain guilt, and the courts' job is to concur and determine punishment. There was guilt, but I never could bring myself to pursue the case. Her husband was an evil man; he saw a vulnerable immigrant and tried to make her his slave. But was it my personal responsibility to right the injustice?

The woman who most possesses my soul is my mother, a figure of great regard among Soviet era Jews. A dissident afraid of nothing, she is my inspiration, and my ball and chain.

Like all good Russian Jewish sons, I am a mama's boy. I would like to please her but it's just not possible. Not always, sometimes, but never always. This is the land that worships the pursuit of happiness. My happiness, not my mother's. Mine. I must follow my pathways. Against her wishes I enlisted in the US Army after college graduation. It was between Gulf Wars.

I hear her annoyance still rattling in my head. "Sasha, Sasha my boy, the Army during peacetime, the Army. Uncle Vanya the Cossack, that's who you are, a true Uncle Vanya." Her words tumbling out of her mouth, her anger filling her thin face with rage, a reddish-purple color covering her cheeks. I cannot escape the color red.

Uncle Vanya the Cossack was a family legend. A Russian Jew who was not conscripted into the Czar's Army but who volunteered, leaving a wife and several children to fend for themselves in a bitterly harsh and unyielding country. His family was spared from death only by the charity of other fellow Jewish villagers. He knew he had wronged his family, but he was a scoundrel and an adventurer. He had places to see and exploits to pursue. When he returned to his family a decade later, he received a deed to the land, an unknown treasure of riches for a Jew during those times. From the moment of his return to his death, he displayed a righteousness that had earlier eluded him. He became a philanthropic man and a devoted husband

and father. His blood flows through my veins and whenever someone in the family demonstrates poor judgment or bad behavior, we are reminded of Uncle Vanya the Cossack in his earlier days.

I love my mother with all my heart and soul, but my Uncle Vanya impulses are hard to contain. After all, what is a dissident? Nothing more than a rebel, a radical seeking revolutionary change. My mother's Uncle Vanya the Cossack's tendencies haunt her life.

When my mother protests my career choice, I respond, "This is America. I am not a member of the hated secret police. I protect and serve the citizens of this New Jerusalem. That's why we left, because here you can be anything you want to be. The pursuit of happiness is guaranteed."

I must remind her, when the heat of the discussion becomes so inflamed that her face turns beet red and her charismatic tongue gets tangled in a mixture of English and Russian words, that it is she who is responsible for us leaving Russia. Our arguments are fierce and so intense you can feel the sparks. Few dare to approach except my level-headed, low-key mathematician father, who meticulously puts out all the flames, somehow leaving the participants to believe that they are both equally correct –a true King Solomon.

As I stand in front of the Atlantis Ocean Theatre with four

steady hands pushing me into a sleek, black car, "I can still crawl back to my place from here. It's not far, the car knows the way," I tell Vasily.

"Not tonight my friend," I feel his hug through my fatigue and alcohol haze. "Take him to his parents," is the order.

"Thanks," I say as the door slams shut.

CHAPTER 4

My car is at the club, which is only a few blocks away, but I walk to the station house from my parents' house I'll take out an official car to drive to Borough Park. I don't know why Hector Diaz called, but I'm assuming it's within my police responsibilities.

The traffic is cruising, this being one of those golden 'tween times' - no commuters, no school buses, just the regular commercial trucks and cabs. The gate is open, and the lights are glaring. The taller son greets me. "Detective Perlov, my father is waiting."

I never mentioned that I was going to visit. He knows me well enough to know how I would respond. Mysteries are the manna for a detective. "Mr. Diaz," I shake his extended hand.

In Spanish, he orders his son to bring us coffee and sweet pastries. My Spanish language skills are minimal, but it's a must for a cop to know the foreign language names of a variety of food staples and, of course, all curses. In New York to survive on the street, you need to know what people are screaming at you during pitch moments of anger and chaos—after all, this is New York, the melting pot of America.

He points to a table and we sit close together; I can hear him exhaling. As immigrants from lands where people live on top of each other, we don't worry about invading personal space. In America, with its gigantic homes of four bedrooms and five bathrooms, personal space is an almost mythical state of being. When you're a foreigner, accustomed to living in cramped, crowded apartments, personal space is an unknown concept. Back in the Motherland, four people were lucky and satisfied to share one bathroom.

"Detective Perlov," he pauses in his broken, heavily accented English.

The tension is intensifying, and I lean my head even closer to his lips, so I shouldn't miss a single syllable.

"I call you," he touches my sleeve, "because I trust only you," he taps my arm. "You I trust."

I gesture with my hand for him to continue.

"You see this," he points to the discolored, deeply wrinkled patch of skin on his cheek.

When we first met, I immediately noticed that scar, its markings so distinctive and crude. Probably, a physically painful memory was associated with it. I knew from my past experiences that government agents provided mementos of their disapproval. That's what I assumed about Mr. Diaz's face because otherwise people told you stories about accidents or natural disasters. These were things strangers shared. But permanent gifts from representatives of the government, those an immigrant kept from outsiders fearing its revelation would mean jail or worse, deportation if the truth were revealed.

But I was wrong. We came from different worlds.

"This, present from drug gang," he gently touches the hardened crevice. "We go from El Salvador because gangs. I no work for them. Never, never, not me. Fear bring me here. Don't go west to California because so many live there in nice weather." He breathes in deeply and I watch his attempts to compose himself, steadying his throat muscles, silently counting backwards.

"Understandable," I say just to encourage him.

"Here I think safe. They go California. Some get deported; some go to jail here in America, but the drugs never stop. Always drugs." He seizes my pale hand and squeezes his powerful, calloused brown ones around mine.

"My cousin come yesterday from home. Very afraid. Gangs after him. They here in New York. You must protect my cousin."

I respond immediately without hesitation. I owe him. "Of course, and your cousin is he here in the shop?" I must think quickly about what I can do to protect this man.

"He hiding near. Yes," his voice is a whisper as he points to the back door of the store.

"Tell me more. What did your cousin actually say?" I ask

since stories get twisted, especially, if they are not speaking directly to you. The value of hearsay is questionable for a good reason.

Even witnesses to crimes are unreliable. People tangle up the details in their heads, and soon instead of giving facts, people report memories that are more dream-like than concrete connections with reality. How often I have heard a description of the fleeing criminal being reported as black, but wait perhaps just dark, there were shadows, the light was poor, and I wasn't wearing my glasses.

"He say gangs chase him. Want to kill him," the anguish grows on his round, frowning face.

"Did he come directly from El Salvador or did he hide in Mexico or some other place like Arizona, Texas or California?"

"I not know; he is here now. Here. You must save him."

"Did he tell you the actual names of people who were chasing him? Did you recognize any of those names?" Facts, not loose ends. Who is doing the chasing and who is likely to commit the killing?

"I love my cousin; he save me when I young," the tears start to well up in the corner of his eyes. He stops a tear from falling onto his shirt with a blackened, greasy fingertip; the engine oil's pungent smell overwhelms all other odors in this tight space.

I owe this man from El Salvador; my moniker is Perlov the Protector, so I have a mission. "Ok, I'll get some protection," I calmly reply.

What should I do? I call my Lieutenant, rather, the new Captain.

"Yeah," he answers with his usual gruff fashion until he recognizes my voice. "Perlov, what's the problem?"

I explain the situation; there's a pause; I can hear him breathing into the phone, but I remain completely silent, waiting patiently and then he replies. "It really belongs to a different precinct, but I'll send over Lewis."

He is my new best friend in the precinct since Jimmy left because we now share an emotional affinity – violently losing a loved one. He's also South Brooklyn's gang expert, part of a salt and pepper team of cops charged with keeping the really bad boys in this part of the city under control.

"Let him interrogate the guy and then we can discuss calling the Borough Park commander for a couple of uniforms," my superior answers with authority.

I close my cell phone. "Mr. Diaz, help is on the way. Why don't you tell me more and perhaps I can meet your cousin? Okay?"

He rises, and I follow him to the back of the store. "How's the boy with the artistic talents?" His youngest son is a budding young painter.

A small half-smile slowly appears on his frightened face. "Good. He having a show. They hang his drawings at Brooklyn Museum. You come?"

I nod my head, "Sure I'd love to come."

"Oscar," he calls out and a small man emerges from the tall shadows of tires piled twelve feet high, the dark rubber pressing against the white ceiling. First his head pokes out, eyes casting about for strangers and then one leg stretches out, finally a whole body visible. His skin is a warm, honey colored shade of brown. His clothes are black and nondescript. His tattoos are so shockingly colorful. Who could imagine green and yellow parrots flying through an equatorial forest of such lushness, almost as if the designs are telling a fable?

I can't help myself, staring in wonderment at his neck and uncovered arms. My mouth hangs open as a child's would in viewing something so brilliantly colorful. As he instinctively flexes his muscles, the birds seem to take flight, the ripples of his well-defined pecs giving the parrots life.

"This cousin Oscar," Hector says in English for me and repeats the introduction in Spanish in a more elaborate style for the other man; the stranger extends his hand in friendship.

I smile and the three of us test the comforts of sitting among the new tires stacked in their orderly places. The two relatives select the smallest of small tires while I check out an economy car model stack of tires. I am certainly not a tall or fat man, but I feel like a giant compared to these guys.

Then I notice the gang tags on the man's hands. My knowledge of gang activity is skimpy, but all cops are on alert for dangerous gang activity; certain tattoos are more significant than others, artistry aside.

My fascination is suspended as another son appears with cups of coffee and muffins meticulously arranged on a cardboard tray. As the guest, I am presented with the first choice.

"From the Kosher bakery down the street," Hector's son tells me.

I do not eat meat or chicken unless I am certain that it's kosher, but other foods are usually acceptable without appropriate kashrut labels. I view following dietary ritual as a measure of discipline and my acknowledgment of being the son of a Jewish dissident. For all the family endured, we must have some tangible display of the reason for those sacrifices.

I don't recall mentioning my adherence to Jewish dietary rituals to Hector, but he probably is assuming because of my association with a nearby Hasid *rebbe*, rabbi, that I strictly follow orthodox dietary rules. No one who lives in New York City mistakes a Hasid with his long, black coat, *payos*, or sidelocks, and heavy, black hat for something else. However, tourists can be confused, whether foreigners or natives from the American Midwest or the South, arriving from places devoid of orthodox Jewry, confusing them for the picturesque Amish. In a city with many strange looking people and fashion tastes, the Hasids blend in as just another oddity.

The cousin begins to talk quickly in Spanish to Hector. His body moves in many directions all at once, a wiry, animated guy; a contortionist. His small frame twirls and turns into a pretzel shape, legs wrapped around one tire and arms around another.

I raise my hands. "Wait. Let's start at the beginning. Help me understand this."

Hector confers with his cousin; their heads touching as they quietly discuss what to tell me.

"OK," is the universal word Hector uses. "My cousin," he lightly pats the top of his hand, which is decorated with a goat's head tattoo. Its piercing black eyes and red blood draping around the animal's neck look amazingly alive. The red is so convincingly the color of blood.

"He in gang, a teenager," on clue Oscar turns over his hand to reveal the palm and I view the Spanish words, which I cannot read.

Hector continues. "We so poor. This long ago.

Government soldiers kill Marxists. Rebels kill soldiers. All them," Hector's extended arm strokes the air, "kill villagers, men, women, children." He stops, and the two men make the sign of the cross.

The two men continue conferring. The tattoos tell a story; Lewis will have to be our interpreter. Perhaps Oscar understands English. It's possible that he is lying to his cousin and this is not his first visit to America. "Drugs all around. Soldiers, rebels all selling drugs to gringos." The men pause to embrace, their arms tangled together. Hector digs his head into his cousin's shoulder blade as if he's a goat ramming into an indestructible fence.

"We do things, bad things to survive," says Hector.

I don't really want to know the details.

CHAPTER 5

The older son reappears. The men all converse in Spanish and I hear the name Lewis. My translator and master interrogator arrives.

Lewis is escorted to this part of the building by the second son. My host and his cousin apprehensively look at the stranger, their eyes darting from Lewis's unsmiling face to each other. Lewis's penetrating, dark eyes draw in every feature as he puts to memory the smallest physical detail for possible later use. Every stranger can evolve into an enemy or a handy snitch.

However, there's a deep well of compassion in that hard-looking man. At just the right moment, unexpectedly, Lewis surprises you with his genuine concern for your wellbeing. Tough and firm, but with a sympathetic understanding of living in the dead-end, high-rise projects of Brooklyn. He is feared by the gang leaders in the Coney Island piss-holes that smell of urine in the elevators and keep the sanitation guys busy picking up the trash dumped out the windows. Yet when a gang war erupts, word is sent to the precinct to find Lewis; they demand his presence as mediator.

"Hey," Lewis spots me and our eyes meet but we don't shake hands. Immediately, he is assessing the situation, the relationship between me and these two men from a perilous place.

Lewis started with the Narcotics Division, the fastest way up the NYPD career ladder and the most dangerous. He has a chest full of medals earned the hard way, confiscating tons of illegal drugs and arresting truly bad boys, men who killed people for the smallest infraction, sometimes just for sport. His arms and right thigh are scarred from gunshot wounds inflicted by various gang members over the last decade. An effective undercover narcotics cop survives by making instant impressions, a false move disastrous, life threatening. A narc who acts quickly, intuitively and successfully, racks up the promotions.

"Detective Lewis," I introduce my colleague and turn towards my host. "Hector Diaz," the cautious man nods his head, "and his cousin Oscar."

The unexpected visitor avoids my colleague's face. I don't even know the man's surname, but that doesn't matter because illegals are unacknowledged members of American society – they don't exist. They silently appear at work sites or in luxury homes as domestics and then disappear into an invisible other world, which no one really wants to know anything about.

Lewis is offered a sweet, which he refuses by waving his hand at the food tray. He is here for business and immediately finds a set of tires to sit on, easily molding his well-developed body into a comfortable position, elbows lightly resting on his thighs. His eyes are memorizing the interior of this room, scanning the location of the piles of tires, the cracks that run along the concrete floor, his nose twitching as he inhales the rubbery odors of the fresh, new tires.

"So, I get the idea your cousin is wanted by some Central American gangs," he announces in English. Then he begins to speak Spanish; I sit attentively watching the body language of the three men, the faces, the jerky motions of the main man in the interrogation seat.

The men huddle as they converse, with the cousin the most demonstrative, his voice lowering to a whisper and then suddenly rising to almost a scream. His has a wrinkled and heavily creased face, filled with the lines of a hard life and poor childhood nutrition. He is expressive and animated as he tells his story. Lewis's brand of Spanish, learned from his Colombian mother, is universally understood by the people he meets in the streets of New York. Oscar doesn't appear to be encountering any difficulty.

There is a break in the discussion; Lewis lifts his body, nods his head and his eyes return to my face. "This is complicated," he tells me, pausing as his tongue settles in the corner of his mouth, a nervous habit. Mine is to unconsciously weave my hands through my dark, wavy hair, my best feature, or so the ladies tell me.

"This man," he points to Oscar while Hector looks on nervously, his finger repeatedly scratching the top of his nose. "He's made some real bad boys very unhappy," a small smile cracks through his tough guy stance. A certain sadism permeates the psyche of all narcotics cops; Lewis likes to see grown men cry and squirm.

My police colleague stands and gets up very close to Oscar's smaller, jittery body. "First, he runs with the gangs, life is tough in the El Salvadoran countryside." There's an unmistakable touch of compassion in the sudden softness in his voice. "Then his wife urges him to give up this life. She's afraid he will land up dead, either killed by a rival gang member or the police." While presumably Oscar doesn't comprehend a word Lewis is telling me, his head nods along with the cadences of the storyteller's voice.

"The gangs don't appreciate dropouts. They really frown on such changes of heart," Lewis winks at Oscar and the man wanly smiles at him. But Hector is grimacing, knowing the likelihood of his cousin escaping the hold of the notorious gangs is slim.

"Now the other problem. Oscar is involved with not just any gang, but the Mara Salvatrucha or MS-13, whose members originally came from places like El Salvador, Honduras, and

Guatemala." At the mention of the gang's name Oscar blinks, you can smell his fear. "The gang itself didn't really get going until they traveled north and settled in the Rampart district of Los Angeles. The idea behind this gang is the same as many similar ones – protection for their own kind against the other mean, nasty gangs in the neighborhood," he laughs.

Lewis enjoys teaching me, the college graduate and law student. "Ah, then they see the light – easy riches, drugs, prostitution, human smuggling, the usual vices and then some. Guys get busted by the LAPD and get deported back to their native countries."

Oscar pays careful attention to Lewis's face although he does not actually understand the conversation. Like a deer caught in the headlights, his eyes dart from Lewis and back to his cousin. Occasionally, a glance comes my way.

"Think of the home countries as the baseball minor leagues, where new members get basic training to come to America, the majors." Americans love sport analogies. I know almost nothing about baseball, although my old partner Jimmy infrequently took me to some minor league games at the Keyspan Stadium in Coney Island. I like the kosher hotdogs and the sunshine.

Still standing, Lewis uses his height to intimidate the frightened man. He casually glances at Oscar and the guy's shoulders drop, making him appear even smaller. "Lately, the Central American governments have become more transparent and less tied to paramilitary forces. This frees them from the blood money of the past and the courts down there are developing independent agencies. They are imposing harsher prison sentences, which they call 'mano dura' or the 'hard hand' treatment for these deportees."

Lewis stares at me and I nod my head, assuring him of my utmost attention. Lewis has a nice delivery – smooth voice level, notching up in volume at the mention of certain words. His arms are folded across his chest, feet apart, like a soldier in an 'at ease' stance. He looks like a drill sergeant offering casual conversation to his troops. I am a soldier in his war against the gangs.

"I participated in a big bust of a group of MS-13 here in New York City several months ago. It was a good operation, complete support from Immigration and Customs. The asses from the FBI were luckily not involved. We picked up 25 but there are thousands of these gang members all over the country. We used to think it was only a West Coast problem, an LA thing, but they are coming east. In that NYC raid, others were picked up in DC, Newark, Baltimore." Lewis takes in a deep breath, cleansing himself of the ugly realties. "These are dangerous sons-of-bitches. Narcotics, gun trafficking, murder and prostitution. And that's just what we know." Lewis kneels next to Oscar. "They are identified by their gang tattoos," forcibly grabbing Oscar's arm to show the symbols of membership.

"Our cousin, while he's scared out of his mind, he's probably not a choir boy. You did some mean, awful things like killing innocent people, maybe raping a few women, selling drugs to school kids," Lewis whispers into Oscar's ear.

Hector translates this last piece of supposition by Lewis. Oscar deftly moves out of Lewis's shadow and quickly stands up, practically knocking Lewis onto the cement floor. "No, no, no, no," he wildly waves his arms at me, grabbing my shoulders in his grip. "No, no," he looks at his cousin.

Lewis inconspicuously bends his index finger, beckoning me to move to another corner of the room. When we are ten feet from the two men he speaks. "This guy is not being straight with me. He's terrified of these gangbangers, but I'm not getting the real reason for his fright. I suspect his cousin is also being lied to."

Lewis's eyes return to Oscar, anxiously huddling with Hector. The two strangers' eyes meet, no one wants to blink first. Finally, Lewis turns his body towards me in satisfaction that he is holding all the winning chips.

"What do you think is really the reason for this

clandestine trip to his long-lost relative in Brooklyn?"

"My best guess is that he took something that didn't belong to him – drugs, money, a woman. And even if he gives it back, he's a dead man. It's a lose-lose situation for him."

We both momentarily focus on the tattoos. If I saw him on the street, fear was not the first emotion I would feel in his presence -- even on a dark night. He looks harmless, but a cop knows that murderers and rapists come in many varieties and motivations. "Do you think you can get the truth out of him?"

"Why would I want to? Unless you think we have some unsolved murder case in Brooklyn and you suspect he's the one, or knows the killer?" Always a pragmatist.

"Doesn't he interest you? Want to know his secrets?" I must know – no loose ends for this cop.

"You're the smart guy with the brains," he playfully but forcefully pokes at my temple. "You've got to know everything," his tone is mocking.

"I assured Hector that I would protect his cousin from the bad guys." I keep my promises. "I owe Hector a debt of gratitude for some help from a prior case." It's my turn to reciprocate.

"He's not some innocent by-stander. That I guarantee," Lewis asserts with complete confidence.

"Still, he's certainly afraid, we should be able to trade

that for something valuable," I answer knowing that's the balancing act we perform with informants.

"Why? What's in it for us?" I feel the intense heat of Lewis's displeasure. "Do you know how many illegals are here with a sorrowful story?"

I open my mouth to speak but he's on a diatribe.

"There are millions of illegals from Latin America and more millions from China and Asia here. All have tough luck stories – bad guys chasing them because of some infraction," he waves his hand in front of my face.

I'm not letting him off too easily, besides I have my new friends at Police Row. "You don't think there's a way to protect him here?" I ask in earnest without pleading.

"Send him back to be killed in his native land. Cheaper that way, no need to send him home in a coffin." The sarcasm is not even masked.

"Come on." I touch his arm. "I promised Hector," my voice filled with urging.

There's a little grunt in his voice. "Let's go back to the beginning. What's in it for the NYPD? We don't have enough officers to provide protection to every scared illegal, but if he has a real story to barter then we're talking about witness protection."

"OK," I say it loud enough that the two huddling men

cast their eyes toward us. "Let's barter," Lewis follows me as I walk back to our host and his cousin.

"Hector." The man looks at me with imploring eyes, "We don't quite believe Oscar's story. He's not telling us the truth. You must demand from him the truth. I cannot help him if he lies to us. We know that he isn't running away just because he wants to get out of the gang. There's a much bigger story behind that statement. Why is he here in Brooklyn?"

Lewis and I sit on the same tires and wait as Hector talks to his cousin. Lewis watches and listens although they speak quickly and perhaps use some Salvadoran slang. Lewis seems to be following their animated conversation, his eyes never leaving the smaller men's. His feet tap in rhythm as he observes the strangers.

Lewis's face cracks a smirk. "Just like I thought," he whispers to me.

Then Hector addresses us. "You right. He not want to share. A woman. I know his wife, and him ashamed but fell in love. She gang leader's woman," he announces.

Lewis whacks me across the chest. I don't cry out but it's painful. "Good, now we're starting with the truth. So, is this woman here in the US? Brooklyn?" Lewis demands.

"In America but not Brooklyn," Hector answers after conferring with Oscar.

"So, we are we talking about protection for both?"

"Yes," Hector replies and both Salvadorans nod.

"OK so for us to help them, we need something in return. Information. What does he know about the gang's operations in the US? We," and I point to Lewis and myself, "naturally, we are especially interested in anything going down here in New York City. Point us to the leaders in NY."

Lewis rests his elbows on his knees and waits.

"They sell drugs," Hector hesitantly answers.

Lewis loses patience, breaking into the conversation, demanding information in Spanish. I can't understand the words, but he is jabbing arms and the tone of voice is harsh. A few minutes go by and I feel Lewis's grip on my arm. "We're going, there's nothing worth talking about." Stumbling, I get to my feet and we head towards the front of the store.

"Wait," Hector screams at us. "Wait," my head turns slightly toward his voice. I see the men conferring and the discussion is highly emotional, arms are flailing, curt words are spoken. Then the gentle sobs begin, Oscar is crying. I recognize remorse - a sinner seeking repentance. How that feeling tugs at my heart and settles in the deepest recesses of my Yehudah soul.

Lewis doesn't turn around. He is ready to go. A hard-headed man requires a greater demonstration of penitence, proof of a change of heart. Deeds not tears are required.

"Please, please," I hear Hector along with a sloppy jumble of incoherent words from Oscar's lips.

My heart is willing to accept a change in the man. I am ready to believe that he is sorry. However, my colleague is still unmoved and his feet march towards the front door. Pinching his arm, his steps slow as we approach the doorway. We wait to hear something – important leads about people, places and events, descriptions of future gang activities and plans, locations of ill-gotten goods, human smuggling routes – something worthy of police protection.

"He knows things. He will talk." Hector cries out to us, a true lamentation echoing from the depths of his soul and Oscar's cries of repentance rise.

Lewis stops, turns his body and faces the two Salvadorans clutched to each other. "What does he know?" Lewis yells out. "I don't have time for this bullshit."

Oscar raises his arm and Lewis gestures to me with a flip of his wrist. We approach.

"OK, let's start from the beginning. And don't lie. I know lies," Lewis tells them. We take back our seats on the tires.

Oscar begins his story and since he is speaking in Spanish, the discussion is lost to me. I can only observe the body movements, the eye contact, the stammering in the voice.

Then Lewis screams at Oscar. "No, no, I'm not interested in the woman. Tell me about the drugs, the murders, the money laundering, and be specific!"

The conversation grows more intense, the muscles in Oscar's neck bulge with tension as the men talk. Fingers point in the air; mouths hang open, voice volume rises and falls. My attention begins to wane, instead I'm thinking about food and something cool to drink.

Someone hears my stomach growling because a son appears at the doorway. He is carrying a tray of cans and pizza. The steam is rising in waves of circular loops from the Italian treat. The smells of cheese, tomato sauce and olive oil make my intestines howl in delight. Nothing among the cold cans appeals to me, but I accept a Coke from the son's outstretched hand. He carefully places the pizza pie on a sturdy box – our impromptu dining table. I see the kashrut symbol.

As I snap a metal tab from the top of the soda can, I whisper to Lewis. "Do we have anything?"

"Maybe. I'll have to check this out, but potentially there's valuable information about future drug drops in New York. The past is useless since he is very hesitant about fingering specific people for crimes. This choir boy," his eyes glance at Oscar with the jaded look of an experienced narcotics detective. "Probably has more than one murder in his resume. Look at his body.

Those tattoos signify his gang activity."

"What happens next?" I ask between bites of pizza, the melting cheese and tangy tomato sauce covering a thin, light crust – perfect pizza. "Good," I smile at the three men, my satisfaction apparent.

Lewis grabs a slice, the pizza too hot to handle without a plate. He studies his food.

I ask him, "Will the Lieutenant, I mean Captain, actually send some uniforms? Are you satisfied that it's worth the protection?"

"Barely, but I'll do it for you." He slaps my back. Even his gentle motions have force. I watch him make the call. The clock moves forward, but unhurriedly.

We sit and eat like old friends at a make-do picnic. Eventually, one of the sons returns.

I bend my hand in a beckoning gesture towards the son. "Is there a police car out front?"

"I'll go check," the young man reports.

Lewis announces his plans. "I'll go out front and look for a squad car."

When the two men are gone, Hector rushes towards me. "I owe you much, much," he hugs me tightly while his cousin looks on with a wide grin of appreciation. "You save him. I love him," he takes his other arm and hugs Oscar.

It's a true aw-shucks moment. Family is all that matters even if you're favorite cousin is an experienced killer and sells drugs to school children. Oscar's an adulterer, liar, thief and probably a drug runner, but family is family. No one understands better than I what a man will do for a woman, rejecting all the rules and reason. I sigh to myself.

CHAPTER 6

Lewis had arranged a meeting with the NYPD gang experts, despite his lack of enthusiasm for Oscar's plight. He was doing it for me and I was flattered.

A call interrupted everything, and I sensed that it was important. Sometimes I took hours to return a call, but today I had this itchy, anxious sense of foreboding. I pulled my car over by the side of the road, not wanting to set a bad example for the citizens.

"Perlov," I say and listen to the voice on the other side of those invisible sound waves. "Detective Perlov," the voice is feminine and although it's somewhat familiar, I can't place a name with its honey tones.

"Peggy Mason, US Attorney Cohen's assistant," she pauses. "We have a very important meeting in his office. It's going to start in 30 minutes. Can you get here in time?"

"I'll get there as quickly as I can. Depends on traffic. What's so important?" I calmly demand, the volume of my voice not rising but firm sounding.

"US Attorney Cohen requests your presence, that's all I can say," she hangs up, no hints, devoid of details.

I am beckoned to make an appearance. My Uncle Vanya the Cossack, the rebel, the unconventional scoundrel, comes alive at the moments when I feel abused and pushed around like a toy, a rag doll. The blood rushes to my head and I suppress the urge to say, 'fuck it.' Uncle Vanya says make a late, grand entrance.

I don't even have a picture of this man, but I imagine him in the flowing pantaloons of a Cossack, sitting high on his white horse, whispering in my ear. "Damn the expected – do what's in your heart. Let the soul answer the doubters." I smile, as I ease into traffic.

This working for two masters has its obvious disadvantages. I am not on anyone's 'A List' of invitees. Cohen must have looked over the list this morning and suddenly it occurs to him, yes, of course, Perlov, the detective, my NYPD 'go to' man for terrorism.

How I miss my partner Jimmy and our chasing around the old neighborhoods – frantic, crazy Coney Island with its Ferris Wheel, roller coaster and Nathan's hotdogs. Of course, there's Little Odessa – Brighton Beach and the Boardwalk.

Once I was an integral part of the station house's ebb and flow. I had a place even if most of my fellow officers considered me an oddball, an outsider. I am physically still there but not part of the action. I know some faces but there is even more reason to treat me as an interloper. My new role is dictated by other forces. I went from Perlov the Protector, Hero of Harbor House, to an afterthought.

"Okay," talking aloud, I gently slap my face. "Stop playing the victim." This is a role I can easily slip into without much preparation. My present assignment is probably the best one I will ever get, terrorism is the new route to promotions and glory. Besides, the government is paying for me to attend law school. Russians are not adept at feeling grateful, too much bitter history, endless cold and lack of sunlight brings out the darkness in one's soul.

I check my watch with satisfaction. I am late. Before I leave the elevator, I look at my reflection in the shiny metal. Not bad looking, not movie star handsome but attractive and a little sexy with my dark, thick, wavy hair, thin lips and angular body. I hear the women whisper about me in the station house. I will never be singled out as the best dresser, but with my polished European manners and intense gaze, the ladies look appreciatively my way.

I approach the door. The receptionist is expecting me and shows me the way, although I am familiar with some of the offices on this high security floor. This is not my first time here, even if they treat me as an afterthought.

"Welcome," US Attorney Cohen smiles as I enter the well-lit, wood paneled conference room. Usually, we meet in glass-enclosed rooms, so the people present today probably do not want to be seen. The US Attorney is saving a spot for me at his right hand. My posture immediately improves at this public display of importance.

"Sorry it was so last minute. I do apologize. I don't know how your name was innocently omitted from the list. Coffee? Bagels?" My mood is getting cheery. I discretely breathe in the aromas of the still hot, steaming coffee and the garlicky smells of the bagels. Brown and crusty, just what I love.

I take my appointed seat and get my first good look at my colleagues around the table. I eye Peggy Mason who gives me a tight, small smile that makes me think she's always constipated. It's no wonder that Cohen never allows her to address a jury.

I inconspicuously glance at the faces around the table. Most of them are unknown to me and I guess this is an important meeting of many federal agencies; no smiles or friendly grins. I pause with half an eye at each suited body, trying not to be rude. One familiar face is from NYPD Police Row, one of the brass but a good guy. He nods at me and I return the gesture.

Then I see him – my mystery man. His dark Semitic features set him apart from the others around the table. Our eyes meet but neither of us gives the other even the slightest bit of recognition. We are men of discretion.

"Let me introduce everyone," Cohen says and proceeds to attach a name to each of the men and two women in the room. "From Mossad," the Israeli secret intelligence agency,

"Dov Amitz," we lock eyes.

He was my confidential informer. Out of a misty morning, he arrived to help me solve my case of a dead Hasid from Uzbekistan. That case remains officially unsolved, although he gave me all the vital clues I needed to be personally reassured that one day, I would learn all the lingering secrets. Still I had loose ends. No case was closed if there were loose ends.

My Inspector Javert tendencies will not let me be satisfied until I discover all the residual pieces of this puzzle. I cannot rest until I know exactly what happened that evening when a foreign assailant stealthily shot to death a father of five from a famous Bukharan family. The deceased was a member of a unique Jewish people from Central Asia with their own customs and rituals. In a twist of fate that leads one to embrace the concept of an omnipotent God, who watches over us, my mother knows this family from our days in an Israeli settlement when we were first exiled from Mother Russia.

One morning, as I was struggling to put the puzzle together, I met this man on the Brighton Beach Boardwalk. He knew where to find me and knew the identity of the killer of my Hasid jeweler. But everything was hush, hush. He was, from that moment we met, an invisible operative. My Mossad contact provided me with the dead man's hat; however, I told the NYPD authorities it was a mystery man who delivered it to my parents' house. That wasn't too much of a stretch, not a lie; I hate lies, a half-truth perhaps.

Now we meet again, strange world we live in. I nod my head, "Mossad, FBI, CIA, DOD, NYPD. This is a meeting of heavy weights." I self-effacingly offer a comment, "And then me, of course." I notice a sliver of a smile on the faces of the NYPD brass and Mr. Mossad.

"Last month, it was just one of those unplanned events. The Building Department in Suffolk County received many complaints from neighbors about a supposedly single-family home being used as a boarding house. The building inspector in Riverhead calls the owner of record. It's a bogus real estate company. He calls immigration and they plan surveillance of the house. Sure enough, just like the neighbors said, young men come and go at all times of the day and night. Perhaps 20 men are living there."

Most people around the table are listening intently with their eyes directly on Cohen, so I am not the only person learning this information for the first time. No one from immigration is present in the room. This is something more than an illegal immigration sting operation.

"The immediate assumption is that this is a plain vanilla illegal immigration ring. No women are ever observed by the Suffolk County police, who conducted the surveillance. There's a collective sigh of relief among the Suffolk authorities because it's not a den of prostitution or some sex slave ring."

Very few police departments maintain friendly relations with the immigration guys because their regulations are so onerous for us to follow. "They plan a raid and," he pauses for a dramatic moment. His hands are out in front of his body. He noisily rises from his chair rattling papers and a coffee cup, his arms fighting the lush carpeting to move his seat backwards, so he can stand. I like this guy's style. Cohen is going to be my courtroom model.

They are met at this house on a quiet, little, non-descript street with blazing guns. They manage to capture fifteen men believing them to be drug mules. Some got away."

Somebody asked if anyone was hurt.

"Nothing serious, but we think that the ringleaders escaped. And who were these fugitives? A small group of Long Island pioneer members of Mara Salvatrucha. You heard of them?" He turns his head to look around the room for name recognition.

I almost spit out the bagel in my mouth, but instantly recover. I don't believe in coincidences. Should I mention Oscar? What is the man up to? Lewis was right, he is telling us lies. I'm uncertain what to share. I do have a responsibility. "I got a frantic call from a confidential informer about his cousin with ties to the MS-13 gang. This guy is looking for some police protection in exchange for providing information. Perhaps he can be helpful." Lend him out to the other agencies but keep him under NYPD authority. This may assure Oscar of police protection.

I get an immediate bite; the FBI agent springs to her feet, the excitement impossible to restrain. "Yes, yes, we've had no luck at all getting close to this organization. We were surprised to find them on Long Island, thought they were only operating in California. We are working with the US Attorney." She gestures towards Cohen. "We are working on bringing racketeering charges against them, but we desperately need informers."

She wags her head like my father's happy puppy. "The fifteen men caught up in the raid, we assume were doing the gang leaders' bidding. Don't know yet, if any rate as dangerous gang members. The ones we captured aren't talkative. We think someone else, no one we have in custody was in charge. Drugs are high on our list of concerns but also human smuggling."

"Sometimes, we blindly stumble into important cases," Cohen says with a shake of his head and the wide-eyed look of a man who won the lottery.

I knew that feeling. It was how Jimmy and I got our detective promotions – lucky breaks. The FBI agent hears enough. "When can I meet this guy?" she asks with the earnestness of a girl scout with only one more merit badge left to add to her green sash.

I can't trust this stranger with Oscar's fate. No, no not

yet. I must stall and dampen her enthusiasm. "Wait. There are lots we need to discuss before jumping into this. This is a big, bad organization, the MS-13. I need to learn more about what's been happening in Suffolk to determine if my informer has anything to offer." Was it possible he escaped from this house in Suffolk and has been running from federal agents for the last 30 days? Finally, settled on his cousin in Brooklyn? It's possible that the events are unrelated. I just don't know.

Our host loudly coughs as he again assumes control of the meeting. "Detective Perlov, this is a complete surprise. Naturally, we are interested in your informer. However, the story is more fascinating." From the intense gaze of those around the table, very few people know the total picture.

Cohen continues, still standing. "In the house, we find these guys. They don't talk. But there's much more to this story," he stops to build momentum.

We look up and he seems even taller, as if he's on his tippy toes. More excited-little-kid-at-the-circus than his usual controlled US Attorney posture.

"Because in this house we also find a woman and she's clearly not from Central America. At the time of the raid, she's discovered apparently living alone in one room in the house. We talk to the men we arrest, and they don't know her. In fact, they are forbidden from talking to her or having any contact with her. She is a 'very special guest,' is what they tell us."

He smiles to himself because he's got a secret that he's going to reveal. "She is wearing the clothing of an observant Muslim; full burqa, we assume she is Arabic or Iranian. If she knows English, she refuses to talk. We bring in an Arabic translator, but she won't speak, like she's deaf and dumb. We bring in a Farsi speaking translator, nothing."

The CIA guy's eyes spring wide open. He starts to speak but someone jumps in first.

My Mossad guy leans towards the center of the table. "We believe that she is an Egyptian. Although she is not cooperative, American intelligence agents were able to get a DNA sample. Neither Israeli nor American intelligence have her in any database. But, her DNA is a familial match to people in our database. If she's from the same family, we should be concerned. We're talking Muslim Brotherhood, a recognized terrorist group. We believe she is related to a terrorist responsible for killing and maiming many in Taba, an Egyptian resort area where many Israelis vacation."

The US Attorney addresses the pack. "This is highly classified information. We have lots of unknowns. Who is this woman? We still are not entirely certain. More importantly, we are very worried that somehow the MS-13 and Islamic terrorists are joining forces. This could be our worst nightmare."

"If they are linked how would they have established that connection?" I ask.

Cohen tells us. "Because this is a perfect marriage of convenience. Who knows how to get in and out of this country undetected more easily than these Latin gangs? Who makes a business of human smuggling? We know after 9/11 that there is an organized network of terrorists. Financing their operations is taking place across the globe. The Islamists provide a valuable contraband product – guns, drugs, in exchange, the MS-13 smuggles terrorists into this country. What could be a better 'win-win' for both parties?"

Is Hector's cousin involved with international terrorists? He hardly seems capable. Doesn't seem to have leadership skills. Who knows? It all could be a great act.

"This woman needs to be interrogated because so far everything is conjecture. She refuses to talk. We are studying her clothing for hints. She is on no Interpol list. The DNA is the only conclusive evidence we have to date." The group waits for their specific assignments.

"Detective Perlov," Cohen stares at me, the others all casting their eyes on my face. The heat is rising in my body; I try to remain unruffled. "We want you to go to Belarus and interrogate the woman," Cohen tells the assembled audience. They all look stunned. The CIA agent is the only one to sit expressionless because he is probably the only one aware of my assignment.

"Me?" I can't contain my own shock. "I don't speak

Arabic, never been to Egypt. What is she doing in Belarus?"

The CIA agent jumps into the conversation. "That's where we are holding her."

"Belarus? Wait. Are you telling me you picked her up in Long Island and then flew her to Belarus for questioning?"

"Yes," the CIA agent answers quickly. "We believe that she is a terrorist or is connected to terrorists. Is she part of some vanguard terrorist cell? Someone has got to get her to talk, force her if necessary. Whatever it takes."

"Wait, wait," I am almost stuttering. "You fly her to Belarus as part of the US government's extraordinary rendition scheme. You wanted to move her to a third-rate former Soviet regime, so you can torture her?" The governments of Poland and Romania were participating until the European Union learned about it and started publicly complaining. Now they move people who they want to torture to other countries where a free press and outside investigating authorities do not exist.

"Why me? Do you think that I support the government's torture program?" What is in my official police jacket that leads Cohen to think I will gladly participate? I am stammering in a state of disbelief.

"We picked you," Cohen tells me in a soothing, reassuring voice, "because you speak both Russian and German. You are known as a great interrogator -- a man who gets the reluctant to open up."

"German?"

The CIA man continues where he left off. "We know there have been Muslim terrorists living in Germany. The 9/11 terrorists lived In Hamburg, Germany. Members of the Muslim Brotherhood have used Germany as a jumping off point in the past. We think if she has links to the Muslim Brotherhood that she has spent time in Hamburg, Germany. We had the labels taken from her clothing analyzed. Certain shops in Hamburg, in the Arab section, sell the same exact items. Although truthfully, these could be sold in dozens of places. She has not spoken at all. We have tried talking to her in many languages including Arabic. But interestingly, her only registered reaction was when someone spoke German. We want you to question her in German and assume the identity of a German federal officer. We think you will appear friendlier than either an American or Egyptian police officer would be."

Suddenly another face appears at the doorway. "Sorry I am late," he tells us in a heavily accented voice, sounding like our Israeli. They look alike in that dark, Semitic way but not quite a member of the tribe. He quickly takes a seat near me.

"This is Mohammed Abdel," one of the NYPD brass introduces him. "He is a guest working with the NYPD from Egypt. Some of you may be aware that we are working closely with the Egyptian government to attempt to stem another terrorist attack before it occurs. This is all part of the NYPD's proactive anti-terrorist plan." He waits for Abdel to make himself comfortable.

Abdel speaks to us. "I assume we are speaking of the woman picked up in the New York area. We believe, we know who she is," then he stops himself, raising his arm.

"Let me re-phrase. Her DNA is scientifically similar to ones we have on file. That DNA belongs to the founding family of the Muslim Brotherhood. These are Egyptian terrorists we have been tracking for decades," he is nodding his head with assurance.

"We wanted her but because of some recent bad publicity, the US government did not return her to Egypt. People would assume that we tortured her. Nonsense. We certainly don't torture every terrorist, but she may hold valuable information. We all want to know," his outstretched arms include everyone around the table. "What is she doing in America?"

"The Egyptian authorities have a long history of following the Muslim Brotherhood," Cohen tells us.

"We have not been able to get the permission of the German government to allow us to interrogate people we know to be Muslim Brotherhood family members living in Germany. They think we don't have enough evidence to carry on interrogations. We haven't sufficiently proven to them that we can pinpoint specific people. They don't want us conducting a raid on a neighborhood where Egyptians live in Hamburg. But chatter we are following indicates Muslim Brotherhood members are hiding in Hamburg. If we have more specific proof then the Germans will be more cooperative," Abdel says.

He glances at me as I respond. "We know that torture is unreliable. Ultimately, the suspect talks but is the information worth anything? The publicity is terrible and democratic countries seem like hypocrites. What's to be gained by torture? There are better ways."

The CIA agent edges closer to the table. Gripping the end of the tabletop he rises. "We had 3,000 dead on 9/11 and if we think that anyone has valuable information to prevent another attack, then it's the government's responsibility to do whatever is necessary. And I mean everything and anything. Man, woman or child, I mean everything. The ends justify the means."

Should I be complacent? Uncle Vanya the Cossack is grumbling in my head and my mother screams out for justice. "For me, this issue of torture is not an esoteric or philosophical discussion." I see a few yawns of disapproval, the ranting and ravings of a naysayer. Maybe they think I'm a liberal, a true curse in law enforcement.

Should I tell them all my story. Would it change minds? When I was a boy, perhaps ten and living in Leningrad, now St. Petersburg, we had visitors in the early hours of the morning. In the darkness, they descended on my apartment with wooden battering rams and they broke down the front door of our apartment.

I heard screams and bodies being pushed and pulled in the darkness. It was a cold night and there was little heat to keep anyone warm, so we were all bundled up in many blankets. I ran out of the bedroom that I shared with my father's parents and saw tall men dressed in black uniforms. The KGB. They were attempting to put handcuffs on my mother and she was fighting like a tiger. A child's horror never is forgotten.

I can picture it. The image never leaves. Someone turns on a light and I see my father jumping on the back of one of these men. My father is a small, thin man, but he becomes a ferocious lion when he is protecting his wife, the mother of his child. He's hanging on this guy's back, screaming and beating the man's head with his fists.

The man is a giant and swings my father's body like a pesky bug and my poor father is slammed against the wall. My grandmother runs to protect him. I see the blood running out of his mouth and nose. My mother is biting the guards and fighting with all her strength. They are going to carry her out like a sack of potatoes, only this package is very much alive.

I run into the kitchen and grab the biggest knife I can find and charge the guard holding my mother's kicking feet. I try to stab him in the chest, but I am a small boy and he is gigantic. He goes to deflect the knife and I miss his chest and stab him in the thigh. He cries out in pain and drops my mother who then kicks him in the balls.

One of the guards points his gun at me. My grandfather drops to the ground, his frail body completely covering me. He screams at the guard. 'Kill me, kill me.' I cannot see anything, but I hear the gun cock. Then a voice laughs. 'Brave little boy;' he laughs again, and more men are heard entering the room. My mother, still screaming, is dragged away. My grandfather does not allow me to see this.

Several weeks later she is returned to us in the dead of the night. Once she had been an accomplished pianist but when she came home, she would never be able to play the piano again. Did my mother's torture at the hands of the KGB stop her fellow dissidents? Did it stop my mother from protesting? Of course not, it made them harder and more determined. Did my mother rat on her friends? We don't know, and she never told me. And what happened to a regime that used torture? It failed; it became decayed and rotted from within. Can these Americans ever understand? I remain silent.

I continue. "If you want me to go to Belarus to interrogate this woman that you may rightfully believe is a terrorist, I will gladly go and attempt to gain her confidence. But I will not under any circumstances participate in the torture of this woman. Keep her in a US military prison, like the government did to Padilla. It must be here in America. I will not leave her in Belarus. And she is not going to be dumped at the prison at Guantanamo Bay to rot."

Jose Padilla was an American citizen, an accused terrorist, hidden away in a military brig in South Carolina. He was labeled an enemy combatant until the US government changed its mind and put him on trial in a civilian court of law. He claimed to have been tortured. Meanwhile, the US government still holds prisoners believed to be terrorists since 2002 at Guantanamo Navy base. None are known to be women.

"These are my requirements. As I said, I am more than willing to help my adopted country. I love this country. It has been very good to me and my family, but I know from personal experience how good intentions can become corrupted. That's the grand, sad story of the Soviet Union."

All eyes revert to Cohen. The Egyptian is stoic, no smiles, no blinking eyes; I receive a cold stare. He views the problem in a different light. My Mossad man bends his head towards his neck, a bone cracks. I can read his mind – 'naïve one'. We all know that Israeli intelligence takes out people it feels are threats.

But for me it is clear. When the Messiah comes, how can I be resurrected and join the righteous if I cannot protect this unknown woman? Besides, my mother would never speak to me if I agree to participate in any action that can lead to torture.

As a good mama's boy, I know whom I must please.

Chapter 7

Women and terrorism, torture and love, Belarus and Lefortovo prison, am I dreaming? My obsession, Olga, in a white wedding gown is dancing and frolicking on the beach. There I am with Vasily, my very best friend from childhood. We fought off the bullies in Leningrad and now we are together in the New Jerusalem. Our trio is laughing and prancing across a deserted beach.

Fragments of one of my mother's dreams haunt me, seeping into my brain asleep or awake. A modern-day Joseph; the Biblical icon in his robe of many colors, the seer of the Pharaoh's dreams, prophesying ancient Israelite's future, my mother sees the family's future. Frightening, yet ever so thrilling, can she truly see my future?

In one of her repetitive dreams the three of us – Vasily, Olga and I are together, playing as if we are innocent children. She is guiltless concerning her husband's death, Vasily is a respectable international businessman not a supplier of guns to rebel soldiers fighting across the globe, and I am not responsible for helping a murderess cover-up a crime. Innocents – we are like the newborn, pure as the first, soft, gentle flakes of a winter snow floating from the sky. Our arms lunge towards the cascading snowflakes.

Is Olga in my future? Her dead, fat husband lies on the ugly, stained carpeting of the living room in Brighton Beach. It is she who changed my life. I know in the deepest recesses of this dark Russian soul, meeting her that summer day is part of a grand scheme, transforming, life altering in ways still unclear.

She is almost famous. I tape her performances in her recurring role as an ambitious immigrant on a daytime soap opera. I share her television images with no one, sitting in the dark, watching her, studying her, scrutinizing her every movement for a sign that she needs me. But I never call, and she never calls me. Sometimes in my dreams, she and Dr. Marina, my lost fiancée, take hands, their fingers interlocking, skipping along the rotting wooden planks of the Boardwalk in the Rockaways near my house.

What's the jingle, jangle noise? "Stop," I scream out to the empty bedroom. "What?" I yell to the walls. "The noise, what is that piercing sound?" I shout to the sleeping gulls outside my window. "What, what?" I cry in the near darkness of my room.

My eyes, half slits, concentrate on the yellowish lit dial of the alarm clock, 4:19 a.m. Now I see the source of this incredible disruption. My phone is ringing and will not stop. My startled heart starts beating faster and faster through my thin tee shirt. "Oh my God, what can it be?" I ask the night table. My mother is mature but not old and sick; my father is fit and trim. "An accident, it must be an accident," I tell the pounding phone.

Or could it be my Olga calling for help? Marina is calling from the grave offering me atonement.

Painstakingly, I lift the handle from its cradle. I hear the words, "Perlov." Whose voice is this? Male for certain.

"Perlov, it's me Sarge, Perlov," he is insistent but composed.

"Sarge," I am so surprised. "What's wrong? Is it Jimmy?" my heart is breaking, the muscles pulling away from the ventricles, the blood leaking out of its chamber. "The Lieutenant, I mean Captain?" my voice pleading.

"Murphy's been shot," he says with resolve but calmly relaying the information.

"Is he dead?" The worst nightmare for a cop, shot in the line of duty. You get a nice funeral; the mayor shows up and cops from other places come in their dress uniforms to demonstrate solidarity, but you are cold meat. I guess the showing is for the widow, children and parents to make them feel better, at least for that moment. Dead is still dead.

"No, but it's bad, the Captain wants you here. Can you get here by 5?" this is an order.

"You bet. Where's Lewis?" his partner.

"At the hospital, Murphy is in surgery. They've got a team of doctors working on him."

"Which hospital," I ask because a fallen cop deserves the best and where you go matters for your survival. These things I know from my lovely Dr. Marina, a chief resident in Emergency Medicine.

"Downstate," he replies, and I can picture the Sarge's big head nodding in appreciation.

"Great," it's the best in Brooklyn, my sweetie's former hospital. I do miss her -- those strong, firm hands. God, what is in store for me? Where is the sign from Hashem? Those dreams, I think they were dreams of Lefortovo prison where my mother rotted, the beach with Olga, a silver sliver flying towards Belarus. I am still half-asleep or am I in shock?

The Sarge continues. "Got the whole trauma team working on him."

"Is he going to make it?" I ask, rubbing my eyes several times to focus because her white wedding dress is still filtering into my thinking. The cold, stone walls of the prison with the strong, steel bars are still lingering.

"We can only pray. Get your ass in here." The Sarge is finished with me and hangs up his phone. I hear the silence. He is calling all the names on the roster. Perhaps, he's going alphabetically so next is 'Q.' No, we have no one named Quincy or Quinn. There are a few Italian guys with names starting with R, even the new Spanish kid. What's his name – Rodriquez?

I forcibly shake my head; forget the bullshit I tell myself, quickly dressing, literally throwing on a shirt and pants. It doesn't matter if my clothing is perfectly matched. Any shoes will do, black socks; it's a good thing I retain my mother's habit of folding the socks together, easy to grab a matching pair. No time for a shower. We are about to start the search for Murphy's assailant, cops together, united to find the bastard who attacks one of us. No one assaults us without dire consequences.

A starry night, I glance up before jumping into my car, heading towards the precinct house. Luckily, my little Amos is with my parents. How could I walk him with duty calling at 5 am?

Taking the bridge, I glance over at the quiet bay separating the isthmus of the Rockaways from the more massive Long Island. The birds are still not stirring, roosting in their nests. My adrenaline is racing through my blood vessels calling all those nerve endings to attention. Hunting a potential cop killer is unpredictable and always dangerous to both the one being tracked and the hunters. But the sleeping gulls are indifferent to the pains and anxieties of humans.

At this hour of the early morning, the earth is in perfect harmony, awaiting the dawn. Oh, the glorious morning, at the exact moment when the sun breaks across the horizon, the glittering gold of that first light, redemption is at hand. Today, I may experience it once again -- that precise instant of Hashem's majesty. I will need its splendid and cleansing presence because I am a soldier, an enforcer, a deliverer this morning. I bring order and control to the unruly masses that strike one of us, the core of stability in the neighborhood. Aboard my chariot, my sturdy car, I drive across the bridge heading for the stationhouse to perform a service to my fallen comrade.

Once I arrive, many familiar faces greet me. The Sarge's message got out to a dozen of us. Ascending the battered concrete steps to the station's lobby, I feel a powerful grip on my shoulder. Quickly, I turn to face the responsible party.

I feel the tears welling up in my eyes from pure joy. "Jimmy, Jimmy, my main man," we hug in the semi-darkness as our fellow officers laugh and clap. For their amusement and our delight, we perform a clunky, clumsy jig, neither of us with an ounce of Irish blood.

"Hey champ," someone gives him a playful jab.

"So why are you here?" I ask in complete amazement but pleased.

"Hey, when one of us gets shot aren't we all brothers. Murphy is a great guy. I owe him and Lewis. Where's Lewis?" Jimmy asks the small crowd congregating near the station house entrance.

I whisper as we climb the steps together, "You aren't a police officer."

His hand disappears behind his back and pulls out his Glock. "Today I am." He points to the fine-looking pistol. "It's registered."

I know he is preparing for an important fight in Atlantic City. "How did you find out about Murphy?"

"I heard it on the police radio that I have in the house. I still keep it on. Crazy I know. Earlier I finished arranging to go down to the Jersey shore for some intensive training. I was wide awake, thinking about the fight, the girlfriend, my father. You know how it can get. I'm restless, tossing and turning, lying in my bed, staring at the ceiling – all jittery."

He smiles that classic Jimmy grin, toothy and expansive, those baby blues staring at me. "I'm thinking, thinking," he taps his temple. "Should I get my own apartment? Should I buy a house with my first winnings? Stupid shit like that. Then I hear the news." He sticks his finger inside his ear, poking at the cartilage. It's a habit of his –finger in the ear for emphasis.

"I get up quickly and call the Lieutenant," he apologizes. "Captain," a thin blush of red fills his round cheeks. "And beg him to let me join the response team. I have to do a little persuading, but I'm here."

"We're together again, on a case. How sweet," I add as we embrace. How can you explain to civilians what it's like to have a great police partnership? It's more rewarding than a happy marriage or a successful business relationship. You depend upon this person to save your ass, watch your back, prepare for the worst, and if necessary give up their life.

"Hey, the champion is with us," we hear the catcalls,

hoots and hollers of the others welcoming Jimmy back to the station house.

My friend and fellow law school colleague, Sergeant Roberta Sullivan is one of those called to duty on this early morning. Jimmy and Roberta have an uneasy relationship, but she smiles at his presence and he returns a welcoming glance.

Sparkling eyes, sharp and alert, neatly attired, stands our leader, the man whose commands we gladly obey. We all circle the newly appointed Captain. His Irish chin juts out in defiance; it is an act of desecration to shoot a fellow officer. Unless the cop is a snitch for Internal Affairs, we stand in unity. A strike at one of us is an assault against all of us.

The Captain doesn't try to console us with words but with action, orders, motion, activity. "Lewis radioed with the suspect's name, Charles 'Cha Cha' Smithe, with an 'e' at the end." For some reason, we all laugh at the name; anything to break the tension.

"I have the warrant for his arrest," he dangles a piece of paper into the air, waving it as if it were a coveted flag. Even with the Patriot Act, we can't go knocking down doors in the wee hours of the morning without the proper paperwork. This asshole would never qualify as a terrorist except to the residents of the housing project where he calls home.

"We think he fled to his girlfriend's apartment in Surfside Gardens. All of you know that housing project." The Captain looks across at his select group of hand-picked police officers, who will comprise the strike team to hunt down Murphy's attacker.

"Do we have a plan?" I ask and all eyes stare at me.

"That's why you're here Perlov, get us a plan." My commander barks and I am ready to assume leadership, especially now that my Jimmy, my right hand, the yin to my yang, is back with me.

"Do we have an apartment number?" I respond. Let's get to the basics. All the officers surround me.

Roberta steps forward. "We'll get someone to track down her name and exact address," she authoritatively adds.

"A computer geek, is one available?" I trust them with the details.

"I'm here," Harris raises his hand, our nerdy, completely competent computer expert, who has developed his own shortcuts to gather information from the enormous NYPD databases. The department is making huge investments in technology to help street cops corral and subdue criminals. It's simply incredible how effective these machines are in analyzing and pinpointing crime trends, patterns and hints that the human eye could never reveal, or the human mind alone absorb.

"Find me the location of her apartment and blueprints of the project," I tell him as he composes mental notes.

"Then if possible, I want to know exactly where the windows of this apartment look out on -- in terms of the project courtyard, surrounding buildings and the street," I add.

"Okay, it won't take too long if it's in any system," he confidently disappears upstairs to the dank attic that the computer geeks call home.

Our Captain looks at his assembled group. "If we can proceed in the darkness before anyone is stirring in the projects, we have a better chance of nailing this guy without anyone getting hurt. We don't want any innocent bystanders caught up in a police firestorm. Surprise is essential."

"Who is this bastard?" Jimmy inquires, trying hard to contain his natural enthusiasm and proclivity for action, feet moving, guns cocked, sirens blaring. He begins to pace and we all recognize his discomfort with the inert; we hate waiting while a cop assailant is breathing unimpeded.

"A gangbanger from the neighborhood. Two rival pieces of shit are fighting over drug territory and Lewis and Murphy walked into their argument. They should have just let the two sons-of-bitches kill each other and who would care," Nelson says. He works in the projects along with our two gang experts. He has a good story, up from the projects, the son of a single mother working as a Licensed Practical Nurse, keeps him away from the gangs. In this new multi-cultural NYPD, there are more people like Nelson among our ranks.

Nelson produces a grainy photo, which we all stare at, memorizing all the fine details, the tattoos representing a secret gang code, the large scar on his cheek, the bushy hair, evil eyes. His image is frozen in our collective brains.

"What about the girlfriend?" someone asks.

"No record, but we think there are a few kids involved," another cop provides more details.

The Captain immediately realizes the danger. "Kids, we've got to be very careful. No accidental shooting of any children. That would not look nice in the tabloids or on the evening news." We all nod our heads in agreement.

Running down the steps at full speed our computer man arrives on the scene, short of breath and excited with his findings.

"Beautiful," I say as we review the blueprints of the apartment, where the front door is in relationship to the other rooms in the one-bedroom apartment. "Here," I point to where the windows are. "When we come through the door if we catch him in bed half asleep, he should be easy to subdue, and no one gets hurt. We must be invisible."

I take the other images he has produced. "Look," I point to the diagrams. "We've got to post people on the roof near where the fire escape ends and under the apartment where the fire escape drops into the courtyard. Roberta, as the sergeant in charge of the uniforms, will be responsible for posting them around the periphery of the building. We don't want anyone accidentally stumbling into mayhem," I tell my audience.

Sergeant Sullivan knows the routine. "I 'll have uniforms at all the entrances to the buildings to keep people from coming or leaving, and around the pathways to the courtyard. We'll get an ambulance parked out of sight but available just in case."

"Okay, are we ready?" the Captain asks.

We all nod our heads. "No sirens." I add.

The Captain moves close to Jimmy. "You don't fire a shot unless someone is going to kill you. Right?"

Jimmy is pleased just to be part of the assault team. "Absolutely."

"It's now 05:25," I announce and everyone in the room sets their watches.

"We'll assemble at 05:45 and let's be prepared for anything. Vests, extra firepower, radios all operating," I like barking orders at others. The Captain is encouraging me with a half-smile.

"Ok, we know what to do," I say with a demanding tone of voice. All heads nod in unison.

Jimmy follows me down to the locker rooms where I hide my private arsenal inherited from my days in the US Army, SWAT unit, and now as a detective.

"Here take this," I hand him a vest, which he puts on as I adjust mine. Preparation is the key to success, so I strap my small pistol around my ankle. My knife is strapped to my thigh. Then he helps me take out two high power rifles, which are standing upright in the locker.

I wrap these beauties in fine cloth, clean them religiously and hope that I never need to use them. There's another locked away in its hard leather case sitting on the floor of my locker, but that's my US Army issue champion competition marksman rifle. I don't need that one this morning.

"You think you'll need these," he asks as he pats the barrel of my SWAT rifle.

I give him a shotgun. "Just in case. The Captain said you can return fire if you think you're a target."

With the armaments secured in my arms, we eagerly proceed to an unmarked squad car. Jimmy's head is bobbing up and down, the tension is palpable, electric sparks invisibly energizing all of us on this mission. The raging anger is controlled by the need to be precise and focused. No dead kids for the evening news, only a murderous gangbanger.

We step into the early morning cool breezes, which sprinkle my face with mist that feels invigorating. The skin's pores open to receive the cleansing salty moisture of the mighty ocean just blocks away. The overhead streetlights cast a hazy blur as the fog remains heavy.

Breathing in deeply, I smile at Jimmy. "It's so great to be back together. The Polish Shaygetz and the Russian outsider.

The fearsome duo, everybody's favorite backup team," I tell my former partner.

Jimmy 'Smiley' Sutton responds with his biggest, widest smile lighting up his eyes. He is ready. The middleweight boxing contender returns to his first love, the streets of New York.

CHAPTER 8

We are on course driving to the desolate housing projects of Coney Island. Too many families are lost or scattered, emotionally scarred and too brittle to accept too much responsibility. It's a world where children are raising parents, old women raising great-great grandchildren.

In the stealth of the early morning light, we position ourselves. Roberta directs the uniforms to each project building entrance, including the basement steps where the super hauls out the garbage for collection. He is probably the first one up each morning.

I am thankful that the fire escapes are located exactly as indicated in the drawings. You can't always trust thirty-year-old blueprints. The place looks like the computer images.

Surprise is our best weapon and we quietly move up the stairs, six of us. Jimmy just behind my heels. I'm in the vanguard, with my neck artery pulsating; it throbs with each step I take. I race up the steps, two at a time. One uniform is posted at the elevator doors. Another officer holds the battering ram. These project apartment doors are quite sturdy. It may take a few powerful, swinging jolts to bring down the door.

The guy next me whispers. "Should we call out police?"

"Police," I almost whisper as two uniforms carrying the

metal pole hold it tightly, reach back and then with a forceful action strike the door. Two officers are at opposite ends of the corridor to prevent any residents from leaving.

Screams are heard from inside the apartment. Then a masculine voice calls out. "Don't come any closer. Got a gun pointed at her. Two kids in here. Don't come any closer," his voice trembling and nervous, but loud enough to be heard through walls and a door.

"Oh shit," I say; he was alerted somehow. We were so quiet, slipping up the stairs like cats on padded paws, no noise until the moment the ramming pole struck the door. If the guy was in a deep sleep this noise wouldn't wake him. Perhaps he was waiting for someone else, a drug accomplice who is going to help him escape the city and the heat from the police.

"Now what?" the guys with the battering ram ask.

"Put it down," I say, and I make the unhappy call to the Captain. He replies in seconds. "We've got a problem," I report, my voice firm and calm. "He's holding a woman with a gun, or so he says."

"Shit," I hear and then a pause. "Do you think he is actually holding her? Maybe it's a ploy."

"Do we chance it? He seems to have been up waiting. I don't think he was expecting us but maybe a fellow drug dealer. I'll alert Roberta that the uniforms need to be totally invisible in case this friend shows up."

"Sure, but about the woman? Is this the girlfriend?" The Captain's concern is clear. "We don't want any bad publicity about an innocent citizen being shot in our pursuit of a cop assailant."

"I'll try and tease out the information," I respond.

"I'll contact Roberta, you concentrate on the woman. Are there children involved?" His anxiety is rising with the possibility of small bloody bodies on the front pages of the newspapers.

"Yes, he says there are children inside." I reply but my anxiety levels are under control because while the problem is more complicated, the stakes higher, the experience is even more exhilarating. I thrive on this level of intensity.

"Ok, see what you can do, but refrain from any shooting except if your life is in danger," he warns me.

My attention shifts from the Captain to my assailant and would-be child killer. "Madam, Miss," I scream out. We hear crying, clearly the sounds of terrified children.

"Charles," I call out to the man behind the door. "Listen, we don't want anyone to get hurt. Send out the children," my voice is relaxed and clear.

The crying gets louder. "Shut up," he screams at the small voices. "Shut up," his anger continues. Then we hear what sounds like a woman's weeping voice.

"I got a gun and I'll kill her," he belligerently yells out to us.

I call back the Captain, "Yes, I think we have a hostage situation."

"I'll be there in minutes and we'll call for the hostage team," our leader informs me.

I go back to our suspect. "Charles, listen to me. You're in big trouble but it can be fixed," I tell the skittish invisible man.

"I killed a police man. I'm dead," his voice fills with anguish although not regret.

"No, no, Charles. You didn't kill anyone. You shot a cop but he's in the hospital. He's quite alive. No, no, we can fix things. Listen," I pause for a sound of recognition.

Teary voices can be heard; small children are inconsolably wailing and crying. It's a piercing, unrelenting sound that would drive anyone nuts.

"Charles, the children are probably frightened and hungry," I say checking my watch, the wee hours fading into the brightening sunlight -- that element of surprise somehow eluding us despite our stealth.

"I know their crying is driving you nuts, send them out to me. I'll get them some food. Does one of them need their diaper changed?" I don't know their ages.

"You cops are going to kill me," he responds as his despondency and fear increase.

"Charles, remember what I said. Nothing is bad yet. We can fix things. Is the door locked?" A uniform goes to touch the doorknob, but I grab his hand.

Whispering I say, "Be careful. He could shoot you through the door."

"Charles, open the door. We won't charge inside. Open the door and step away, back inside the room. Let the children walk out."

"No, you'll shoot me if I go to the door," he answers in defiance.

"No Charles, we're putting our guns away," I say.

Two of the uniforms start to put their guns back inside their holsters but Jimmy smacks one on the wrist. "No, no," he tells our guys. "That's the message for the fool inside. You be prepared," he reprimands the men.

"Charles send your girlfriend to the door, let her open it. Then let the children leave."

"No, you come in and get them," he screams.

A woman's voice shrieks, "Help me, help us."

A loud crack is heard, quickly followed by a yelp as if a puppy was being hit. Sobbing turns to inarticulate cries of anguish.

I'm losing patience and the hostage team is not to be found. Sighing deeply, I continue. "Charles, let her open the door. Then she can step back, and I'll come in and collect the children."

"You leave your gun outside," he demands.

Jimmy whispers, "You crazy, you're going inside to get the children?"

"Don't worry he won't shoot me," my confidence rolls off my lips and my 'kick ass' smile shines across my face.

"Yeah, you're so sure," Jimmy answers while my fellow officers simply stare at me. Among our little group is a motorcycle cop wearing his official garb of helmet, high boots and thick gloves. For some reason Roberta has him on her 'go to' list for emergencies.

"You got a death wish?" Jimmy mockingly asks.

"Hey, isn't this why we love the job? The action," I snap my fingers and Jimmy reverts to a boxer stance jabbing at my chest.

"Charles, come on, send someone to open the door," we hear feet scuffling and some grunts. The children are eerily quiet.

Then it happens, the door latch is released. I signal to the uniforms to step aside bracing themselves against the walls, invisible to the suspect, pistols ready, adrenaline high. This is why I joined the department - to experience this surge of energy shooting through every vein of my body, all my oxygen filling the vessels and producing such a high. Jimmy tugs at the motorcycle cop's helmet and gloves and the man quickly removes them.

"Put these on," he insists. Some extra padding that may

be useful depending upon what kind of bullets Charles has in the chamber of his gun. I obey; there's no harm in minimizing risk.

I bend my knees, squatting, my elbows resting on my thighs as I slowly push on the front door of the apartment. I make myself a smaller target. In this seemingly uncomfortable position, I enter the room. The children laugh at my acrobatic stance and funny attire. Charles is distracted by my appearance and their sudden laughter. Beckoning to a toddler and a boy of about three or four, they quickly respond and run towards me. I step backwards towards the safety of the hallway. There are moments in my police work that I am ever thankful that my mother sent me to ballet school in Petersburg. My limited ballet talents find use in the strangest places.

The motorcycle cop gathers up the children in his big muscular arms, grabbing their confused little bodies, pushing them to safety against the hallway wall. Jimmy hauls me out of firing range by seizing the back of my shirt and pulling me into the corridor. I fall on my ass.

Meanwhile, the door is still open, the gunman distracted. I turn over onto my stomach, and crawl towards the open doorway, hand on the pistol wrapped around my ankle. If I can wing him in the shoulder, this crisis will be over. Just as I twist myself into position, a clear shot possible, the wind hits me in the face, stirring up the dirt and dust on the floor as the door loudly slams shut.

"Ah, ah," I groan in disgust. "If I was only faster we might have put an end to this situation."

"Hey," someone announces in relief. "We got the kids. I doubted that would happen so easily."

I'm about to call the Captain when I see his large physical presence in the hallway.

Getting to my feet, I approach him. He slaps me on the shoulder. "Good work, at least we got the kids. Now we have the hostage team arriving in minutes and, unfortunately, the press knows."

"I've got an idea. When I was in the room, I caught a glance at that front window. Let me see if I can find the right angle with my gun scope across the courtyard." I don't stop for an answer, running down the steps, Jimmy following me.

"Where are you going?" he stammers as he runs to catch up with me, inches from my feet.

"To the car," I reply as I jump down the steps. "Company?" I sarcastically ask our uniforms at the elevators. They smirk as we both see a few unfamiliar faces. The hostage team has arrived to save the day.

Roberta has the television cameras and reporters on the sidewalk, not too close to the housing project building. She has ordered up a dozen more uniforms to patrol the periphery to keep the press out of danger and from interfering with our operation.

I run to our car and open the trunk. There is my most beautiful rifle, resting silently, waiting to be tested, to demonstrate its power and strength. This is the one designed to kill from a football field distance.

Roberta comes to my side. "What's your plan?" she asks while she watches me carefully take the rifle from its concealed position. "The Captain told me to do nothing but keep the courtyard free of people, pets and by-standers," she adds.

"I have the perfect plan," I answer as I raise the gun to my chest. I kiss it; gently rub the cold metal against my cheek.

She smiles in appreciation. "Yeah?"

"I'm going to the roof, across from the apartment," I point to a nearby building. "I want to know if I can really see inside that apartment. I think I can locate the exact window.

The three of us look at the apartment building where the hostage is waiting to be rescued. We have a mission to complete – serve and protect.

Roberta, one of the true brains in the station house says, "I called for some nifty equipment from a sergeant I know. I think we can get a small camera attached to a retractable pole to the edge of the windowsill. I've got a guy right under the window, on the fire escape. See him?" As the sun is rising, we notice a figure, standing, waiting for instructions.

"Good plan," I say and tap her gently on the shoulder.

"I'm going up there," she follows my finger as I point to the adjacent roof.

"Me too," Jimmy follows me as we both race across the courtyard towards an entrance. With my heavy gun cradled in my arms, we still manage to move silently and quickly.

Meantime, I see from the corner of my eye that Roberta is directing more reinforcements towards the other building to prevent any foot traffic.

"To the roof," I tell Jimmy and we move like graceful cheetahs tracking our prey, nimbly sprinting towards the highest point in the complex. We don't use the elevators, too slow and urine soaked. Instead, we choose the claustrophobic stairwells, the industrial colored paint peeling, the tiles permanently stained with dirt, caked crud, old blood blots and yesterday's garbage.

On the roof, I gesture for Jimmy to get on all fours so we're invisible to any stray eyes. Like wild cats defending their hard-earned meal, I protectively tow the rifle under my armpit across the asphalt roof to the edge. Glancing over the top, I quickly determine the location of the window, the cop under the window as my guide.

"There," I whisper to Jimmy pointing to the location of the cop, assailant, and his hostage.

Conveniently, there's a slight dip in the wall surrounding the roof; my gun sits perfectly in the spot. Carefully, I place the rifle on this slight ledge and peer through the scope, scanning the building's windows. With the gun's powerful magnification, I see the pole. Then I slowly lift the barrel towards the target. I see our man and the frightened woman. From this distance, I can see their animated arms and assume they are arguing.

"Perlov," the voice on the police radio calls to me.

"Yes," I don't recognize it, but it feels authoritative.

"It's Deputy Inspector Monroe. Where are you?"

"I'm on the roof across from the apartment," I tell him, my hands steady although my heart is wildly pumping blood to my brains and lungs. I can hear the thumping.

"What can you see?" the rest of his words cutting out; despite 9/11, these radios are second rate.

I answer, hoping that he hears me. "I see our guy and a woman. It looks," I stare into the scope, "like they are tied together. It's not handcuffs, a rope or some heavy string, too thin to be a belt."

His voice returns. "Does he have a gun?"

"Yes, he is pointing it at her and she is resisting him. They are tugging at each other." I blink to wet my eyes and continue to stare down the scope. "What do you see with the camera Sergeant Sullivan has placed under the window?" I ask.

Now the radio is working better. "It's as small as a dime. It looks like the one that a doctor sticks up your ass to do a colonoscopy. The magnification is so intense everything is fuzzy in the room," he adds in disgust at the new technology, obviously not field-tested.

"How's the hostage negotiating going?" I know the procedures.

"Like shit. You stand ready. The Deputy Commissioner asked me if we needed the SWAT guys, but I said I got the best marksman in the department right here."

"Yes sir," I answer with respect.

"Can you see clearly? Are the windows clean enough?" he nervously asks, his voice stumbling over the words.

"Looks like the Housing Authority's maintenance team has been doing an exemplary job. Crystal clean," I answer.

The voice goes silent. I let the instrument of death go slack, my finger off the trigger. Jimmy hands me a stick of gum. It's cinnamon, my favorite. I breathe in the fragrance before unfolding the silvery covering and place it gingerly on my tongue. Dependable Jimmy, he knows my habits.

"Let me go down and find out what's going on. I'll call you," my former partner tells me, not one to enjoy just sitting. He takes his cell phone out of his pocket, ready to contact me. I take mine out and place it on the asphalt roof floor. "Keep it," he leaves the entire packet of gum.

I sit alone but alert and ready for a call. Bracing my back against the wall that protects people from accidentally falling off the roof, I wait for my orders. This is the life of a sniper, perching on roofs, lying on grassy knolls looking up through an opening in the bushes, hiding in trees, waiting for the precise moment to make a kill. It requires skills beyond those of a mere marksman; the sniper is a patient, trained killer.

Mr. Yushko, a jeweler I met on a case, was a sniper. A 'zaichata' during the Great Patriotic War, as we Russians call World War II. Mr. Yushko was a disciple of the great Vasily Alexandrovich Zaitsev, who was a celebrated marksman, killing Nazis by the hundreds. Yushko was there during the great Battle of Stalingrad and it was my grandfather who gave him that opportunity, to sacrifice everything for the Motherland. Although as a Jew, Yushko was preparing to forfeit all to keep the Nazis from exterminating all his countrymen. If the battle had gone the other way and the Soviet Army defeated, there would be no Jews in Europe.

"Rrrr...rrr," my cell phone rings. Some people attach music to their cell phone's rings, but not me. I prefer a jarring sound; there's nothing soothing about being summoned to my job.

I glance at the number, "Jimmy, what's happening?"

"It's not going well. They called the guy's mother, put her on some kind of speaker phone and she started screaming at him for being a no-good son-of-a-bitch, he deserved to die," he reports, and I can picture his nodding head.

He continues. "Meanwhile, the asshole insists that he

killed Murphy. The PR lackey called the TV stations and had them create a special message that Murphy was not dead, but the guy refused to turn on the tube." My former partner is still my most trustworthy and reliable source.

"You got your eyeball on the scope all this time?" he asks.

"I take breaks but then get ready. My cheek is pressed against the barrel of the rifle and every few seconds I take a glance to check out the scene. I might see something before anyone can call me." A good sniper is prepared for the inevitable.

"They managed to get audio. Got some kind of thing – looks like a suction cup that actually amplifies the voices in the other room, cool. That Roberta has contacts in the techie world. The camera sucks but the voices are pretty clear, so they know what he's saying. You got a clean view of him," my inquisitive Jimmy needs to know.

"Usually, because while he's tied to her, the rope or string is loose so there's give. He's not holding the gun to her head every second." I blink once and set my eye to the scope to review the scene, don't want to be giving out false or misleading information.

"At this very minute he looks agitated. The gun hand is up in the air. His mouth is open wide, probably he's yelling. This woman never stops screaming; her mouth never closes. I would be tempted to kill her just to shut her up." She's a skinny thing, wearing tight jeans and a long sleeve thin sweater.

"I'll get back to you," Jimmy says as his voice fades and then disappears.

If it takes all day and all night, I am here, ready and willing. Although my hobbies never include activities requiring lots of patience such as chess or mathematical puzzles, which my father loves, I do have some ingrained ability to sit completely immobile and concentrate. I could consider becoming a Buddhist monk. But I do not require any props to focus, no bells or repeating some mantra. I can just focus, drawing every muscle to a state of absolute calmness. At first my heart rushes like a speeding car on a racetrack, but then a serenity settles in and my pulse becomes steadier. I patiently wait.

Glancing at my watch, I notice that it's almost lunchtime. The sun controls the skies and it's directly above me, warming my body, the heat rising from the black colored rooftop. If it were August at noontime, your feet would sink into the melting, black sticky goo, the tar clinging to your heels. But lucky for me, it's a cool September day with the ocean breezes floating through the canyons of this housing project; the temperature thankfully is not a problem.

I replace the hardened gob of chewing gum in my mouth with a fresh flexible stick. That immediate sensation of the new gum is refreshing, lubricating all the dry crevices of my mouth. Closing my eyes for less than a moment, I chew slowly.

"Perlov," I hear the commanding voice on my police radio.

"Yes sir," I immediately reply.

"The situation is deteriorating. What do you see? Does it look like he is threatening to kill her?"

I look. "He is dancing around the room, dragging the woman. She never closes her mouth." It's amazing what I can see so clearly from so far way.

"Stand ready. If you think he is going to kill her then you have my permission to shoot him."

"Yes sir," I repeat his message. "I now have your permission to shoot to kill," I reply.

"Yes. But can you shoot to wound?" The commander asks with a lingering hope that death is not the predetermined outcome.

"No. I have only one opportunity. If I wound him and he can fire his gun and harms her, what have I gained?" We are taught only to shoot to kill. One shot is what we assume.

"Okay," he utters the word slowly and painfully.

"I am ready," I answer.

Placing my eye securely on the scope, I take a moment. "Hashem, forgive me for what I am about to do. I only do this to save an innocent life."

My eye blinks, my finger rests on the trigger. I see him and her. I wait for the precise moment when I can clearly shoot to kill. The seconds turn to minutes. There he is. His arm is around her neck, pressing against her throat as if in a wrestling hold but the gun is pointed slightly away.

I hold my breath, squeeze the trigger, and release. This new weaponry is so advanced that the gun has no kick. Immediately, I look at my handy work. The man's body rocks forward by the bullet's impact and the woman is out of sight.

Then through the scope, I see uniforms bursting into the room, the apartment door knocked off its hinges.

"Great work Perlov," I hear the Deputy Inspector's voice on the radio.

"Is she alright?" I confidently inquire, sure of my perfect handiwork but nonetheless wanting to have official word about my success.

"The woman has a great pair of lungs. She's still screaming but she's unhurt. You saved her life," my superior answers with relief.

I smile to myself as I disengage the firing mechanism. I hear his footsteps.

"Sasha, Sasha, you did good," Jimmy gently jabs me first with his right hand and then his left. His fists merely skim the surface of the cloth of my jacket.

I offer him a stick of his own gum.

"What you did is very cool. Death at a distance. But I always loved beating the shit out of suspects. Professional boxing is ritualized and regulated, it's not the same thing," he answers.

Jimmy likes it best when it's up front and personal. We both enjoy those next minutes sitting next to each other. I don't hesitate to share. My sounding board is sitting by my side. "I've got a most fascinating case. Very hush, hush, this terrorism thing is crazy."

"Yeah, what kind of case," his interest is piqued.

I shouldn't share too much but I can't resist. I put my finger to my lips. "They picked up a foreigner, a woman from the Middle East with a gang of illegals from south of the border." I add. "Shhh...So the big issue, is she a terrorist? What the hell is she doing in the USA with a bunch of gangbangers?" I shake my head up and down.

He looks up at the brilliant sky. "A woman, really, is she attractive?"

I poke him. "Attractive, of course that's the first question you would ask. I don't know, I haven't met her yet," I answer.

"Okay. We've got gangbangers and a Middle Eastern woman, crazy. You said it. You think they smuggled her into the country? And if so, why? Beginning of a new business model? Sounds like some sort of conspiracy. You love conspiracies. What's that Russian dark soul think? Yeah," he grunts out the last word.

"I'm thinking conspiracies. I got this feeling," I rub my stomach with my open palms.

"You go with those feelings. Your instincts are the best. Nine out of ten times your instincts are right." He nods his head. "When I first met you, you told me about these feelings. I thought 'what kind of sissy shit is that all about?' But I was wrong. Go with them," he pokes me a few times on the forearm.

We are so different but made such great partners, complementing each other's personalities. It was boxing that brought us together, our mutual love for the sport.

"If you ever need anything - support, another opinion - you know you can count on me," he elbows me.

Once I stand, I give him a big Russian bear hug. "You're going to win in Atlantic City. I know it," I touch my fist against my heart.

"Yes," he answers with self-assurance. "Then it's Las Vegas. Your pal Vasily has got me doubled with that Russian heavyweight. The Polish Shaygetz and the Russian Bear."

Life is so strange. My Jimmy's career is under the control of my oldest friend Vasily. Boxing and gangsters is just the way it is; Jimmy doesn't care.

"I'll buy you a drink," I check my watch. "I guess it's too early. How about a cup of coffee and lunch," I ask as we bump each other in a playful, silly gesture, adolescent boys in men's clothing.

"I've got to get to the Jersey shore but sure, a cup of coffee," we walk down the staircase.

CHAPTER 9

It pains me to watch Jimmy leave. It's as if the air was forcibly sucked out of my lungs. The hours together were just like old times. He told me to stay with my instincts; I trust him, he knows what it takes to be a good cop. My eyes follow him as he enters his car and we wave as he drives to Jersey.

I need a partner on this case, someone who understands these gangbangers. I'll call my new Captain and arrange for Lewis to assist me. He's alone spending too much time in the hospital. Cops need partners and to keep busy.

My conversation with the Captain lasts only a few minutes. He agrees. Lewis should not be spending all his time in his partner's hospital room. He has skills needed in the streets.

Since my true love was taken from me, I've learned to hate hospitals; the constant din of dull, repetitive sounds, broken by the jingle jangle of jarring noises, bright, glaring, corrosive lights, probing fingers and ill-fitting uniforms of all colors indicating hospital status. She wore the color white, a physician, a healer with her strong hands and searing eyes. She sought knowledge, always concerned about the welfare of her diverse patients in a large Brooklyn hospital, even trying to help the crazy one who killed her.

Her still body dressed in white, on a bed of pure white, if not for the blood. The redness, its brightness several different shades of crimson. The blood covered the sheets and her uniform. And the stillness; I can never get that picture of perfect stillness out of my mind; no flickering eyes, twitching lips, chattering teeth; absolute nothingness, life shut down completely.

The disturbing images follow me. Where do I find my solace, my escape from the numbness of her death, but at the door of an immutable force, never tiring, forever constant – the sea? While the gulls sleep, the pounding surf remains as a reassuring, continuous sound. As the first glimpse of light beckons the opening of the day, the dawn, the eternal beginning, the silence is broken by squeals from the birds fighting over a few crumbs remaining on the sand. The surf speaks through the wet irregular trail it leaves behind. The tiny birds arrive, the sandpipers, following the crooked path, quickly eating the miniscule bacteria left in the path of the returning waves.

I think these thoughts as I arrive. Murphy is a patient in her hospital, a major trauma center, so the driveway is filled with ambulances, fire rescue vans, police cars. A security guard directs me to a special official parking lot. From the moment of your arrival, you feel the urgency and chaos of the place. Noises

– angry, grating, strident noises strike at you; headache-producing sounds surround you as you enter the busy lobby. I know where to go, but I read the signs painted in a flashy, neon shade against the plain, bland colored wall.

The doors open, I enter the packed elevator, riding to the tenth floor; inaudible names are heard through the inferior public-address system. Is it any wonder that doctors don't immediately respond to an event? How can they hear their name being called?

Arriving on the ICU floor, I don't want to disturb the nurses studying charts, peering at computer screens, chatting among themselves. I just wander down the wide hallways and listen as my leather-heeled shoes chafe against the recently polished linoleum floor.

Murphy's name appears on a piece of cardstock inserted into a small metal plate next to the door. The paper will be tossed when the next patient occupies the room. This is the ICU, so he doesn't have to share the room.

I hesitate before knocking. A tall woman, her ebony skin a brilliant contrast to her light green uniform, steps in front of me.

"Yes?" she demandingly asks.

"I'm here to see Detective Murphy. I'm from his precinct," I defensibly say, the sight of the uniform making me self-conscious.

She looks me directly in the eyes. "I know you?"

I study her, a statuesque woman, taller than me; her coffee complexion dazzles in the dull hospital lights. She doesn't look familiar, my face no doubt displaying a dumb expression.

"You're the police officer that saved those babies. I saw your picture on the TV. You did a great job. Those poor little children," she nods her head. "What's your name?" She requests in a soft but authoritative way.

"Detective Sasha Perlov," I say, my self-confidence returning.

"You're a good man Detective Sasha Perlov, a good man," she tells me.

I feel the heat rising as my face reddens. "Thank you," is the best that I can manage.

"I hear it in your accent. You're an immigrant. I'm from Jamaica. Eastern Europe?"

"Russia," my fading Slavic nationalism returns.

"That man you shot, a nasty man. No one, especially those poor children, will miss him," I feel her firm hand on my shoulder as she opens the door to Murphy's room.

"Do I need to wear protective clothing? You know those funny-looking uniforms, mask and bootees for the shoes," I point towards my toes.

"No," she laughs as she shakes her head. "No problem

with infection." She smiles, and laughs again, a warm, contagious sound. Another immigrant with a story, probably filled with sacrifice and hardship. Still smiling, she closes the door, protecting our privacy.

"Perlov," Lewis approaches with an outstretched hand.

We shake hands and he grabs me around the shoulders, pressing them together. I don't want to protest since this is clearly meant as a sign of camaraderie.

Mrs. Murphy breaks off our little cozy display, so she can tightly hug me. Her head slumps onto my shoulder; she is a tall woman her chin could easily rest on my shoulder.

"Claudine, it's great to see you," is my only response to soothe her worry and anxiety. I don't know too much about her except her name and that she is from the French side of the Caribbean island of St. Martens.

"You got that bastard," Lewis adds, slapping me on the back.

I look at poor Murphy; there's not a part of his body that isn't tied to tubes or medical devices. His head is barely visible, there's a hose in his nose, and wires are attached to the top of his head. He looks like a creature out of a science fiction story. I hesitantly move nearer, with so many objects sticking out of his body I don't want to disturb anything.

It must be difficult to sleep here at night. There is no moment of total quiet. The green lights flash on the display panel, the machines beep and snort out unintelligible noises. The bed squeaks. The glaring lights make it easy for the nurses to check your vital signs but hurt your aching eyes.

His hand moves, beckoning me to approach, which I slowly do. I gather his fingers into my hand, his response surprisingly strong as he squeezes. His wife reaches over his limp body and removes the suction piece in his mouth. I lean forward as he whispers, "Thank you," I faintly hear. I'm good at lip reading.

"We got him. He won't be harming any more cops or women or children," I confidently announce.

"The son-of-a-bitch found a vulnerable spot," Lewis excitedly explains. "Murphy was wearing the vest," he points to his chest. "The bullet got inside the vest," he raises his arm to demonstrate. "The bullet entered under the left armpit," he touches his own armpit. "Murphy got shot in the chest, but the bullet managed to avoid the important organs. He looks a lot worse than he's doing." Lewis warmly smiles at his supine partner.

I wanly smile at his discombobulated body. "It can always be worse," I offer.

"But the bad deed was punished thanks to you and your crackerjack eye," Lewis gushingly says, with a clown-face grin while Claudine touches the sleeve of my shirt with her hand, pawing me like an overeager puppy in gratitude.

"Nothing is done alone. It was a joint effort. We all got involved and a bad guy is gone. He won't be threatening the neighborhood." I want to talk about Jimmy helping but I don't mention his name. Lewis and Murphy are a great team; gazing at the helpless Murphy, it's possible their police partnership is at an end. I don't want to express any reservations about their future or share my own feelings about Jimmy's departure.

Claudine presses her head against my shoulder. "Sasha, you're the hero. You like West Indian women?" She jokingly asks with a small smirk. Everyone in the station house knows about my tastes— I follow the rules of kashrut at least publicly in my choice of women. I wear my *Yiddishkeit*, Jewishness, on my sleeve so no one must guess or gossip.

I play along. "If I did, I would come to you to ask for an introduction."

There is a gentle knock on the door. "Mr. Murphy needs his rest," the Jamaican nurse apologetically tells me.

"Yes," I look for a clear spot on Murphy's body, so I can display my good wishes for a speedy recovery. If he were *mishpocheh*, family, I would plant a wet kiss on the top of his head. Instead, I squeeze his swollen, dangling fingers. His body must be filled with fluids.

"Listen," my lips are close to Lewis's ear. "Can we talk? I need a favor."

"Of course, anything," he yanks my shoulder again. I'm

certain my muscles are bruised from all his friendliness.

"There's a cafeteria downstairs. Let's grab a cup of coffee," I suggest and kiss Claudine on the cheek. Leaving the beeping room, the machines bid me good-bye with a few groans and electronic moans.

"Be back soon," Lewis informs Murphy and smiles at Claudine as he closes the door.

We head towards the cafeteria on the lobby floor. Lewis is the lead dog on the trail for a table. Cops learn to look for inconspicuous corners away from the prying eyes of the public. Quiet is not necessary, libraries are too silent, but spots with good views are valuable. We find a table in the far reaches of this cavernous cafeteria with the humming artificial lights flickering above us.

"What do you want to eat?" I ask heading for the food station, leaving Lewis to mind our table.

"If they have a corn muffin and some butter. Cup of coffee," he answers in a hushed but audible voice.

It's an off-peak period with just a few customers examining what's left on the shelves -- none too appetizing to look at or smell but hopefully still edible. The coffee looks like sludge, not fit for anyone, even a cop on an all-night stakeout. I find the muffin and get myself a bagel with a crusty crust.

"Can you toast this?" The food service clerk indifferently takes my purchase to the circular, rotating toasting machine;

fascinating how it slowly moves, the radiant heat browning the bagel. I pour out hot steaming water into two cups, grabbing a tea bag and a powdered substance labeled hot chocolate. I doubt it has any real cocoa in it, but the packaging looks pretty. I take my bagel from the outstretched hand.

I quickly return and observe Lewis's distracted face staring into space, lost in another world, probably worried about Murphy, his partner of more than five years. "Hey, the coffee looked like shit so here's something else." I hand him the package of hot chocolate, muffin and a few packets of butter. The butter looks like the real stuff, turning mushy from the heat of my hot bagel.

"What's the story? How can I help you?" he bites into the muffin. "Good."

"It's Hector and his cousin Oscar?"

"Our Salvadoran drug dealer turned escapee. Sure, what's up?" he pauses between bites.

"It's all so strange," I begin and then my eye is sidetracked, a balloon is caught in the ceiling light fixture. In seconds it explodes. Lewis doesn't flinch at the sudden noise while we hear screams from the middle of the room, even a crying baby.

"You know I'm working for US Attorney Cohen," I'm telling a man who rarely forgets details.

Lewis sips his drink and nods his head. "Spying on the

spies for the NYPD."

"This group I'm working with is interested in the possibility that MS-13 gang members are working with terrorist groups to do who knows what. They picked up a Muslim woman living with some MS-13 in Riverhead, Long Island. I'm thinking could this woman be the one our friend was talking about?" I reply between sips.

"And you need me to be the translator, play the bi-lingual interrogator again?" he asks with a half-smile, part-smug smirk.

"Yes, the Captain is authorizing it, but I want you to agree." I wait for a sign.

He nods his head.

"I want to keep the feds away from Oscar until I know for certain if there's any relationship between him and my mystery woman." I don't mention the part about this woman being swept away, out of the land of the free and the brave to Belarus and my new assignment.

"You got a list of all those that were picked up in the raid. Any people talking about missing pals, the ones who got away? Anyone mention Oscar's name?"

"My understanding is that some of the guys are missing and no one claims to know anything about this secret woman," I report.

"The mystery woman and the Latin gangbanger—weird but life is full of bizarre situations. Why not this one?" he laughs.

If a relationship exists, can I learn something about her from Oscar before I go to question her? Could Oscar be the leverage I need to extract information from her? He could know her little habits, her pleasures, what she hates, food she loves to eat, music, dance, something that can give me an immediate insider's view of her, make it seem that I know her. Lovers' lips utter words of insight but also the potential for betrayal, pretense and falsehood. Could he think she betrayed him? Or better, could she think he abandoned her? So many possibilities are here, the gangster and the Muslim terrorist, a story for the tabloids, a TV movie of the week.

"Maybe her lover or just a messenger," Lewis says. "He didn't seem to me to be too bright, but who knows? Acting like an idiot could be part of his role." His nodding turns to head shaking as his interest grows from doing me a favor to solving a case.

"You're going to help me?" I ask, assuming I know the answer.

"Of course, I owe you, besides this has lots of angles."

"Great," I reach across the table and playfully smack his hand. "There's more. Tapes of the surveillance of the Riverhead house by immigration. I'm going to track them down and maybe Oscar's face appears."

"When do we start?" my eager partner asks with

renewed enthusiasm.

I have a few other stops to make. "How about I call you later?"

"Okay, we're partners on this case," he hits me on the arm for good measure.

CHAPTER 10

I have loose ends. I'm waiting to hear from someone in NYPD about the surveillance tapes. As I drive back to Brighton Beach, I shake my head to myself, thinking about this case. Oscar and his mystery woman -- perhaps the distance drew them together; both strangers, foreigners in an alien culture, afraid, lonely, ambivalent about their choices. Sadness, or regret, possibly it was the first recognition that she could not follow through with her dangerous assignment. She was weak, and he was stronger. She knew it was a mistake to volunteer to be a martyr for Allah.

The idea seemed preposterous. She spoke Arabic and German. He spoke Spanish and an uneven version of childish English. It was impossible for them to communicate. Oh, but love or sorrow or hunger for some emotional attachment made words unnecessary. They simply had to stare into each other's eyes with longing, their hands touching, maybe their lips; physical intimacy solved many of the problems of star-crossed lovers, at least temporarily.

My women clutter my brain. Zipora – I need to call her. We are not meant for each other but there's an attraction, we can both feel the vibes, the smoldering eroticism just under the prim and proper attire. A Hasidic woman and a NYPD detective

– oil and water but she is attractive, and I know the feelings are mutual.

But the image that drives me to total distraction belongs to her, my Russian widow. I try with such a weakness to erase her from my consciousness. Olga, my obsession, those blue eyes. I see them in the sea as I stare from my balcony on misty mornings. I secretly tape her appearances on the soap opera where she plays the Russian seductress, those blonde locks lightly touching her shoulder, the lips slightly apart. There's no pout, it's a firm mouth, a determined face, the struggling immigrant trying to make her place in this strange land. Ah, this New Jerusalem, welcoming but be wary because of the hostility just resting an inch below the surface, ready to rear its ugly head in the form of immigration bashing. We love immigrants, they reshape and revitalize our cities, but we hate them – their ambition, their children who take first place medals in competitions, their pushy ways, and their demands for a proper place in society.

The call comes suddenly, "Perlov?" An unfamiliar masculine voice asks.

"Yes," her face wants to linger, the haunting crystal-clear eyes, but forcibly I strike her image. I am listening to the voice on the phone; luckily, duty calls me away from her.

"Howie Stein, the police video guy. Are you the detective who I'm supposed to show those tapes from the Suffolk County police stake-out for the illegals?" The uncertainty causes his voice to quiver at the oddest point in the question, the double 'l' ringing.

My attention is on the caller, "Yes, Howie. Yes, I'm the one. What do you have?" I ask trying to decide whether I should view the tapes before I question Oscar. It could be hours of tapes resulting in nothing.

"I got many tapes," the 'm' and 'n' hang on his lips for emphasis.

"Well is there something I can view quickly because I have an important appointment later but there's a small window open right now," I add.

"Yeah, you can start with the raid that's maybe 60 minutes."

"Good, are you downtown?" I know there are dozens of police offices.

"Hell no, we're the cheap suits in the low rent district. You'll find me in Long Island City." He tells me precisely how to find him in the outer borough of Queens, in one of New York City's ever changing up and coming neighborhoods, this one formerly home to abandoned warehouses and junk car lots.

"I'll be there in less than thirty minutes," I reply, slipping the keys into the car's ignition.

"I'm not going anywhere. See you soon,"

His directions are excellent; I arrive earlier than expected. I find a place to park on the street, scanning the low-rise buildings surrounding the address: solid looking, working class and light industrial with a smattering of warehouses – some are brick, the industrial places more likely aluminum sided, largely windowless. How depressing. The hundred-year-old wood frame houses are well maintained; the paint looks fresh and the gutters hang in perfect order. Except for the thick shadows cast by the Citibank building, thirty stories high, this is a pedestrian level place. What's missing is retail –no coffee shops, grocery stores, can't find a bottle of wine or a pack of cigarettes. The main boulevards are wide enough for the biggest trucks to rumble down the neatly paved street, but where's a guy going to go to eat dinner?

The innocuous-looking police building could house anything. I show my badge. Cameras follow your every movement, sensors and signals precede your footsteps. I expect that the next improvement will be a machine that will identify me by the lenses of my eyes.

Howie Stein is a known entity in the building. I am escorted to the video room by a fellow officer. We do not speak. I have a job to do, while he is bored by his assignment.

We don't knock as we enter; Howie does not rate any formalities. There he sits, a much younger guy than his voice would suggest. He's not wearing a suit but a pair of khakis and an open collared shirt, no tie, worn sneakers and no shoelaces. This is the NYPD's version of a techie nerd.

"Hey," he doesn't offer a hand in friendship, but a rolling padded chair. "Sit," there's playfulness in his voice.

"Thanks," I easily slip into the seat.

"What should I view in my limited time?" I know the answer but maybe he decided on a different tape.

"Well, here's the thing," he scratches his bushy mane. "We got these tapes from Suffolk County PD and the quality varies so you need patience to look at them. Right now, we can start with the morning of the raid. By that time, they figured out that they may have something interesting and worthy of better equipment. However, someone involved in the raid is filming so it's quite cool – avant-garde verite," he nods his head in approval. He's a guy who enjoys his job.

"You're a film student when you're not here?" I figure he looks the part.

"I'm studying film editing at NYU," he immodestly replies, but without haughtiness. I may be sharing a moment with a future editor of a Sundance Film Festival entry.

"Why not a documentary maker or indie film director?" I teasingly ask.

He knows I'm just shitting with him. "I don't know if I can come up with a brilliant idea, but I can make images brilliantly merge together into a coherent story." His tone is more boastful.

I like this guy, another outsider at the NYPD. "What is your current project?"

"I'm working with a guy making a documentary about the Boardwalk," he tells me.

"Coney Island?" a place I know so well.

"Hell no, the Rockaways. You been out there?" he enthusiastically asks.

"In fact," I straighten up in my chair. "I live there." We toss very approving glances at each other, immediately admiring each other's tastes.

"Me too, in Belle Harbor,"

"Oh, you live in the best part of town. I live in the middle of the Peninsula,"

"You surf?" he eagerly asks because there's no better place to surf in the New York City area than the untamed, aggressive waves of the Rockaways.

"Not well, but I do," my trusty surfboard is in the garage of my house minutes from the surfing capital -- Beach 90th Street.

I am clearly leaner and wiry rather than big-chested and muscular like he is, but surfers come in many varieties.

"Any chance you were a lifeguard?" he skeptically asks; we are connecting.

"Yes sir, right near where I live, dangerous middle

section of the Rockaways with rip tides and hordes of stupid people who don't know how to swim deciding to jump into the water. I can't put a number on how many adults and kids I've saved from drowning," I confidently tell him.

"No shit," he reaches out to touch my arm. "Me too, but in Far Rockaway near the beat-up concession stands. Wow, I got to admit you don't look much like an ocean lifeguard. Kinda thin," he stares at my chest.

"I'm powerful," I close my fists and bend my arms like a silly circus strongman, puffing out my chest.

"You Russian? Jew?" he hesitantly asks.

"Yes sir," I smack his arm and gently pull out of my buttoned shirt the gold Star of David hanging around my neck. My accent forever gives me away as a foreigner.

"I'm a Jew, not many of us in the NYPD. You're the only Russian I met who was a cop; a couple of the computer guys but not a cop," he bobs his head up and down.

I smile he keeps nodding his head.

"Cool, *mishpocheh*," grinning as he says the Yiddish word for family.

"What should we watch? We do this together. Right?" I stretch my arm to grab the top of his chair, drawing him closer to me.

"Yes, I'm your guide," he pulls out a tape from a file drawer.

The tape is pushed into the appropriate slot and the screen lights up with images. Buttons are pressed, white and green lights flash and then a pretty clear picture emerges on the large screen. "Whoever is holding the camera is running so the images are shaky, but we got audio shot with a decent quality camera. We're picking up the voices of Suffolk County PD and immigration folks. The suits are immigration, the cops are all in uniform. The people running are the illegals. See," he touches the screen, "how they all run in every direction to avoid apprehension." He plays with some dials and the image becomes sharper.

"Have you reviewed this?" I want a crash course in its contents – time is my enemy.

"No, not really. I just quickly put it in to make sure that there's something here, not a blank tape or completely useless, totally fuzzy images," he flicks a few more dials. This is far more complex and elaborate than my DVD player.

I take my cell phone from my pocket. "Here is a picture of a guy I'm looking for. Do you think we can tell if he's among those fleeing?" I show him my photo of Oscar.

"Give me that," he takes the phone and produces a small cable from somewhere that leads to a computer. In moments, my phone picture appears on a nearby screen.

"Great," I respond with delight and surprise. This is a perfect set-up, Oscar's face on one screen and the running video on another.

"As you can tell," he touches the video screen, "most of those fleeing are wearing hoods and long sweat pants. What we are seeing are people's backs so it's difficult to capture a face, but two sets of eyes are better than one. You've got to concentrate," he informs me We exchange glances. I am his willing student.

"If there's anything you see that you want a close-up, that's fine. The camera that took this was OK, but my video reader is exceptional. I can get in real close if there's something that catches your eye. Even an exposed hand if there are gang tags, we can lock-in a view," From another drawer he pulls out two candy bars, offering me the larger one. He has manners, a guy who knows how to share.

At the sight of the snack my stomach begins to rumble. I'm hungry; it's past my dinnertime. "Thanks," and we begin our staring contest. Who can find something valuable?

He is extremely patient, studying each image, his eyes hardly blinking.

"I'm also looking for a woman," I inform him, my mystery challenge. "Do you remember seeing a female figure?"

"Like I said, this is my first time looking at this tape in its entirety," he chews very quietly. Women must appreciate his polished manners.

This is boring, but I try to pay attention. Howie is my role model. Minutes become more minutes; I am tempted to glimpse at my watch.

Then the magic break happens. "Wait, wait," he screams in excitement and he touches a bunch of dials. "Look," he points to the screen.

There she is. No doubt a woman's figure. My initial reaction is, "Wow. Yes, it's a woman with a head-scarf, but not the full-length burqa I was told she was wearing. You know those complete body covering outfits Muslim women wear," I quickly say.

"Maybe they found it in the house. I imagine it would be pretty hard to flee wearing something so long," he suggests.

Before I can request it, I see the figure become magnified and we are staring into the eyes of my mystery woman. "That must be her," I answer.

For several seconds our eyes are glued to the screen. "Is there a way for me to capture that image," I ask in ignorance.

"Sure, sure," he responds with the eagerness of a Boy Scout earning his most accomplished merit badge. His hands dance across a computer board, the buttons and dials answering with whistles and flashes of brilliant light. "Look," as she appears on the computer screen.

"Nice, nice," I touch the screen as if some magical information, Ponce de Leon's secret of agelessness, will be passed to me through osmosis; eternal truths find their way through my skin, flowing from my nerve endings to my brain. A flash of sparkling light will solve the mystery.

"I can make an actual print of this face," he glances at me for approval. "But the best image will be seen on a computer screen. I can send you this image through an e-mail. What's your address?" I give him one. I have a handy laptop for this job.

"This is fabulous," I am more satisfied than I ever expected when I sat down. We both quietly sit and chew the remainder of our candy bars.

Our eyes return to the running video. "There's someone next to my lady," I observe.

He stares at the woman and in a matter of minutes we focus on this one image. There is a short person wearing a hooded sweatshirt close to her.

"Do you think we can get a better view of this guy," I touch the screen, my fingertips leaving a residue and my DNA identity. "Maybe he's my subject of interest, Oscar." I am hoping against the odds that it's him, but at least I have a picture of the woman to show Oscar later.

He moves the dials and the image changes directions, gets smaller, then larger. Several more views are attempted, but the result is the same – a clear view of a face does not appear.

"It's pretty blocked. I can't even retrieve a proper view of the person's hands to look for gang tags. Nothing," he shakes his head in disappointment. "Every angle is too shadowed. All we've got is a sweatshirt, the hood closed tightly. I think he's wearing a cap under the hood." He tries once more; a persistent man is one that I admire. "I can't see what he's wearing on his feet," he replies. "Sneakers are clues, but the camera is not pointed in the right direction. This cameraman was an amateur, too many wild angles and not enough focus."

"Anything distinguishable about the sweatshirt?" I ask in frustration.

The computer reworks the views once again and then the magnification begins. "Look," he points not wanting to touch the screen and perhaps dim future views with fingertips, a lesson for me to learn.

I stare at the screen, squinting, my nose practically touching the screen. "What's that?" I ask.

"Russell Athletic that's what it says," he responds with confidence. We have identified the brand of the sweatshirt.

"Very ordinary, at least a million sold last month," my voice registers my unhappiness.

"Yeah," he says, "but you have an article of clothing to use for identification. My advice is to find this sweatshirt."

He's right. "Yeah, when I see him, I'll look for the sweatshirt." I glance at my watch.

"My friend, thanks, thanks a lot," I tell him with genuine

appreciation for his attention to my cause.

"Just doing my job," he answers. It's a tag line that I use. We have yet more in common. I reluctantly rise from my chair; I like this guy – Jewish surfer and former lifeguard.

"Wait before you go, I want to show you something else." He gets off his chair, returning with a box of tapes.

I look at what could be a pile of junk.

"Stay just a moment. I'm not sure what these are and if they're not part of your case or any case, I'll toss them. We've got people just dumping things here all the time. If you don't want them, give me the OK and they'll go in the garbage. You'll be doing me a favor."

I owe him a favor. "Okay," I can be a little late. Oscar isn't going anywhere.

Randomly, he selects a tape from the cardboard container and inserts it into the machine. I watch his hands as they expertly retrieve an image with sound.

We both stare. The voices are sharper than the pictures. It's from the inside of a police van and the people are laughing.

I sit down. "Hell, I know that face," it's the young woman from the demonstration.

Howie takes a seat. "What's going on?" he goes silent as we both attentively listen.

There are a half a dozen bodies inside the van. No one is shackled or in handcuffs. Clearly, they are enjoying themselves, laughing and cackling like chickens. Then we both see the badges.

"Shit, they're police, undercover cops," I am devastated, sinking into my seat.

"Yeah, you're right. Undercover cops on a sting, drug bust," he answers.

"Shit no. I arrested that woman at the recent anti-war demonstration," pointing to the one with acne.

"Cops pretending to be demonstrators?" he asks.

I intently look at him. "Crap, you're right. I remember that they separated some of the demonstrators."

"The real ones go in one van and get formally charged, while this other group of spies is released," he answers with a laugh.

It's so clear. "Shh...it. That's exactly right. We didn't know. We," and I point to myself. "We cops at the demonstration were in the dark about this undercover operation."

"That's why it's undercover," he replies without any emotion. "Instead of narcotics or vice they're on political duty," he chuckles, no outrage is on his lips.

"Not right," I shake my head. "Not right. Those were just ordinary citizens protesting," I reply with a heavy heart.

"Nothing is right since 9/11. It's an insane world and the cops have become as paranoid as the federal government. It's the mayor and the police commissioner. It's just an overreaction, insane," he calmly says.

"This woman," I point to the one I arrested, refraining from touching the screen, preventing my perspiration from fogging it up. "Can you get a sharper image?"

"Sure," and he does. "Good now?"

"Very good," I reply and we both stare. The tape continues to roll.

"Listen," I say, both of us quiet.

"Jackie," a voice says. The others on the tap wait for her to speak.

"Stop it," I scream, and Howie stops the tape.

"Jackie, her name is Jackie." I tell my guy who nods his head in agreement. "How can I find her? I must talk to this woman, find out what's going on. The NYPD is sending its own to act as spies."

"Can you read her badge number?" I ask in a hopeful voice.

He turns the tape on and moves the video forward then backwards, magnifying the image. "I don't know," he says.

I glance at my watch. It's getting late. He reads my need to leave.

"You can't get rid of those tapes," I insist.

"Hell no, this could be part of a civil lawsuit. I'll continue viewing it. This is fun," he is amused. "But how many female officers named Jackie work for the department? I've got a friend. If I give him the name Jackie, he'll be able to find her once I describe her. This is really cool," he whistles.

I appreciate his enthusiasm, although I am sickened. These are the shenanigans of police in the Motherland, not the New Jerusalem. "I'll be back," I gently slap him on the top of his shoulders.

"I'll be here," he continues to study the tape. "Could be lots of interesting things recorded on the other tapes," returning his attention to the box. I am pissed, but Oscar waits for me.

CHAPTER 11

Oscar is still at the tire store and not at a safe house. The NYPD bosses have not decided about hiding Oscar, but the tire store looks like it's under arrest; the police presence is heavy with alert, uniformed officers patrolling the perimeter on foot. The two guys selected for duty could be actors from an action-packed movie; the heavies, broad brawn with flexing muscles bulging from their police-issued uniforms. There's an additional squad car out front, with its officers probably personally assigned to watch over the store owner and his cousin. I don't immediately see Lewis, but I notice his car on the street. It's hidden; squeezed between two junky neighborhood vehicles; his is a flashy type, brilliant neon red, huge engine with a roaring sound, and a muffler that is deliberately kept loud and noisy.

I look like a cop in my Sears suit and sensible shoes; I wear my badge on my belt, showing it to the officers. They don't even crack the smallest smile, but the taller one's head turns ever so slightly, giving me permission to continue inside.

Lewis knows one of the guys inside; they are amicably chatting, the two under police protective custody invisible.

I wave my hand and Lewis acknowledges me with a head turn.

"Hey," is all I can think of to say as I approach.

"This is Perlov the Protector," Lewis introduces me to the high-ranking uniformed officer.

We shake hands and he gives me a big smile. "We know your reputation Perlov, protecting your people and everyone else. Your defensive shield covers little kids being held hostage by lunatic cop shooters. Good work," he slaps me on the shoulder.

A blush of embarrassment rising to cover my cheeks, "Thanks, I've got a soft spot for screaming kids, and I hate guys who would even think about capping a cop," we all nod our heads in agreement.

"We are babysitting some possibly high-level informant." He asks, "should I be expecting the FBI?"

Lewis grimaces. "I don't know how much this piece of shit is worth."

The other officer chimes in, "You both realize that a tire shop in the middle of a residential area is not an ideal location to be holding an important witness or informant. Too many people, too many kids. Somebody needs to make the big decision and we'll move him."

Lewis answers. "Tonight, we either cut him loose to face the consequences of his bad choices or we put him in witness protection."

"Okay, let's go talk to our guy," I suggest.

"Hi," I say. Hector's face immediately lights up with a big grin, highlighting his wide, flattened cheekbones, a Central American of Indian extraction. Oscar is more cautious; he doesn't know me well although I'm the cop offering him the possibility of redemption. He is being given the opportunity to publicly confess his sins, promise to make amends, and in return, he is being provided the keys to a new life.

Lewis simply barrels into the room and though he's not a physically massive man, he commands attention; the wide strides of his step, the unsmiling, tight face, the swinging arms. He means what he says, and he expects you to listen.

Lewis looks directly into Hector's eyes. "You aren't really needed," he gestures with his index finger for our host to leave the room.

"No, no," he responds, at first thinking Lewis is joking. But he notices his elevated arm is not budging.

"Go," my new partner announces, directing with his finger towards the doorway. "Close the door on your way out." "Wait, wait." Hector doesn't rise from his chair, instead he moves his arms in many directions at the same moment in utter exasperation.

Lewis's tone of voice hardens, darkens, the harshness becoming more apparent. "Go," he repeats, again pointing in the direction of the door. "Now,".

Oscar gives his cousin a gentle elbow and they speak in

Spanish. If Lewis is listening, he remains nonchalantly unmoved by the discussion. Hector reluctantly leaves the side of his long lost relative, constantly turning back to watch the three of us at the table. Lewis sits immobile, waiting for Hector to disappear.

"Okay, let's talk reality," Lewis says in English and then he begins a loud discussion in Spanish. Something being spoken results in Oscar lowering his eyes, perhaps in embarrassment or shame. I observe the body language like a graduate student in a psychology behavioral experiment.

Finally, I get impatient. "What are you asking? What's the drama about?" I poke Lewis's arm.

"He's talking generalities. If we are going to get anyone to give this piece of shit protection, he must do a lot better. I need names, places, descriptions. Can we stop some of this bad shit from happening? So far, he is keeping too close to the vest. I demand facts," his fist slams the table. Oscar's shoulders rise just barely, his face showing no emotion, but I bet his heart is wildly beating.

"Here's what I need from him," I say, "I must know if he is somehow involved with that MS-13 immigration raid in Riverhead. Did he miraculously escape or is he a fed informant gone AWAL? And most importantly, does he know my mystery woman?"

Lewis's body leans back. "Right, the Riverhead connection, yes that's your thing. I've just been messing with his head."

"I've seen a tape of that raid, but I can't pick out Oscar. I really don't know if he was there at the time of the raid, or ever there. His links to human smuggling and drugs as a member of the MS-13 are not my main concern. That woman is my interest," I reply.

"No problem. I'll tell him we got his face on the tape from the raid in Riverhead and see his reaction. You want the names of those guys in that house?" Lewis is thinking on a new track.

"Yes, that's a start," I answer. "But the woman is the key. Who is she? What's his relationship to her? Yes, tell him I've got his face on tape."

Lewis grabs Oscar's forearms, holding them flat against the tabletop. The smaller man frowns but doesn't cry out in pain; that would be sissy stuff – a coward, not macho. Our Oscar's tattoos indicate he's some type of tough guy.

At first, they speak calmly, then with greater agitation; Oscar struggles to be released from Lewis's strong grip, but the cop holds tightly to the man's reddening arms. I say nothing. Gangbangers may need a little more persuasion, more loosening up than ordinary suspects. Lewis screams in his face and, still holding onto him, shouts in one ear at a deafeningly tone. Oscar is strong, but Lewis keeps the man pinned. Then the physical pressure gets more threatening as Lewis grabs Oscar's throat. The squeezing is aggressive but not life-ending.

The faces of both men are bright red. Lewis has done this a thousand times before and Oscar is no choir boy. When Lewis resumes shouting his words are sprinkled with spit, Oscar's face receiving a misty film. Lewis suddenly releases him, and his limp body falls against the chair. They resume with more civil speaking tone, Lewis firing questions and Oscar returning the missiles with short answers.

I hear Oscar say the universal word, "OK," then, "Si," followed by a list of names. One doesn't have to speak the language to recognize that the words are names.

Lewis reports, "He did live at that house."

"I hope he's not lying just to save his ass," I answer in skepticism.

"Well, we'll assume he's telling some half-truths, never the full picture." Suspects rarely reveal all. "He's afraid of somebody, really scared shitless, someone whose name he is not telling me yet. But he wants to live and bring his wife and children here. That's the carrot; bring the whole family to safety. We're dangling a real incentive for him to cooperate."

"I'll get a recorder, so we can tape this discussion. Let him describe some of these guys. Then after I can match them with what we can see on the tapes and who we have under arrest. The bigger news is not who's in jail but who's in the house that we don't have under lock and key besides him," I point at Oscar. We exchange glances; mine is not tight and stretched like Lewis's but friendly. I'm going to play Good Cop.

I'm up on my feet as the two men stare at each other, Lewis explaining that I'm getting a recorder.

"Well if nothing makes sense and we conclude he's giving us bogus stuff, then we cut him loose. He must figure that we're not total fools; if he doesn't deliver something meaningful, he's dead meat out there." When I return with the machine, the two men are exactly in the same position. I return to my seat. "How did he escape?" I ask.

They confer in Spanish. The tension is still present but there are no exaggerated gestures, no great modulations in the voices; a conversation like anyone might have with an acquaintance.

"He says in the confusion, cops everywhere, immigration suits, he was able to escape through a back door and disappear into the neighborhood. He stole a car and drove here," Lewis tells me.

It's all logical, although it could be complete lies. "How will we know if he's telling us the truth? I have an image from those tapes of a hooded man next to my mystery woman. We still need to know about her."

"Well, we start with the list of names. We can compare the guys in prison and their supposed names with what Oscar says right now. We've got fingerprints, DNA on those in custody.

Somebody is comparing these with the national database. It won't take too long to figure it out," Lewis says with absolute assurance. "Most of these guys have some criminal record either here or back home or both places. We'll know about the assholes he was with in the house. As for the woman, well, she's probably not in any database. You think he speaks Arabic?" Lewis laughs and glances at our gangbanger.

"It's the woman who I want information about. Does he know her? Were they lovers?" I pull out of my pocket the grainy photo I got from Howie Stein.

I push the photo in front of Oscar's eyes. Our informant's face doesn't register any emotion, his eyes don't blink. I ask him in English, "You know her? Lover? Girlfriend?" I shove the picture until it practically touches his nose. "Your woman?"

He is very quiet, his eyes filling up with the image of her face. He nods his head.

I jab Lewis's arm, "Ask him who she is? When did he first meet her?"

This time the discussion is fully animated with deep sighs and moans from Oscar. Lewis turns to me. "Shit, she's from the Middle East. He doesn't really know her. She was kept isolated in one room by herself. She just appeared one day," Lewis informs me.

"Were they lovers? She appeared one day out of the blue from where? Did she arrive by car or in a van? I need more information about her. Push him," I demand of Lewis.

Lewis moves into Oscar's personal space, hovering over his head, his finger pressing against the smaller man's chest. Then he takes a dramatic break, sits back several feet away, his voice much softer. He's laughing. Lewis moves again, forward towards Oscar, but his voice is a whisper and his smile grows larger. I see the beginning of a grin on Oscar's face.

Lewis turns his head towards me. "I'm praising Oscar's manhood and his prowess with the ladies," he winks at me.

If they are lovers, words are certainly not the glue that is responsible for bringing them together. I shake my head at both men. Oscar is blushing; Lewis must be getting details about their love life.

Lewis returns his attention to me. "No, not lovers. She wore clothing that covered her. He was told to treat her like a saint, no getting close. His job was to deliver her to a location. He was waiting for instructions," he reports.

"Who was to give him those instructions? This is someone of great interest to me. Could we be lucky and have this guy in custody? I need a good description." I ram my elbow at Lewis's arm.

Lewis must still be heaping praises on Oscar's way with the ladies because he's still smiling. Lewis turns to me, "He got calls."

I get up from my chair, "Phone, you have cell phone,"

and I place my cell phone to my ear. "Phone?"

He seems to understand and says, "No," then he says something in Spanish.

"In the raid, he lost his phone," Lewis repeats.

"How was this guy going to contact him? By phone? Phone he lost? We must go over everything the immigration guys found at the scene or in the yard. Do you believe him?" I ask as the evidence is frustratingly unavailable.

"No, if some big boss was calling me, I'd hide in a sewer if the feds raided the place," Lewis replies.

"Ask him did anyone ever come to the house to see her, anyone even a child. Details, I've got to have details," I demand.

Lewis nods his head and his voice volume rises. He gets a little more physical with Oscar, moving his chair closer, his hands on Oscar's shoulders, squeezing. I see Lewis's fingers kneading the informant's flesh.

Lewis announces to me, "No, no visitors. His orders came via the phone he lost in the raid." He pushes down hard on his shoulder blade.

"He is afraid of this man. The description could be any gangbanger. You need to get Oscar to a line-up and let's see if we have this man in custody. His responsibility was to get her special food and make sure no one got close."

"You believe him. There's a boss man? Could Oscar be the boss man?" I am skeptical.

"No, I don't think Oscar is that smart to be the boss." Lewis flashes a malevolent smile towards Oscar. "My guess is that Oscar is so afraid because he failed in his mission. The woman is in US government custody. He was responsible. There's going to be payback for this failure. He figures that they will come for him and kill him. He's now a liability."

"I need this guy. We find him and maybe we know more about this budding relationship between foreign terrorists and MS-13. If Oscar is really involved with that woman, he will be protected. No question. But is he shitting us to save his ass?"

Lewis and Oscar go back to another round of discussion, painful negotiations. Oscar's shoulders are probably red and sore. "He claims his orders came from phone calls. If your first concern was whether our Oscar was at that house in Riverhead? The way to check it out is simply to find out if any of the guys we have in custody knows Oscar. We take him to where immigration is holding the others."

"Okay," I smile at Oscar. "If they know him then he is very valuable to me. US Attorney Cohen will get him protection. It's no longer a NYPD problem."

"I'll make arrangements to get him to the immigration holding center. And I'll get Suffolk police to check all the nearby pay phones, as well as shops where disposable phones can be purchased. I doubt we'll ever find Oscar's phone."

"Oscar," I gently touch his shoulder. "We will protect

you."

I look at Lewis. "I just hope he is the one protecting her and not making shit up."

He reaches for my hand. "Thank you," Oscar says in English. "Thank you," then kisses my hand.

CHAPTER 12

I am more awake than asleep when I hear the unpleasant sounds.

"Perlov, it's time," an unknown voice tells me. "Cohen will give you more details but be ready to leave tonight. And be prepared to stay for an unknown period," the phone goes dead.

My adventure begins. Rising from my half-slumber I seek my redemption. It awaits me. Hashem has put me on a mission of mercy. Save the country, save the woman, save myself.

In a trance-like state of dreaminess and wakefulness, I stand on the balcony and look out. The coolness is refreshing. The foamy surf is hurtling forward towards the dark, hard sand in anticipation of the dawn. A thin sliver of light is just visible far beyond the Boardwalk into the slowly visible horizon. The colors start as an orangey-red, but in minutes they erupt into more brilliance with bright yellows, deeper shades of red and glowing orange.

See me, the sun declares; and the gulls welcome her blinding heat. Their necks lunging upwards towards the warmth; they noisily announce the morning.

"Tell me my purpose. Give me the plan. Show me the way," I scream to the gulls and the deserted beach. "I make my public confession like Yehudah. Saving her, I will save myself."

I hear a chorus of squawking gulls answer my declaration. In high-pitched voices, they offer their support; but also beg for nourishment. I respond by throwing out scraps of bread from my balcony. The feathers fly in all directions; I walk inside and close my door.

The rest is just routine as I prepare for my trip abroad; knowing what this mystery woman looks like gives me confidence. She is real, and this is a real mission.

Luckily, I don't have to be concerned with what to pack. It's so simple being an indifferent dresser, not like my Jimmy, the peacock, with expensive and refined tastes.

Amos is curious. He jumps on the bed and settles inside the open suitcase, sniffing it, checking old odors. He is seeking familiar smells. He gets my scent, but not his. He knows that I'm going away, but does this trip involve him? He's a good traveler, lays on the passenger seat of my car relaxed, sleeping, waiting for the destination's end. He is unfamiliar with air travel and this is certainly not going to be his inaugural trip. He is in good hands; my father loves having a second dog around the house.

I rummage through my top dresser drawer for my passport. After a few excited moments, I find it exactly where I left it, in a leather pouch. I touch it with intense gratification, my fingers gliding across the still smooth surface. I did earn this American identification, although not in a field of battle. My US Army service was between wars – Iraq I and bloody, dangerous

Iraq II, fortunate me. I volunteered against the advice and counsel of my parents. They thought me mad. As it turned out it was a foolish waste of time. However, I proved that stereotypes are often wrong. A Jew from Brighton Beach, Brooklyn, a Russian immigrant, I turned out to be a masterful marksman to the complete amazement of my military superiors. I was being prepped for the US Olympics if only I were willing to re-enlist. I said no, my Uncle Vanya the Cossack guiding that decision.

Besides, my superiors were whispering in the corners the word, "Kike." Unacceptable. No Army career for me.

It was time. I kissed the *mezuzah* on my side door. Who knows when I will return? I must leave Amos with my parents so off we go.

"Where are you going?" my father asks as he sits down with the two dogs at his feet.

"Away on business," I answer.

"Business, what kind of business?" my mother picks up on the conversation.

"Police business, I'm going for training," I try not to lie too much.

"Really?" my mother answers in English.

"You know I have this special assignment, terrorism training," I reply continuing my conversation in Russian.

"Really?" my father answers in English and scratches his own head in mild amusement.

"Really," I answer in English. "Really," repeating myself, emphasizing the double 'l' in the word.

"So where are you going for this terrorism training?" the discussion returning to Russian.

"I can't say, very hush, hush," I press my index finger against my lips.

Both my parents stare intently at my face, my mother placing her hands on her hips. "Please enough with the secrecy. Where are you going?" actually stomping her foot on the tile floor.

My father rests his elbows on the table and gives me a harsh look of disapproval. "We will worry," he says.

My mother lets the vegetables fry on the stove without her ardent attention and she sits next to me. "*Nu?*"

"Okay," I mumble, and they move close to me. I can smell what they ate for breakfast. "The food in the pan will burn," I remind her.

She just waves her hand. "*Nu?* Let's hear," she glues her heels to the floor waiting for my explanation.

"OK, the US government has picked up someone, who is of interest to them. They have asked me to fly where they are holding this person to speak with them." I answer as truthfully as I can.

"Speak with them? Where are they being held? Somewhere close? Cuba perhaps?" My suspicious mother, the prisoner of conscience, a former enemy of the state, immediately answers.

"No, they were picked up abroad," I lie.

"Abroad like Iraq or Afghanistan?" My father chimes in with a question.

"No," I don't quite know what to say and deeply regret having opened this Pandora's Box of half-truths, half-lies.

"You are doing something not kosher," she pounds her chest. "Not good, I can hear it in your voice. Something bad," she empathically says.

"No, I am being sent on a mission of mercy. We live in a dangerous world," I reply. On some level, I agree with my own statement and on another more visceral level, I know my mother is right.

"Torture, you will be involved with torture," she smacks me on the hand – so hard, it stings.

"No, no, no," I vigorously shake my head. "Nothing like that, I'm going to talk to her," I reply.

"Her? You mean it's a woman," my father asks, and our elbows touch on the tabletop.

"Women can be dangerous. You read about female suicide bombers, terrorists. I'm talking about terrorists, who may want to do us all harm in this country, dangerous people," I inform them.

"One person's terrorist is another one's freedom fighter,"

my father the methodic mathematician answers.

"Where are you going?" my mother demands to know, giving me an icy stare.

I can't resist her displays of such displeasure. "Belarus," I blurt out, the word tumbling out of my mouth. Say it quickly so she doesn't have time for it to sink into her brain.

"Did I hear you right? Belarus, the former Soviet republic, the one with the autocratic leader, the corrupt and undemocratic nation in Eastern Europe?" she quickly summarizes her opinion of the place.

I just nod my head.

"Rendition is what you're doing. Taking her to a place where you can torture her. If not you then someone else," she replies as someone who intricately follows news leaks about what happens to prisoners across the globe. She spits on the floor. "How dare you, my son," she turns her head away from me.

My father is the counselor, the mediator. "Wait, wait, Anna, he is going to avoid those things by talking to her. She will be able to reason with Sasha. Right?" he asks.

"Of course, I would never participate in any torture. No, I will not allow this woman to be harmed. I promise," I take her deformed hand, the one her torturers mangled, placing it against my chest. She can hear my beating heart, thump, thump; her son, part of her life, a good mama's boy, incapable of ever being able to withstand her disapproval. I cannot hurt this woman.

"Don't worry Anna, we know our boy. None of that parsing of words, no government rules about intentional infliction of death or organ failure. Our boy knows what is ethical, no stretching of the Geneva Convention's Article 3. Right," he adds with a declaration.

"Right, I will not harm this woman, nor will I allow anything bad to happen to her." I state with assurance and conviction, my hand stomping the table's surface.

"Belarus," my mother doesn't like the sound of the word; her face crinkles up into an unflattering knot of wrinkles at the pronunciation of the country's name.

"I didn't choose the location," I tell them.

"Where in the country are you going?" my father asks as he moves from politics to my travel plans.

"I'm not certain about exactly where. I'm going, that's all I know. I'm getting my final plans later today and then I'm off."

"And when will you be back?" my mother asks – she is softening, emotionally moving from disapproval to mere worry. She is a good worrier; it naturally flows from her pores as a Jewish mother.

"Don't know that either, most of the details I don't know and will probably not know until I actually arrive. As I said, very hush, hush," I make that same gesture again to their mild annoyance.

"How will we know that you arrived safety?" she pleadingly asks.

"I'll contact you either by phone or computer. Don't worry, I will be safe," I don't anticipate any real physical danger.

"I want you to do me a favor, a very important favor if you are actually going to Belarus," my mother calmly announces.

I listen carefully as her steely eyes rest on mine.

"I want you to visit my mother's first cousin. She lives in some tiny village in Belarus but not too far from Minsk. I'm certain somewhere along the way, you will be going to Minsk. I will get you the important information." She quickly leaves the table but stops long enough to shut off the heat on the frying pan.

"This is a great favor to your mother. We were just talking about how we must go visit the old woman. She must be past 90," my father tells me as he stands, emptying the contents of the frying pan into my plate and his. A few scraps are dropped on the floor for the dogs, who very gentlemanly devour the food without an argument between them.

I check to see if my mother has returned. "I will not be torturing anyone. You should know me well enough by now. I am your blood. I would never."

"I trust you, as does your mother. She gets a little

emotional. It's understandable. You know," he softly adds.

We look intensely at each other. He believes me. I take a bite and ask. "Will I remember the cousin?" then stop to chew. It's good; it's hard to ruin fresh vegetables.

"I doubt it but she's the last link to your mother's mother," he says, a moment of nostalgia lighting his face, eyes focusing on some unseen person. Gently he slaps my arm. "You're a good boy. No torture," he shakes a finger at me. His political views take a few minutes of rest while he eats.

"You can trust me on that." I again reassure my father and he grabs my wrist, squeezing so tightly I can feel it going numb; it hurts but I don't wince. I know he's making his views crystal clear to me.

"You're a good boy. It has not always been easy living with your mother. She's been fighting for the right things all her life," he's speaking to himself.

"Of course," I reply, and he releases his grip, he leans over and kisses the side of my head.

My mother returns with an expensive-looking piece of writing paper. On it are a neatly handwritten name and address, and a series of numbers I assume belong to a telephone number. She learned after her encounters with Soviet police how to write perfectly with her other hand.

I place the important paper in my leather documents pouch with my passport, driver's license and American Express substitute money. "Want us to take you to the airport?" my father inquires. He likes to make the trip, watching the silver bullets land and depart, their roaring engines disturbing all manner of animal and bird life. There's a special spot near Rockaway Boulevard where the planes come precariously close to the traffic, the wire fencing shakes in fear. Once the edge of a plane's landing gear almost touched the roof of a large truck, resulting in the vehicle toppling over onto the roadway. What a mess.

"Before all this foreign travel interfered, I was going to see Zipora." I nonchalantly tell my inquisitive parents. My mother is shopping for a wife for me. Since the death of my beloved Dr. Marina, she is accelerating her pace, asking all Russian Jewish women she meets if they know of an eligible girl for a young man with high potential, a law student. She ignores the part about the full-time job as a NYPD detective going to law school on the government's dime.

"Really," my father returns to the English language. They must have gotten stuck on this word. It wasn't part of their vocabulary yesterday.

"The pretty Hasid woman Zipora from Midwood?" my mother continues our discussion in the mother tongue.

"Yes," I respond; they have met her and her daughters.

"Is this serous?" my mother is starting to drill me on my love life. I can feel the pumping beginning.

"I don't know," that's my most honest answer since it's a strange relationship.

"A Hasid woman and you with your odd hours and inability to observe even the basic religious restrictions." She moves her chair very close to me, our knees are touching.

"Actually, she's become less observant and it has nothing to do with me. She's going to college and reading new things, her eyes are opening up to a whole new and exciting world," I tell them. It's her willingness to change that is quite amazing, revealing a flexibility I admire.

My father's head rocks as he listens. The mathematician, he doesn't believe in religion or God although he goes to shul every Saturday with my mother and eats kosher food. It's his compromise for the sake of the marriage. How can the husband of a Jewish dissident not embrace the religion?

"I bet she still expects a future husband to strictly observe the basics, praying three times a day, obeying the rituals of the Sabbath, going to shul every day and studying the Torah, no working on any of the holidays. Not even watching TV is acceptable on the Sabbath. And no driving. Yes?" she stares at me.

"We haven't gotten to those details. She likes me, thinks I'm an honorable man. I found the killer of her best friend's husband. She's attracted to me and I am to her," I defensively answer. I resent and adore my mother's pesky interference.

"Speaking of that widow, Jimmy isn't still going to visit her friend Yana, the dead jeweler's wife? The boxer, the Polish Shaygetz, Roman Catholic, former altar boy, finds love with a Hasidic woman from the Ukraine. Does life get any stranger?" my mother asks with a mischievous twinkle in her eye. She knows from personal experience the strangeness of love – my parents together all these years, simply remarkable.

"It's crazy but the answer is yes. Zipora tells me he comes over offering protection to Yana and to the whole extended family. You know that the two women still live together with all eight children in a big house in Midwood. It was originally Zipora's house, but after the murder Yana moved into Zipora's home. The two widows," we all laugh at Jimmy's blind love and loss of reason.

I conspicuously glance at my watch. It's time to leave. My mother quickly makes up a little *pekl,* so I shouldn't get hungry during the day.

"You have an instant family," my father remarks returning to Zipora. "The daughters seem like nice kids, but girls can be tough. They may take exception to another man taking their father's place." Zipora's husband was killed on 9/11 in the World Trade Center.

"It's been awhile, the little ones don't even remember him. Hasids believe that she should have remarried a year after her husband's death." I authoritatively add. Zipora tells me these facts – not to influence my decision about her but just as information, teaching me the traditions of her people.

"Are you serious about her?" now my mother is fascinated; should she stop hounding all the women she knows about eligible girls? She doesn't want to give false impressions.

"It's too soon. I'm not prepared for such a big change and I love what I do as a NYPD detective. I know how you neglect to tell people about my real profession," the annoyance finding its way into the conversation. I stop myself. I'm going away and don't want to leave on a sour note.

My father breaks into the conversation, first with his swinging arms. He wants peace. "Call before you take off," my father requests.

I kiss them both. Amos seems completely content in their house. I scratch him on the top of the head and he gives me a good-bye lick.

"Safe trip," my father says as they both walk me out to my waiting car. I watch my mother. She's thinking about Zipora that's why she isn't reminding me of my responsibility to uphold the family's good name – no torture.

CHAPTER 13

The sleek, black Town Car arrives; silently, it makes its way towards the international airport known to New Yorkers as simply JFK. The night air is misty and dreary, but not my spirits. Adventure is before me and the tension is good. I am alert, my eyes, ears and nose are focused on all the little details in the car. The smells of a former passenger, a smoker, permeates the leather seats; the carpeting is worn but still plush, while the speckled plastic divider separating me from my driver is scratched as if long nails had meant to leave a signature.

Sometimes the skies above Jamaica Bay are threatening, the clouds and fog so thick no planes can safely land or depart. The driver never speaks, so I just practice my powers of observation. The car meanders through the twisty back roads of JFK airport finding its way to a dark, hidden cargo area. There my transportation is waiting for me - a CIA-chartered, Gulfstream III jet. I wonder who else will be going with me.

The driver effortlessly lifts my baggage, disappearing with it. I walk up the metal steps into the plane's belly. At the top of the stairs stands a uniformed male attendant waiting for me.

"Welcome Mr. Perlov," he smiles as he speaks. He looks

immaculate in the blue uniform, braided golden epaulets on his shoulders, the perfect picture of a high school marching band member. His stare is warm yet distant. He never approaches too closely.

I step inside, the plane's interior, well-lit and unlike any plane I have ever boarded. I feel as if I were visiting a homey office with a built-in bar, couches and cushiony chairs. Two men in their 40's stand up from their seats as I draw nearer.

"Hi," says the taller one, the stockier guy extending his hand in friendship.

I shake the hands of both men.

"We're going to be a little delayed, poor visibility, but sit and we can talk." The taller one appears to be the main man, the other guy watches for instructions. His teeth show the ravages of black coffee and unfiltered cigarettes. "I'm Rob McNulty and this is Peter Wright," he points to his companion.

I sit and open my jacket. Unfamiliar with the proper attire for such a meeting, I wear a gray blazer, long sleeve shirt and casual, wrinkle-free cotton pants with my almost new pair of loafers.

Jimmy had nagged me to get a pair. I refused the one with tassels as that was not my style, although it looked great on Jimmy. I went for the more conservative penny loafers; the leather is shining from my earlier buffing. These men are wearing jeans and golf shirts, but on their feet are loafers, the thicker guy wearing the tassels and the thinner, more athletic man, a copy of my mine.

"You guys from the CIA?" I am new at this kind of interrogation game.

"Yes," McNulty answers for the two of them.

"Are we it?" I ask, my eyes looking around for the presence of others.

"The pilot and co-pilot," the leader responds.

"What's the game plan?" I am still clueless.

"Want a drink, something to eat?" Wright asks with a toothy smile.

On hearing these words, the attendant re-appears and offers me a shot glass of a clear liquid. A platter of cheese and crackers surrounded by green and red grapes is placed in the center of the table. McNulty nods his head, then once again turns invisible.

I gingerly sample one of the grapes and grip the slippery cheese, adeptly getting it to stay on the slender cracker. "My assignment?" I ask while taking a bite.

McNulty takes a file off the floor. "This is what we know, which I admit is very little about this woman." He pushes the small bundle towards me.

I turn it, so I can open the manila folder, its slight contents probably not much more illuminating than what I got from Cohen.

"Who provided this? Mossad? The Egyptians?" I ask. My man with the secrets, Dov Amitz, was probably the conduit for this or perhaps Mohammed Abdel.

"We are not at liberty to discuss our sources," he tells me with authority. "But German intelligence is aware of what you are doing," his voice harsher. "You are fluent in German, that's why you're here. We gave you the original reports written in German."

I view the official seal of the German government. "I thought they were not certain about the Hamburg connection?" I ask.

"We have convinced the German government to let you pose as a German intelligence officer. They are also wary of the Muslim Brotherhood. They don't want their tourist spots targeted any more than the Israelis or Egyptians," McNulty says.

"Exactly what is expected from me?" I remain anxious in a good way – looking forward to this assignment, yet still feeling inadequately informed.

"It's really very simple," Wright unexpectedly speaks. "We have a woman in custody in Belarus; you know that she was picked up in Riverhead, NY. She's from, well – we're not certain. She appears to be a member of the Egyptian family that founded the Muslim Brotherhood. They have camera footage of someone looking like her in an Arab enclave in Hamburg. The people living there are not legal residents. We think she may have children living in this enclave in Hamburg. He folds his hands very neatly like a clergyman would before delivering the sermon.

"My job is to find out what was she doing in Riverhead. What's the connection between her and the El Salvadorian gang MS-13? And is she a member of the Muslim Brotherhood?" It all sounds so elementary, but grilling a suspect is rarely easy. Those that effortlessly confess are usually not guilty.

"We want to know about her family – does she have family? Where are they? Germany? Egypt? America? Find out as much of her personal history as possible. We want to construct a terrorist profile because we fear the landscape is changing rapidly and we are unprepared," Wright continues.

"I'll do my best," is the only response that I can think of at this moment.

McNulty reaches inside an accordion file by his feet. "Here, these are your identity papers," he hands me a packet.

I slowly open it, taking a hard look at the passport and other official documents.

"You are Karl Erdmann, a German national and a member of German intelligence," he tells me.

I open the passport, finding my picture with a new name. Inside the document folder is also a driver's license with my picture and new name. It's a good photo; I look quite intellectual, a small smile on my face not indicating smugness or conceit but oozing with confidence. I like this. "Where did you get my photo? It certainly doesn't look like my police photo or even my New York driver's license."

"We want you to live the part of this German intelligence officer. Naturally, producing credible documents is required. Are you carrying your own passport?" McNulty asks and extends his arm.

"Yes," I instinctively touch my attaché case resting next to my leg.

"Can I have it?" his arm rests in midair.

"Why?" I press my ankle against the case.

"Just in case," he nonchalantly replies.

"Why? Why should it matter?" suddenly this assignment doesn't seem so innocuous.

"You may be searched when you enter the prison. This avoids any confusion," his arm remaining in its same demanding position.

"I just won't carry it on me at those times," I answer and wrap my feet tightly around my attaché case.

Wright gives McNulty an arched brow. "No, we must have all your own identity papers. All kinds of unexpected things can happen. Please," his impatient fingers wiggle in the air.

With reluctance, I give him my own passport and police identity card as well as my New York driver's license. I feel naked, "Here."

"Thanks. Look further inside that envelope I gave you," McNulty directs me.

My fingers grab onto other items. "Wow," I pull out a wad of bills – Euros by the dozens and currency I don't immediately recognize. "Belarus rubles?"

"You may need to pay for information. The CIA is renting the prison and the guards are locals. Don't hesitate to use the money because we can get you much more," the top man tells me with eagerness. "Buy people meals, drinks, anyone who you think might be useful,"

"Okay," I like the extra spending cash.

"Any other identity cards?"

"I do have this," I reach inside my case and show them my money.

He quickly retrieves it from my hand, "Thanks."

He offers me a smile and I reciprocate not certain how to respond.

"Are you wearing a weapon? Are you armed?" Wright calmly asks without any threat of menace in his voice.

"No," I had no intention of bringing one of my guns into a foreign country.

"Good because we can't have you carrying any firearms," Wright says. I have the feeling that he wants to immediately pat me down.

We share a silent moment, my eyes gazing at the two

strangers. We are all trying to determine each other's trustworthiness.

"Can I look at your clothing," Wright asks with some hesitancy, but the resolve is evident in his voice.

"Why?" I can't understand this crazy process.

"We can't have you wearing clothing with American labels," he answers and although it sounds logical, it's stupid.

"Why not? You don't think German nationals shop for American clothing. They love to visit New York just for that purpose. With the American dollar worth so little abroad, America is a shopper's heaven. I can have US labels," my determination is greater than their rationality.

The two silently confer; I see the eyes dart. McNulty gives the instructions. "No, everything goes including your underwear. We will replace what's in your suitcase with products sold in Germany."

"You're kidding?" Their faces do not show any frivolity.

"We don't mean right this moment but before you leave the plane. We'll keep these things for you and when you return from this mission, it will all be returned. Don't worry, it'll be in good hands," Wright speaks while glancing at McNulty.

I don't smile; this is not amusing, but I will not be able to leave this plane with my own clothing.

"Are you my handlers – will both of you be going to the prison with me?" I don't have an opinion whether that will be good or bad.

"No, we're just delivering you and providing some basic instructions. There's a point man you will meet tomorrow at the airport who will take you to your hotel near the prison. We will say auf wiedersehen tomorrow," McNulty adds with a slight smile, his eyes crinkling up a bit. "We may be returning you to the US. It's not been determined,".

"That's the spy business, right?" I chuckle. They don't smile, but McNulty's lips separate, almost a grin.

"Look these over. We have kosher food for you. Eat, drink some vodka and get some sleep. There's a sleeping area in the back, the chair moves down to make a bed. There's even some cotton PJ's and your own bathroom, shower, sink. Once we arrive, you will hit the dirt running so enjoy the rest of the night," Wright says.

"Kosher food, really?" I am amazed and frightened because that means they know so much about me while I know nothing about them.

"We understand that's your preference. We aim to please," McNulty says with a wide smile, his friendliest of the evening.

The pilot informs us to get ready for take-off and the attendant suddenly makes another appearance, this time leading me to my compartment behind some wall. The walls are thin, so I can hear them mumbling to each other despite the sounds of the jet getting ready to ascend, but the exact words escape my comprehension and thirty minutes later, I don't care. The food is great, the file's contents more questioning than informative, the reading is boring and before too long my eyes close.

When we land it's daylight. I can read the name of the company on the plane – Global Cargo Service etched in red paint. I walk down the steps and glance back at McNulty and Wright waving good-bye. A new person emerges from the tarmac to lead me to the next stop on this adventure – another stranger whom I will need.

"Hello, Tom Castillo," he has an enthusiastic demeanor pumping my hand as we shake. A man of medium build, there is nothing distinguishable about him except for the big pinky ring, with a big enough diamond that a woman would be envious.

"Where are we?" I ask because we are not in Minsk or any other major city; it's clearly a rural place.

"It's an old Soviet airbase. We're not too far from our destination," he helps me with my baggage. "You got your papers?" he asks as he lifts my bag into the car's trunk.

"Yes, I am a German national, Karl Erdmann," suddenly being someone else is apparently very important for my mission.

"Good because that's the name you will use with the

guards at the prison, with the people in the hotel and anywhere else you travel," he adds while opening the passenger front door for me.

Should I give him a tip? I laugh at my own silent joke. He's too busy running his eyes across the landing field to notice.

"You with the CIA?" I ask to be friendly.

"Hell no," he quickly answers and although there's no traffic, he drives very cautiously.

"So, who are you with?" this spy game is not what I expected.

"Contractor," he slips his free hand into his breast pocket and emerges with a thick business card. "Thomas J. Castillo, Consultant. Worldwide Security. Nice card, right?" he shakes his head like a kid with a shiny, new toy.

"Consultant," I parrot his words. "You are going to be my 'go to' guy here in Belarus. Do you speak Russian or Belarusian?" I ask with my level of concern rising by the second.

"Hell no," he matter-of-factly answers without any obvious concern.

"But I depend on you for some guidance here. Yes?" I'm afraid to hear his answer.

"Hell no, we both wing it," he starts to laugh hysterically. I turn to watch the tears roll down his perfectly round face, the brown eyes filled with liquid.

I am stunned but what can I do, I'm here. "Do we have a handler from the CIA?" Hopefully someone else is in charge.

"Yes, but we won't see much of him. My orders are simple. I take you to your hotel—Soviet vintage. I could find you a nicer one in Minsk, but that's a distance from the prison. I was instructed to keep it close. As for Minsk, we will be visiting there for dinner and drinks, but it's easier to roll out of bed to get to the prison. I'm only your chauffeur. You will be hearing from the big guy sometime soon," he confidently answers.

"And who is this big guy," I hope he has more useful and instructive answers.

"Former Navy Seal, tough guy but really I think he's full of crap. The truth be told, my friend, you're on your own. You do have marching orders," he turns to face me as we wait at the stop sign. We are in some agricultural area, meadows and forests surrounding us.

"A name?" I ask.

"He calls himself John Smith. Rubbish, right? What an asshole, but when he comes to town we go to the most expensive places," my companion tells me.

"What are your plans for me today, right now?" I can't conceal my growing unease.

"Well actually you get a choice. I can take you to the hotel, or if you trust me with your personal items, I'll deliver your bags and drive you directly to the prison. What's your pleasure?" he smilingly adds.

"At the prison who will I find? Who is in charge at the prison?" I can't believe that the operation is so loose.

"You're in charge of this operation. As far as I know it's you, the prisoner and the Belarusian prison personnel. You are the boss," he lightly slaps my shoulder.

"Do you know the guys from the plane who brought me here?"

"Yes, scary bunch, real CIA. I heard that about them, but certainly no one directly speaks to me about those guys. I think McNulty, the tall one, and his sidekick Wright are in the torture business. The stuff they euphemistically call extraordinary interrogation techniques," he laughs. "I heard someone say they oversee all these extraordinary rendition prisons. Notice everything is 'extraordinary.' I would not consider them drinking buddies."

CHAPTER 14

As the car makes it over a hill, I see the prison in view, dark, dreary stone, rows and rows of barbed wire and guard towers. It feels like a scene from Soviet times visiting my mother in prison. The former Soviet Union must have had only two or three prison designers. It could be the same outfit from Russia.

"Who else is in this prison? It certainly looks like it can hold hundreds of prisoners," as we draw closer its size becomes more apparent.

"No idea, this is the first time I got this close to the place," he confesses.

"How did you get this job?" I can't imagine because of some expertise in interrogating possible terrorists or familiarity with the country.

"I went to college with the son of the head personnel guy in Fairfax, Virginia. I'm a card-carrying Republican and Bush man," he replies without a trace of absurdity about his lack of credentials.

"Okay, let's proceed onward towards the prison. Do you also act as my valet, removing my clothing from the bag and hanging them up in my hotel room? Check for wrinkles?" I respond with mockery although I keep a straight face.

"If you want me to, sure," he replies without

acknowledging any sarcasm on my part.

"Do you wait for me here when I go inside?" I can't believe that I'm expected to run this whole operation.

"No just call me when you want me to pick you up," stopping the car in front of a wooden guard house. He hands me a piece of paper with his cell phone number.

"Use this," he hands me a cell phone. "Not much works here but this does. I can assure you of that," he fervently nods his head – a confident young man.

I get out of the car and stare at my new surroundings. Perversely, this looks vaguely familiar. I would never have dreamed that as an adult I would return to such a place.

A big, powerfully built guard wearing a Belarusian military uniform greets me with a waving arm. His rifle across his chest, he stands guard over the entrance. I reluctantly leave the comfort of my companion. He drives off leaving me alone in this isolated place.

As the guard approaches, I see the trail of dust as Tom speeds away towards the hotel.

At that moment, I realize that I must act as if I am in charge moving without hesitancy, knowing what dogs learn as pups, never show fear. Take those long strides and let confidence exude from every pore, I am the boss man.

"Karl Erdmann," I tell the guard.

He looks me over. "Yes," he tells me in halting German,

then says nothing more.

My trusty old Belarusian language skills come in handy. "I'm here to see the female prisoner brought in by the Americans," I tell him, although I'm not certain that it's the correct scenario.

"Yes, come this way," he says in his native language. "You speak pretty good Belarusian," and he looks carefully at my facial features. "Are you originally from Russia?"

"I am a German national," I quickly reply. "But I was born in Petersburg; my father was German, a government official. There are many former Soviet citizens now living in the united Germany," I give him a warm glance, my smile grows wider.

"I would like to live in Germany," he answers with a yearning in his voice.

"Not much here, but we're not far from Minsk," I reply accepting my chauffeur's information.

"Not much in Minsk either," we arrive at the front entrance to the prison.

Another more senior officer meets us; he is wearing a higher rank on his uniform. His pockmarked face shows no evidence of friendliness.

"Karl Erdmann," I reply and open my breast pocket to show my identification card from German intelligence, BND.

He stares at the papers without blinking. His decades-old, untreated acne must have made him an outcast among his classmates. I wonder what his wife looks like because I notice a wedding ring – perhaps Beauty and the Beast.

In an awkward German, he asks me, "Mr. Erdmann, we must search you. Are you carrying any weapons?"

In my much more refined Belarusian, I reply. "No, my friend I carry no weapons, no contraband, nothing. Please do whatever is necessary. I can drop my pants and you can put your fingers up my ass." I assume the macho man position – act threatening and intimidating, keep these people at bay. My knowledge of German intelligence officers can fill a thimble, but I act with complete authority.

The subordinate guard smiles but the boss man shows no emotion. He personally pats me down and, accidentally on purpose, pinches my balls. I should wince in pain, but I remain steady. "You're fine," he announces to everyone in the room.

The first guard becomes my personal tour guide as we enter the maximum-security prison with its luminescent lighting, smooth flooring and dull paint job – institutional gray-green. The floors are spotlessly clean and waxed.

"How many prisoners are here?" I ask.

"Only one," he replies as he directs me to the proper location.

"You're kidding," I realize my reply is in Russian, similar languages Belarusian and Russian, both East Slavic like Ukrainian but with different nuances, especially with the slang and colloquialisms.

He understands. "Yes, the American's woman is the only prisoner," he smiles. "It's good we have her because what else would we be doing. There are dozens of people working here minding only one person," he nods his head up and down, smiling in gratitude.

"Well, were there many more prisoners here before?" I can't believe this huge complex is devoted to holding one individual.

"Not really, not since Soviet times has there been a need to lock up so many people. My understanding is that the Americans bought the use of it sometime in late 2001 and we've been happily employed ever since. They were going to close this old behemoth down, but it was rescued by the American authorities."

"You mean since the September 11th incidents it's become an American property?" What times we live in.

"I guess," he hesitatively replies.

"Were there many prisoners brought here by the Americans?" I quickly grasp this man's importance as one of my best informants.

"Maybe a dozen a couple years back, but not lately. Who cares? The money comes in and we're paid," he shrugs his shoulders. Why question or analyze a good thing.

"Am I the first German here?" Let's see if someone else

has used this ruse.

"Yes," and he grins. "Germany and America together in their terrorism war," he laughs.

Not a believer in this new international war my guard, but rationality and logic died a long time ago. "Okay, show me the prisoner," several yards later we stop in front of a cell. I peek in through the narrow slit.

"Has anyone else come to see her," I ask before he opens the heavy metal door.

"Yes, when she first arrived, but no one since," he informs me.

"How long ago was that?" my bare facts need some enrichment and verification.

"About a month ago," he claims, and the door opens.

She does not move despite the noise and intrusion. In fact, she seems immobile almost like a mannequin. The room is windowless and completely bare. I quickly observe the small camera in the corner near the ceiling. The lights are bright but artificial-feeling, too glaring and harsh to be like the softness of the sun. The lighting fixture makes a low, monotonous, buzzing sound that could easily be ignored and forgotten after a while.

I have no name for the prisoner, if she's a member of the founding family of the Muslim Brotherhood I have a surname, so I just announce myself. "Hello," I try and get her attention. I fail. Her eyes look down at her hands although she is not cowering. She is not showing fear, just indifference.

I move closer but not too close, speaking quietly in German. "My name is Karl; I'm here from German intelligence. I am trying to negotiate your release from the Americans. I just have a few questions to ask," I stand three feet from her.

She remains motionless. Her head is covered by a scarf and she is wearing a loose-fitting Middle Eastern-looking garment that she must slip over her head. Although she is alone, she must know that she is constantly being watched. There is no bathroom just a toilet seat and a small sink. The only furniture in the room is the bed where she sits.

I start. "What is your name? We have you as a resident of Hamburg, Germany but not a citizen. Can you verify for me your name?" I stand motionless

She doesn't speak or even pick up her head.

I continue. "I'm sure you want to get out of here. I need your cooperation, so the Americans release you and I can take you back to Germany. You do want to get back to your family in Germany?" I am assuming she actually was living in Germany and has a family. My voice is calm and wait for her response.

If she is blinking, I can't see from the bent position of her head.

I want to approach and forcibly pick up her head, but I don't want to seem threatening, not yet. Instead, I sit on the floor across from her.

"I have lots of time. Do you want to spend the rest of your life in this windowless room because the Americans will not let you go until you answer some of their questions? Who are you? What were you doing in America in the company of Latin gang members?" My tendency is to build up to a crescendo, moving the words at a slow pace at first and then rapid-fire. But I constrain my instincts, continuing to speak slowly.

She says absolutely nothing. Her fingers do not budge as she keeps them tightly wrapped together in her lap.

"I can make your life worth living, give you things, get you out of this place. Lipstick, maybe you crave a drink of something besides water. What about a Koran?" I watch for her reaction.

She moves. Her face lifts and I see her warm, dark brown eyes. We are locked in a longing glance. Finally, I hit the right nerve; there is a weakness that I can potentially manipulate.

Still she doesn't speak. I wonder if she feels comfortable talking in German, but I don't comprehend any Arabic. Understanding a language and conversing in it are two different skills. As a non-English speaking immigrant, I appreciate that dilemma.

"I will bring you one when I return but we must talk. Do you want me to find an Arabic speaking translator?" I ask as my voice becomes more pleading.

She stares at me but doesn't speak, her long eyelashes barely fluttering. Her powers of stillness are simply amazing, a truly learned behavior, completely unnatural; our bodies instinctively twist and turn, our hearts pound and pulsate, the nose hairs quiver with each new breath. She is like a statue and I find it unnerving.

I press my back against the wall and say nothing, although my body cannot perfect her ability to sit motionless. I close my eyes and imagine that I am standing on my balcony off my bedroom in the Rockaways. The roaring surf pounding the packed sand in the early morning hours, leaving a trail of salty foam and billowing holes as the underground creatures suck in air and watery nutrients. I focus on the waves, the uneven line of white caps. My body is transported above that very choppy sea. My heart beats slower and my pulse decreases, unhurriedly, I open my half-slit eyes to observe my suspect. She is watching me.

She makes no movement to affirm an agreement. She simply stares at me. We stay in this position for what feels like hours but probably is no more than thirty minutes.

"I'll be back. We have much to discuss," I stand. I remain fixated on her eyes and then she reverts to her former behavior, eyes concentrating on her hands in her lap.

The exit door is several feet in the distance and I slowly walk towards it. I slam my fists against the steel door, it rattles like aging metal does when neglected. The prisoner hardly moves. My friendly guard looks through the slit. I ask him in Belarusian, "Open up please, it's time," I leave the prisoner to her own thoughts, which I haven't a clue about.

"Talkative?" he asks and laughs.

"So, you know that she never speaks?" I ask.

"Don't know anyone who has actually heard her say one word, not even in her sleep. She is so quiet we sometimes think she's dead," he answers.

"Perhaps she is trying to will herself to death," I reply. I have heard about such things. "Strange," I say to no one in particular, and then I am wordless. We noiselessly travel through the corridors to the entrance. At the desk, I wave good-bye to my hosts. "I'll be back soon," I announce.

Outside the walls of the prison I call my 'go to' man in Belarus.

CHAPTER 15

It takes Tom Castillo only ten minutes to pick me up at the half-circle curving entrance. He is still smiling, singing to himself and gets out to open the passenger door for me like a good chauffeur.

"Dinner?" the always helpful youthful associate asks.

"Sure," I lean my head against the neck rest; the car is not a familiar brand but reasonably comfortable. "Where can I get a Koran? Do you think there's an Islamic bookstore or a mosque in Minsk?" my voice tentative.

"Doubt it," he looks my way as he drives.

"What do you suggest?" I inquire with anticipation and high expectations since he seems to know his way around the neighborhood.

"Internet, that's the best way," his tone convincing.

"Really?" my initial reaction reluctance because I don't want to believe that a computer is superior to purchasing a product directly from a human being.

"We'll go online, there's an Internet cafe in town, we can order it right now. It may take 24 or 48 hours, then you'll have it. I wouldn't trust any other way," he nods his head completely satisfied with his idea.

Since I have limited choices and he seems so

reassuring, I agree. "Okay, I'll use my credit card," instinctively, I touch my breast pocket, then remember I don't have any credit cards with me. I left them all with my true identity in New York; I can't even use my own passport.

"Oh, no, no, I have a credit card, which we can use. My job is to make our trip as successful as possible. I'll take care of it and we'll have it delivered to your hotel." He whistles as he drives into the small crowd of emerging drivers.

He easily finds a place to park on the street as we head towards this Internet café. The computer is a universal helpmate found even in the deepest reaches of the former Soviet Union; the place even has a decent menu and the waiter brings us to a large table in the corner.

"How about a beer?" Tom asks.

I hate beer but if someone is watching me, what good German doesn't drink beer, so for the sake of my role-playing I respond. "Of course."

The signs in the café are in Belarusian or Russian, but here and there something is written in English. It takes no time for Tom to make our purchase and we toast when the drinks arrive.

"Here's to a profitable venture." He salutes the air and then takes a huge gulp as if his throat was parched from the desert heat.

I gingerly sip my drink; it is cold and refreshing. "What is next for you?" I try and make small talk.

"I like this assignment. I hope you stay a long time," he answers.

"What did you do before?" I inspect the tuna with my fork, turning it over and checking the color of the fish before I take a bite.

"I was in Iraq as a contractor, not a soldier. Still, what a dangerous place. I mean I was so scared. I'll admit to you," he almost whispers but draws near so no one else can possibly hear. "Many times, I thought I'd pee in my pants. The incredible noise, the bursts of gunfire, bombs and massive waves of smoke, never knowing who to trust. This is a great assignment compared to that," he swallows the rest of the contents of the glass and gestures for another.

"I bet this pays less," I answer assuming higher combat pay.

"Sure, but if you're dead, what good is money? I like this just fine," he licks off the foam from the second beer.

My new companion is smarter than he looks and not too greedy. We eat, and he drinks a third beer while I nurse my first. I share as little as possible although I pump him for information about contractors in Iraq. And what more does he know about my plane companions from the CIA – the torture directors? Dinner lasts a couple of hours. Neither of us have another place or activity that demands our attention.

When I am returned to my hotel, I report to my superior in New York with my super spy phone. Cohen answers himself.

"I got nothing to report, the prisoner never spoke a word to me or to anyone else it seems. But I hope to use my powers of harmless persuasion to get her to talk," I reply. My tone isn't flippant, but he could interpret my playful words for such an attitude.

"Keep me posted daily even if you have nothing new," he curtly responds, his words clipped and short.

"I understand my guys who brought me here on the plane oversee torture in these rendition prisons. What do you know?" I ask Cohen.

"Don't worry about them. You have an assignment. No torture by you or anyone else," he quickly replies. "Stop worrying about that and get me answers to more important questions. Is the city under imminent threat?"

"I hope no one is expecting instant results. This woman will not be easy to crack. I'm not even certain that I can get her to talk," I answer.

"No one is expecting miracles just get her to talk. You are the master of persuasion."

The key must be children, I hope she has some. I can't imagine as a mother she won't miss them, although if she volunteered as a suicide terrorist attacker, she is expecting death. In the next life, she may anticipate seeing them again –I hope not.

The next day the Koran does not arrive in the post. I ask the desk clerk and anyone I can find. There is no package for me. I find it interesting that Tom is staying in another hotel, but I don't inquire. I don't know if it's important, I let it go without explanation.

The car is ready, and he is eager to start the day. "Back to the prison?" he asks with bubbly enthusiasm.

"The package did not come." I'm disappointed and he can hear it in my voice as well as observe the long frown on my face.

"Don't worry it will come. Trust me," He tells me about some obscure baseball statistic that means nothing to me, but I wanly smile. I depend upon him, at least for the moment. We have nothing in common except for the important fact that he needs me, and I need him to accomplish our mutually symbiotic task.

The guards are waiting for me and Tom stays well outside the barbed wire perimeter, never venturing too close to the entrance. Obviously, the prison makes him uncomfortable.

My friendly guard is there. "Naturally, she is waiting for you." He laughs as we walk through the security gates and the hidden and visible sensors. I am no longer subjected to any pat-down.

"I don't intend to see her today," I tell him in Belarusian. I want to return to her when I have something to give her – the damn Koran. "Is there a surveillance room?"

He brings me inside a windowless, cool, dark control room filled with screens but only one is operating – there is my prisoner of interest.

"You keep this camera on all the time?" I ask the man in his native tongue. He is sitting by the screens, only the one flashing with activity. "Yes, 24/7," he quickly responds, looking at me, studying the foreigner who speaks the language so well. "Each tape covers 24 hours," he adds.

"It looks like she does nothing but sit on that bed," we all stare at the screen.

"Yes, she is incredibly disciplined. She does not speak or move. We have prisoners who pace and claw at the walls, but not her. What you see is just typical," he adds with a measure of admiration.

"Since the time when she was brought in here, this is what she does, nothing, nothing?" I shake my head in disbelief, but we all observe her doing absolutely nothing, simply breathing.

"Do we know if in fact she can speak? Maybe she's deaf and dumb," I ask, although I know that she reacted positively to the mention of the word Koran. But I'm testing the guards. How responsive are they to the prisoner? Perhaps they have important observations to offer me.

"Well, we know that she hears because she responds when we bang on the door to hand her food," he answers with certainty.

"The food she eats meets Islamic standards of purity?" I'm thinking about what I can manipulate. What can I take away and then give back that's important to her, so she'll be more pliable, more willing to talk.

"We were told that Muslims and Jews eat similar food. We get her food from the Jewish church in Minsk. You know the people with the long beards and black coats. They bring us food for her and assure us that it would be acceptable," he answers, pleased with their gesture of consideration.

"You mean the Hasidic men," I ask, demonstrating their unique appearance by pulling on my chin, creating the illusion of a long beard. "There is a Chabad House in Minsk?" I know that the Hasids are everywhere in the former Soviet Union, bringing back the old-time religion. I'll check on that because I would appreciate a good kosher meal on Friday night – *Shabbes*.

"Yes, that's what they call themselves, Hasid," all the men in the room nod their heads. I notice the return of the senior guard; he seems to have just materialized, perhaps afraid of being left out of the conversation or unfamiliar with my new demands.

The presence of Hasidic men could be unsettling to the locals. I'm expecting an anti-Semitic remark, but they are noticeably quiet. Perhaps they think I am Jewish or that all Germans are publicly supposed to be sympathetic to Jews since the Holocaust.

The men stand ready to answer any more of my questions, alert, some rocking on their heels, waiting for the opportunity to respond, displaying their best behavior, wanting to make a good impression. Everyone is committed to satisfying my requests.

"You keep the tapes here?" I inquire because I don't see any cartons of tapes or much of anything else in this spotlessly clean room. I could touch all the screens with a white glove and find no trace of dust or lint.

"Yes," he points to a black, metal credenza. "Inside," keeping his index finger floating in midair.

"Can I see the tape from the day that she arrived?" I nod my head for further emphasis.

Immediately, he responds by moving from his cushy chair to a tall, metal storage cabinet, retrieving the tape, which appears to be labeled with the date of her arrival.

I stand next to him. "I understand that the prisoner has received a few visitors since she arrived. Do you have the tapes from these dates?" I request.

"I have to look at the book and check the dates. Every

visitor to this prison is logged in just as you were today and yesterday," he moves to a compact desk. He quickly finds a soft-covered black book and checks the dates, his finger moving down a page. Without any hesitation, he returns to the cabinet and finds the tapes, handing them to me.

The head guard is carefully watching the proceedings. "I have a room nearby where you can view the tapes," he informs me in his official voice, flat but commanding.

"Can I take them with me?" I ask although I don't expect an affirmative response. The orders must be that no important evidence can be removed. I assume to get my way, my tone of voice must be harder, sharper and more threatening.

"Of course," he instantly says. "You are the boss," looking directly into my eyes. "Just sign in the book," he points to the dark object.

In my role as boss, I then proceed to make more demands. "Do you keep the lights on all the time in her cell?"

"Yes, no one said anything else," he defensively responds; his mouth looking pinched, with a worried frown making a new appearance.

"Okay," the words nonjudgmental but quickly I reassert my status as boss man. "I want you to more closely mimic the real world. At 7 PM, I want you to start dimming the lights until by 9 PM there is only a little light—just enough that you can still see her. At 5 AM, I want you to start lighting the room so that by

7 AM it is more like daylight. Can that be done?"

"Certainly, we can do that," he answers, and in fact appears delighted to be following orders, a small smile emerging.

"The room has no natural light, no windows. Do you have a cell with windows?" I would like her prison stay to not be too comfortable, but there must be some rewards, some incentives for good behavior for her talking to me.

"Yes, we do, in another part of the prison," he dutifully replies.

"Good because if she starts to talk, giving me useful information, then I want her moved, but not yet." I raise my finger into the air for emphasis.

"Of course, anything you want," he respectfully answers but not subserviently. This man is someone who holds power and authority in my absence. He directs and expects his orders to be fulfilled. His deference towards me is a mere survival technique since presumably as an officer tied to the Americans, indirectly, I am paying his salary and everyone else's in this remote location.

He hands me my package of tapes.

"Thanks. I'll review them and return them to you," I tell them as I ready myself to depart. My friendly guard is right at my heels, escorting me out of the building.

He doesn't leave my side even as I make a quick call for

Tom to retrieve me.

He stands close to me, available to answer any questions that I might hesitate to ask in front of the group.

"Tell me why does the Belarus government help the Americans? I thought the country is an ally and good friend of Russia's but not America or Germany" I don't know how political he is, but I ask out of curiosity.

"Money, everything is now about money," he rapidly replies without indecision.

"Still is that all there is to government relations – money?" I act like the stupid one.

"Well, it's true that we are best friends with Putin's Russia, but we need to maintain our independence. By taking in American prisoners, we stick it in the eye of the Russians, a bargaining chip. There are those in the government eager to make nice to the Americans." He answers with authority but checks over his shoulder to make certain there are not ears listening.

We both see the approaching car. He waves and disappears back into the giant fortress.

"Where to boss?" Tom asks in his usually cheery voice.

I like this feeling of being in charge, although in truth, I realize this status is tenuous at best. If I don't get her to talk to me, my role is finished and I'm back to being the almost golden boy, just another ambitious NYPD detective.

"Can you get me a VCR to watch these tapes?" I show him my bounty.

"No problem, I'll get the concierge to find something for you to use," he confidently drives back to the hotel. Using his cell phone, he calls ahead for food and a compatible machine for my tapes. By the time we arrive, everything is arranged. Tom asks, "Want company while you watch the tapes?" He has that sorry eye look that my dog gets when he's been left alone too long.

"Sure," I answer, two sets of eyes may be useful. Besides, he may recognize and know something about the visitors.

"Should I bring the popcorn and beer? I got the food here," he asks with a happy smile, big wide eyes.

CHAPTER 16

I was anxious to get the interrogation going. How to motivate her? The Koran was the dangling carrot. When I went to the desk clerk and asked about my package, my hanging hound face told the story of my disappointment.

"No Herr Erdmann, no package," he was apologetic although he was not responsible.

When Tom came around to fetch me in the morning, I was pissed, my face a deep frown.

"Hey, still nothing," I tell him even though he couldn't miss my aggravation, no loopy smile on my face.

"No problem," he cheerfully said. "It will come tomorrow. Want to go back to the prison for more tapes, "I'm going sightseeing," I declared. "Can you get me a car?" with the thought that this was the perfect opportunity to go visit my grandmother's cousin Nadia. I got directions from the Internet and received the go-ahead from my mother back in Brighton Beach, Brooklyn. The cousin was fine with any time, no formal invitation was necessary; she was going to be home for the foreseeable future – just show up at her door.

"I can drive you," Tom quickly responded with a happy, smiley face like that silly, yellow symbol.

"Hell no," I abruptly replied, and he immediately realized

that this time I was not in the mood for his merry company. The smile faded but never entirely disappeared from his face. "Okay, if that's what you want," he was saddened by my decision but not permanently. "You can use mine," he gently smacked the door. "It's got a full tank of petro," he reached into his wallet and gave me a gasoline credit card.

"Thanks, but what will you do without any transportation?" I returned a toothy smile; he tried so hard. It was difficult not to like him despite his many limitations.

"No problem," he said. "I'll get a ride to Minsk and look around for a mosque. I might get lucky, you know. Besides, we could always use two Korans, right?" he seemed so confident.

Here was a man who spoke not a word of Belarusian or Russian. He knew nothing about the country or its culture. He probably would recognize a mosque from his days in Iraq, but his moxie was so comforting. That was the most disquieting thing about the incompetent – fools never realized how dangerous their lack of abilities was to everyone else.

"You want me to get the concierge to pack you a nice box lunch?" he continued his deferential ways.

"No, I think I'll try and experience the whole adventure – roads, food, the big picture," I spread my arms apart making a giant 'V.'

"Okay, be careful since these are winding roads and the police aren't all that dependable except when they have their hands out," he shows me a beggar's position. All he needs is a tin cup.

"Okay, I'm on my way, don't wait up for me," I jokingly add.

"Have fun," he waves as he returns to my hotel's lobby.

I drop a sweater on the back seat and begin my journey home to a past that I know nothing about, and until recently did not care to know.

The actual mileage was relatively short, according to my Internet map, but as Tom was quick to note these were roads of uncertain condition. The major cities were being revitalized with state money and some limited private funds but the countryside – long neglected by all the leaders, past and present, was in a far more delicate situation.

I was making this journey to please the most important person in my life – my mother - but as a student of history, there was another dimension. I was curious about what happened to Belarus since the death of the Evil Empire. The exploits of my grandfather, the Hero of the Battle of Stalingrad, were described in the old Soviet textbooks, but this maternal side of the family was foreign to me.

I realized because the roads were narrow in parts and totally absent of any overhead lighting, I would have to return long before nightfall. I didn't want to be traveling strange roadways in darkness. I was told to expect a small village without any modern touches. I remembered visiting my grandfather's dacha in my youth. We drove through the rural countryside to get to his rambling, decrepit wooden house with the fish pond and nearby roaring brook, part of the former estate of a low-level member of the czar's family. It was a gift from the Soviet bureaucracy to a genuine hero.

I expected the cousin's village to look like the ones we passed on the way to the dacha; humble in origins, a modest farming community, although how much agriculture was being produced today was probably limited. Poverty remained a problem for Belarus, especially in the rural areas. She was an old pensioner paid by the Russian authorities but supported by her financially successful sons living in Moscow.

The day was perfect for 'taking a ride' as my father likes to say. The temperature is just right – not cold and not hot. I look for posted mileage signs telling me distances and the speed limit, not wanting any reason for a police officer to confront me. I trust that my papers look genuine, but why test them? On my journey, I must live the lie of Karl Erdmann, German intelligence officer. But once with my cousin, I can reveal my real self—this spy business is very straining on the memory cells, keeping you on your toes, never able to let your pretenses drop.

The drive is most pleasing and soon the road sign is

before me. Here was the village and it looked like nothing, the same as many others that I past. As I drive into the center of the village, everyone stops to catch a glimpse of me. Women with packages in their arms drop their bundles and stand on the side of the road. A tractor moving slowly through the main street comes to a halt and allows me to pass. Since I had actual directions to her house, it is unnecessary to inquire from strangers where she lives.

I stop my car. There she is sitting on a porch, rocking in an ancient wooden chair as old as she is, which is close to a century my mother says, a big dog by her side. When she stands, I realize how teeny, tiny she is, the dog on four legs practically as tall. The two approach me, she is waving enthusiastically while the dog's tail matches her motions.

Her thin, spindly legs bring her to the yard's front fence. With outstretched arms she embraces me and kisses both my cheeks as I bend to her height. "Sasha, Sasha, oh my good boy, Sasha, Sasha," I feel her tears of joy, the salty trail making its way down to my chin. The huge canine watches and the tail movement slows while he determines my relationship to his mistress. I must seem like a friend because he certainly senses her delight.

"Cousin Nadia," I say, reciprocating with kisses.

We are introduced. "This is Boris, my big boy, isn't he beautiful? I named him after our country's savior – Boris

Yeltsin," she wraps her slender arms around the dog's narrow neck. The dog's tail reacts immediately, rapidly and with vigor, the wagging producing instant air-conditioning.

"Welcome my boy. Do you remember me?" she squeezes my hand with a strength that defies her small stature.

"I do, really I do," I take her hand in mine and we stroll towards the house.

"It's been many years, your grandfather's dacha that was the last time," she shakes her head, bouncing with each step. "Many years, so long ago. Yes, a lifetime," she had that distant look, recalling the past, which in her case must be close to 100 years.

"I remember that time and several others, but always at the dacha," I say as I try to recall back to that last holiday.

"I was taller then, and perhaps more gray than white," she chuckles. It's hearty and her whole mouth is exposed; remarkably, she seems to have all her teeth. As she laughs, she pulls at the strands of her very white hair.

"I didn't forget," I repeat myself to assure her of my sincerity.

"You were an adolescent. Now you're a grown man," she pulls at my arm. "And what a handsome man," she turns to take a full-length view. "You have our family resemblance. Your grandmother was a beautiful woman, dying so young. Oh, oh, we Russians, such suffering," she bobs her head up and down.

"What a life of sacrifice," she doesn't need my assistance walking up the four steps. Her faithful canine is right at her heels, his pointy, slender head bobbing up and down the same way as hers.

The door opens with a slight push. The dog runs out in front to check for any enemies inside. He scouts out the rooms to make certain that it's safe for her to enter.

She pets the top of his head. "He's part Russian Wolfhound," she pets his side, touching his silky coat. "The thinness of a Greyhound but taller, similar pointy snout but with curly hair. Luckily not a pure breed because they don't bark," she directs me to the largest chair in the big room serving as living space and dining area. "Sit," she orders me.

"I didn't know that about Wolfhounds," I reply. The old can always teach the young.

"Once, and it was only once, someone tried to break into this place. Not a villager, that I know for sure. When they heard Boris growling and barking, they ran away. He might have frightened them by pressing his big head against the window and they saw his huge size. That was the only trouble I have ever had here." He knows that she is praising him so licks her hand in gratitude. She rewards him with a dog treat. He gobbles up the biscuit in a couple of seconds, leaving not a speck of crumbs.

"You're not afraid of dogs, are you?" she asks worrying

about how we will all get along.

"Oh no, I love dogs. I have a dog, a little one but I love all kinds of dogs, mutts included," my smile is open and friendly. The big dog approaches, sniffs my hand and licks me. "See, we're all friends," I say and together we laugh. Even the dog grunts his approval.

"Sasha, Sasha, oh excuse me, I forgot your real name," she is suddenly remorseful, her warm smile fading from her small face.

"Fyodor Illich," I quickly add. "But call me Sasha, everyone calls me that. In America, I use that as my first name. When I became a naturalized citizen, I called myself – Sasha Perlov," I playfully report, my hands making jerking motions like a perky child. "In America, you can remake yourself, get a new name and a new persona," I report as one who believes in the power to change oneself.

Her eyes brighten. "I think about how exciting it must be to live there, but this is home." She smacks the steel stove. "I have lots of good things for us to eat. You, me," she touches the dog's nose. "Boris," his tail pumps the air.

"Good, I'm hungry," I testify as my stomach juices moan for nourishment.

"You can smoke," she tells me as she moves pots around the stove's top.

"I gave it up," I rise from the chair and approach. "Can I

help?"

"Oh no, Sasha, no, no. Go sit my boy," she gives me a slight shove.

"Set the table?" I ask as a good mama's boy, I am quite handy in the kitchen.

"Look it's done," she informs me, her body continuing to move me away from her stove as if she's a border collie and I am a frisky goat.

I walk towards the only table in the room, which I assume is where we will dine. I pick up the plate, its gold trim etched smoothly around the edge. I turn it over and read the inscription. 'Fine China.'

I take a seat at the dark, wooden table. This way I can rise quickly if she needs me. "It must be lonely here, just you and the dog," I ask out of ignorance but also concern.

"Oh, no Sasha, I love it here. When the great empire fell, I decided to return home to die," she pinches her arm. "I'm still alive. My husband died in 1990 and my sons didn't need me anymore. They were grown with their own children. I wanted to come home and this is home," her eyes staring at me for added emphasis.

"I understand," I say although I really don't.

She comes closer. "I doubt that you understand," she replies as if she is reading my mind.

"Well it is a little hard to understand. This is really an

isolated place, far from family and old friends. You used to live in Moscow with your children. Moscow is a great city, a cosmopolitan center with fine hotels, excellent restaurants, world famous theaters and the ballet. I may be prejudice coming from Petersburg, so I can say it's not as grand as Peter's city." I feel my unconscious nationalism returning.

"I liked Petersburg; I didn't go often but occasionally, more of an arts center than the busy, bustling Moscow. Didn't I see you there?" she inquisitively asks.

"Perhaps, but all I remember is you and your family visiting the dacha," I answer scratching my head. I could be wrong, it's been awhile.

"It doesn't matter." She returns to the stove. "Come here," she says with a big voice, one accustomed to giving out orders.

I immediately get up and move towards her. She hands me a bowl of red liquid. "Borsch?" I ask.

"You like it, every Russian eats it," she matter-of-factly tells me. I take the second bowl for her, placing them both on the table. The steam from the dish is blowing circles of heat into the air. I like my borsch cold, but I say nothing. Being a perfect gentleman, I pull out her chair. She gracefully glides onto the seat as I push it close to the table's edge.

"Thank you, my boy," she gives me an impish smile. In her youth, I imagine a coquettish young flirt.

"I guess you were seeking a quiet life," I wait for her to take the first sip.

"It's more than that. I am the only Jew here. I'm not really a religious woman, but I feel that Hashem, the Holy One, did spare me from the Nazis so that I may bear witness. The czars, Stalin, the Nazis, the Communists, we Jews are still here, here in this very village. I live here to prove that try as hard as they might, they could not exterminate all the Jews." She pounds the table with a closed fist and then takes a sip. "Good?"

"Very good," I answer taking that first sip, impressed by her convictions; she is so sure of the clarity of her thinking.

"*Ess,*" she says as she hands me a basket filled with home-made bread, warm from the oven.

"Don't you miss your children, or even appreciating Jewish life if you're the only one here." I ask as I blanket the bread with creamy butter.

"You're a good son. I understand how you might think a mother should stay physically close to her children. But we are together more than many. For the High Holidays, I go to one son in Moscow and the family joins us. We go to shul and pray in the newly renovated synagogue. For *Pesach*, I go to the other son staying at least a few weeks each time. Then I go shopping, to the theater and the ballet in Moscow. I do all those sophisticated things. In the summer, this is our family dacha, they all come to visit and stay for weeks. The grandchildren sleep in those tents that pop up from a trailer, inventive. I am still close to my family," she rises from her chair.

I stand as a polite guest.

She retrieves a bottle from a cabinet and shows it to me. "A little vodka for us. I don't want people to think I'm a *shikker* but for a big, important meal we need the proper liquid refreshments." She hands me two decorative glasses. She generously pours out the liquid. "You drink vodka? Know a little Yiddish?" she peppers me with questions.

"Yes, I love vodka and I speak a little Yiddish, *shikker* is a great word for drunk." I add and lick off the residual liquid on the lip of the glass.

"It's funny how the collapse of the Soviet Union resulted in all kinds of unintended consequences," she watches me drink. "For example," she continues, and I stop to stare into her all-knowing eyes. "The best vodka in the world is made from potatoes," she categorically says, her fingers pressing against the top of the table.

I pound the table for emphasis. "Exactly right. Exactly, what I say," deciding not to contain my enthusiasm.

"So where do you find potato vodka in today's crazy world of different kinds of vodka, colored ones, American imitations?" she asks.

"Poland," I instantly answer.

"A connoisseur," she responds with the brightest of bright smiles and our glasses clink as we toast. "*L'chayim*, to life," she proclaims.

"A hundred more years to you," I reply, touching the tip of her glass.

"One hundred, why not 150 more," she teasingly adds.

"Sure, why be so cautious," I say while she blushes, must be the strong liquor.

We finish the contents of our glasses and sit contentedly. So relaxed are we that the place could be the site of a bombing raid and we wouldn't care.

I look around the room and then speak to my hostess who is lovingly staring at me. "Do you get along with the neighbors?" I am curious about this potentially combustible mix of people.

"Well, at first they were suspicious about my return. I didn't help the situation when I took some of them to court to fight for my rightful property ownership." She holds tightly to her now empty glass.

"A big mess?" I can picture the round-faced peasants angry and petulant, like badly behaving children.

"It was solved the way most disputes get solved," she rubs her fingertips together. "With a *shmir* here and a *shmir* there," she uses the Yiddish word for bribe.

I laugh in appreciation. That's an old Soviet trick and one

that still effectively works in America.

"But my oldest son is a smart one; we need to fix this place up before I can move in, no indoor plumbing, the walls too thin, a mighty wind could cause such drafts. He hires the local villagers," she informs me.

"Good decision," I add with a nodding head.

"Exactly, now they come to see me as a money maker for them. I am valuable alive and in good enough health to live here on my own. He hires them for everything, maintenance for the house, keeping the outside property looking nice and neat, helping me with the garden. Two years ago, I was able to tend to it myself," she shakes her head. "But no longer, and I love fresh fruits and vegetables. A man and woman from the village are my expert gardeners."

"He keeps them on retainer for you, a constant stream of revenue," I catch on quickly to the ploy.

"Yes, and now we are all friends, but wait till I die," she bangs her palm on the table.

"Yes?" I am inquisitive.

"I get lots of other support from the Hasids in Minsk, the *Rebbe* is an American from Brooklyn," she watches my wide, expressive eyes.

"Borough Park I bet," I suggest.

"I don't know but that sounds good. I go to them in Minsk and stay in the *Rebbe's* house. I had trouble at first because they didn't want to take Boris, but I insisted. Since my son gives them money they relented. I go there frequently, and his yeshiva boys come every two weeks with kosher food and books, anything I need from the city. They were all afraid of Boris, but I taught them to differentiate vicious fighting dogs from my Boris," he is at her hand waiting to be petted.

"An important lesson," I laugh and touch the dog's fury head.

"When I die, this place will go to the *Rebbe* in Minsk," she roars in laughter.

"Really? Don't your sons want this place after all the fixing they paid for," I ask in amazement.

"No, my lawyer has all the papers. As long as my sons are alive and want to visit, they can with their children and grandchildren. After that it belongs to the Hasids, not to one particular rabbi, but the Hasidic community in Minsk. A poke in the eye to the gentiles. The Jews have returned and in great numbers," her slight body shakes in amusement. "What a change after fifty years," she is rocking with glee.

I join her.

She stands and returns to the stove. "Now I could use your help," she beckons to me with a crooked finger.

I am on my feet in seconds and the dog right next to me. I assist her serving as the waiter, carrying the main platter with its poached fish, lentils and fresh vegetables to the table.

The smells are mouth-watering, the flavors pouring into my nostrils, my stomach aching for the delectables. "Oh, everything is going to be delicious," I say. She hears my genuineness, perhaps even my gut screaming for food.

She arranges the dishes on the table in a very precise way, which I do not disturb. Each dish belongs on a specific spot on the table. She smiles at her creation, then serves me a hearty portion while the dog sits nearby licking his chops in anticipation. I fill our glasses.

"Boris, you be patient, I never fail to feed you." She stops to pet the dog's head, taking her seat too quickly for me to play the role of well-mannered guest.

"Well here's to a long, long life," I raise my glass.

She practically empties the glass in one gulp and pours us both refills. "I have lived a long life," she laughs. "Good vodka helps and watching what you eat, not too much. But you can't live forever." She serves herself a small portion from the ample offerings before us.

I taste the fish. "So good," realizing despite her age she is still a good cook. Fish can be a tricky dish – never cook too long or certainly serve raw.

We eat for a few quiet minutes but we both crave conversation.

"I dream; my dreams have been my messengers always in my life. Hashem speaks to me in those hazy hours of the darkness. They saved me from the Nazis and the Communists. I know, not exactly the moment, the day or the month or the year, but in my dreams, Boris and I leave this earth together." The dog moves closer to her upon hearing his name, wrapping his lean legs around her chair.

"No, no," I protest.

"Yes, yes, its fine. We all must die someday. I don't actually see my death, but Boris and I are together." She smiles in a sly way, an all-knowing way, a keeper of secrets that others cannot possibly ever know.

"Don't be so maudlin," I urge between bites; it's the vodka talking.

"Oh, it's fine really. I would wager. Are you a betting man?" she laughs and then tastes her own creation, pleased with the results.

"Yes, what will we bet on?" I ask as I finish a mouthful of lentils.

"My death – in a car accident. You should watch how those yeshiva boys drive. My eyesight is old and not as functional as it once was, but they don't know the gas pedal from the brake." She wildly swats the air with her hand in a display of angst from recalling the experience.

"Don't drive with them," is my recommendation.

"I just hope that they don't get killed or kill anyone else," she adds completely assured of the dream's meaning.

I shake my head and my finger at her. "No more talk of death," is my warning.

"If I am wrong," she speaks softly, not believing that is possible. "I have my sons promise to take good care of Boris if I go first. They made a vow to me. You understand the importance of such a thing for a Jew?" she asks in a most serious tone.

"Yes. It says in Numbers – 'if a man makes a vow to the Eternal or takes an oath imposing an obligation on himself, he shall not break his pledge; he must carry out all that has crossed his lips.'"

She pokes my hand with her deformed finger. "Good boy, you know your Talmud. I am impressed."

I luminously smile, the blush of the vodka covering my face.

"Your mother must be the inspiration for your biblical studies. She is a dreamer of visions. I always remember that about her. I'm certain while in prison, counting the days and weeks until her release that it was her dreams that assured her all would be right in the end. And see, it is," she gently jabs me in the arm.

"I guess," then I think about some of those dreams. Oh, how they disrupted our lives, especially, the ones about reburying all her dead relatives. They all had to rest together in the old Jewish Cemetery in St. Petersburg, everyone together in eternity – all but the dead child that was one of my mother's secrets. She was a keeper of all kinds of secrets. It was the Hasids from Borough Park who made it possible despite the costs and the seemingly endless delays. Ultimately with the desired end. "The Biblical Joseph is my mother," we both laugh.

My cousin the keeper of the family history speaks. "Her mother also possessed that special power. It's in the genes. She knew she would die during the Battle of Stalingrad, she told me before those horrific events, but she was not afraid of death because she heard God's message that enough of the family would survive. And it did. Right?" she tells me as one equally possessed.

"I remember near the end of his life that my grandfather also had vivid dreams. There was one – he dreamed it repeatedly. The giant bear, he interpreted that image as representing the fate of the Soviet Union, fatally shot. On his dying lips, words of love for the Revolution despite its obvious failings. My mother received second mention.

"It was said that his mother was called a witch. Her dreams always came true and she frightened people with those dreams. Remember, we lived in ignorant times before the Revolution. So maybe your grandfather always dreamed vibrant dreams but kept it to himself because of how people reacted to his mother."

She cuts a big piece of fish, dropping it daintily into her

small mouth.

"Umm...mmm," is my reaction to the vegetables, roasted ever so lightly.

"Sasha my boy, do you have dreams of prophecy?" she asks with heightened interest.

"No, in my dreams I don't see the future, but I have this intuitive sense," I softly thump my chest. "I feel it in here," I touch my heart. "As a cop that often makes my job easier, although it's tough to explain to my superiors why I think certain ways."

"I understand, perhaps in your old age, the dreams will come to you, it's a certain family trait on both sides," she takes my hand. "I know after your mother's experiences with the KGB that naturally she's not pleased with you being a police officer. But we all remind her that her father was a good public servant, a government official, dutifully obeying orders that he didn't always support." She shakes a finger close to my nose.

"I like my job as a cop, often solving riddles, determining people's motivations -- not just that someone committed a heinous crime but why. It teaches us about ourselves, who we are. Really, the truth is that humans are not more compassionate or pious than your dog," I stop to pat his head; I am rewarded with some wild tail wagging.

"Yes, I can imagine that it is interesting and dangerous in New York City, all those murders and such," she manages to neatly stuff another large mouthful of lentils into her mouth. She pours us both another round of drinks.

Finally, I am forced to admit, "I'm stuffed, I don't think I can eat anything more," patting my stomach.

"Oh, later we'll have dessert," she says. Already she is preparing the scraps for Boris who waits patiently.

"I'll help with these," I start to remove the dirty dishes form the table.

"Don't bother, tomorrow a village woman comes here to clean and straighten up, no problem, just leave everything in the sink, that's good enough." She watches as Boris cleans the plate so not the tiniest morsel of food is found.

"Should I give him these plates and we won't have to wash them?" I ask with a short giggle; dogs are so amusing to watch.

"Maybe except for the fish bones," she informs me in utter seriousness.

I perform my limited tasks. "Anything else you want me to do," I try to be helpful.

"No, just sit and talk. I love Boris, but he doesn't talk so I'm glad to have some human company, especially my family that I don't see often." She allows Boris to drink water from a bowl off the table.

She joins me on the couch and we sit near each together, centimeters separate our thighs.

"My mother told me that you were a partisan during the Great Patriotic War, fighting the Nazis," on hearing my words she grasps my hands.

"Yes, that's true. It couldn't be helped," she adds.

"Oh please, you are a brave woman, courageous to do those sorts of things," I reply.

"No, no, I am not brave, pin no medals of courage on my chest. It was a matter of survival - that simple. I was not afraid to die, but I didn't want to die at that point in time," she answers.

"Can you tell me some of what happened," I respectfully inquire,

"So long ago," she sighs, the depth of despair still residing in her heart.

"It's true that not all Jews went to the gas chambers like sheep," I add.

"True, very true, especially in the Russian territories where locals—Jews and gentiles and Red Army units mixed together in support of each other. Many of the Red Army units sent out in 1941 in response to the Nazi invasion were captured. Still others managed to escape and regroup with the help of local people." She recounts a history lost to most westerners.

"What a mistake for Stalin to trust Hitler, so many innocent people died because of that disastrous decision." I shake my head in disgust at the poor choices made by former Soviet leaders.

"So much went wrong in 1941. But my survival was revealed in a dream," she tells me.

Dreams can be dangerous and enlightening. I suppose also life-saving. "Before Operation Barbarossa?" I ask her, referring to the name given to Hitler's invasion of Russia and its republics.

"Yes, in the early spring of 1941, just before we were visited by the agents of hell, when Jews were still alive in the millions in their villages, towns and cities across the great Slavic plains. Before the Nazi madness," she says with a sadness that time will never heal.

"What do you remember?"

"I knew death was near. In my dream, my dead grandfather spoke to me. 'Take the children away from danger. Go now,' he told me. My husband was in the Red Army on the western front. My mother thought I was mad, ranted and raved in anger, but I traveled to Moscow. I had to do it despite the distance," she emphatically tells me with a strained strength.

"Were you in Moscow in the summer?" I ask.

The invading Nazi armies overwhelmed the Red Army at the start of Operation Barbarossa, part of the Nazi plan of controlling what they called Ostland, the Baltic states of Estonia, Latvia and Lithuania and neighboring Belarus. With the start of this phase of the war, millions of Russians, especially Jews suffered, thousands murdered at a time.

On June 27, 1941, Bialystok in northeastern Poland became Nazi territory. The Jews were herded into the Great Synagogue like cattle, the holy place torched, 800 innocents burning to death. Another group of Nazi divisions captured Minsk on that same day. Whole Red Army units were surrounded by the 200-mile Nazi advance, and while almost 300,000 Red soldiers were captured, more than 250,000 escaped to continue the bloody fight.

The Nazi Army got to Moscow in December 1941, as far east as they would ever come, but they had underestimated the resolve of the Red Army and the citizens. With no shelter, lacking supplies and unprepared for a brutal Russian winter, the German troops bunkered down near Moscow while the casualties mounted due to the determined Red Army forces and the frigid weather.

"I managed to get to Moscow and leave my children with old friends; two of my sons survived, the youngest died. I was trapped. I could not get back to this village with the approaching Nazi armies," her voice lowers while her hands turn to ice.

"War divides families," I say.

"Yes," her voice grows very tiny. "I joined with shattered Red Army troops, local villagers, even a few Jews who managed to escape the rampage. Remarkably, I was able to make my way west, but it took more than two years." She rests her head against my shoulder for support both physical and moral.

"I can't imagine how difficult," I offer condolences.

"When I get here," the tears come pouring out, an unleashing of a reservoir of regrets. The sobs come forcefully, her thin shoulders shaking with the sobbing.

"Don't say any more," I hug her, afraid to squeeze too tightly.

But she pushes away. "You can't know, dead all dead. Those bastards had the Jews, my mother, my father, my sister and all the children, all the children, all the innocents, what did they do?" and her tears cannot be reconciled. "Dead, empty of people, all gone," she stops, the tears falling onto her lap. She sits crying, quietly. I am silent, respectful to all the dead --so many dead, too many to count, although the Nazis kept meticulous records.

Finally, moving closer, I hug her tighter. "It was a long time ago," I soothingly say.

"Dead, all dead," the tears show no sign of ebbing. "They poured lye on the dead bodies, some still alive. They knew, those Nazi bastards; they knew that they were committing evil, heinous acts, not human. One cousin did manage to survive, hiding under dead bodies; he saw, so many dead that they could not bury them fast enough," unexpectedly some strength returns to her speech, a new tenacity. "It's why I stay here, a reminder, a witness," she wipes her eyes. Her fingers are damp as is her face; the cheeks shiny from the moisture, the salt finding home in her deep crevices.

"Tissues?" I ask hoping that she is feeling better.

She points to a dresser. I hesitate to leave her even for a moment, but I see the mucus dripping unflatteringly.

I locate the box, an American brand, and hand it to her; she gracefully manages to repeatedly blow her nose and clear her passages.

"I'm sorry," she is apologetic.

"Don't be silly," I say, clutching her hands.

"I don't know what got into me, the vodka perhaps," the impish smile returns. She touches the edge of my chin with her thumb, turning my head in one direction and then another. "It's the way you hold your head; it reminds me so much of my father. The moment I saw you today as an adult, his image flashed into my brain; it's the little things. Let me show you," she rises from the couch to retrieve a photo album. She delicately places it on the sofa. She sits down and turns the fading, thinning pages.

"Here he is," she ever so gently strokes the edge of the crumbling photo.

I stare and see the resemblance, the chin. I can't see the eyes too clearly. "Yes, I do see it," I add.

Rising she says, "Look it over. Let me get that dessert.

You sit and look through the pages. I have several more books. Maybe you will find a few that you like and take back to your mother."

I smile at her. "My mother would like that," I nod my head as I notice her still studying me.

"You look over those pages and I'll tell you who they are. Most are relatives, long gone, but some are of villagers. I even have a couple of gentiles who are still alive here in this village. You're going to stay for the night?"

I glance out the window. The light is starting to vanish. Darkness comes quickly.

"Of course," I immediately answer. Should I call Tom? Hell no, is he my mother? Oh, but the car. "Excuse me for a minute, I need to call someone. I'll just walk outside on the porch." Plus, there's my nightly call back to New York to US Attorney Cohen.

CHAPTER 17

Tom is waiting for me as I emerge from my room.

"Nice trip?" he asks, his mouth partially open, his puppy dog manners returned. "I've eaten, and I need to run a few errands. Can I leave you on your own for about an hour?"

You want to come with me?" he asks. I hand him the keys and he takes them into his palm, rubbing them as if they were a magic amulet. "No thanks," I quickly reply. I am not hungry for his company.

Before I venture outside to find an open café, I go to check my mail. The desk clerk is happy to see me. "Herr Erdmann, your package," he smiles as he hands me the small, tightly wrapped parcel.

I stare at the finely typed words. The address is Saudi Arabia. "Thanks," I don't know why but I hand him several crisp euros. His smile grows so much larger, his smoke-stained teeth show.

"Oh, Herr Erdmann, thank you, thank you," he quickly hides his gift.

I decide to open my prize in private, leave the hotel and start walking down the avenue. I know something about the area. I feel things are going to change for the better. I now have something to offer my recalcitrant suspect – a reward for good behavior.

I hear the footsteps but don't turn around. It could be anyone.

"Herr Erdmann," the deep, unfamiliar male voice says.

I instantly turn to face the source calling my new name. I don't know this man, but his buzz cut hairdo immediately leads me to ask, "Mr. John Smith?"

"Yes, can I join you for breakfast?" he asks.

I extend my hand in friendship.

He physically withdraws. "Let's keep walking. Go straight ahead down this block and then take a quick left. There's a little café, take a table in the rear," he disappears into a small alleyway.

I don't know if I like this spy business, but I follow his instructions. When I arrive at the small restaurant, I point to a back table and the waiter lets me find my own seat. I slip onto the hard, wooden chair. The table-cloth is spotlessly clean, the floors recently washed, remarkable considering that the general ambiance is shabby, old and worn. There's out-of-date lighting fixtures, windows in need of caulking, cracked tiles, a sense of failure and exhaustion pervades.

Within minutes the stranger joins me, his eyes darting, searching for something or someone. I don't speak, waiting for him to make the first move.

"Okay, this is good," his accent is flavored with the

strong, consonant tones of the American Midwest.

"Lots of mystery," I add with a widening grin.

"We should be careful," he admonishes me.

"So is John Smith your real name," I inquire with my grin increasing.

"Hell yes, I'm not covert for Christ stake, I'm the field operations guy. Shit," he shakes his head in disgust but then stares into my eyes. "Don't get me wrong. I like NYPD cops. I'm very pleased to finally have some professionals to work with on this case."

"If this is not a covert operation what's with all the darting into alleyways?"

"This is a former Soviet state, they think like Soviets so it's best to keep a low-profile, that's all," he reassuringly tells me.

"OK," the universal response.

The waiter moseys over to the table, tiny pad in hand ready to take our order, and asks in Russian, "Gentlemen, what can I get you?"

John seems to understand that he is asking about food. He looks to me for advice. I turn towards him. "Eggs, sausage, something like that?"

"Anything breakfast like," he answers and closes the menu, which apparently, he can't read.

I tell our waiter in Russian. "One order of eggs with

sausage and potatoes and the second order, poached eggs, two cups of coffee and orange juice." "What do we know?" he returns to business.

"So far nothing. I have been unsuccessful in getting her to talk. What do you know about her?"

"German intelligence says they think she's been living in some Arab enclave in Hamburg. There's no camera footage specifically identifying her, but then again, these women have so much clothing on it's hard to see faces. Her DNA is supposedly genetically very similar to members of the Muslim Brotherhood whose DNA and fingerprints they do have on file. That's really the only tangible evidence we have. She could be a wife, sister, cousin, daughter, who knows. That's why you're here."

"Doesn't German immigration have something on her?" I ask.

"No, they are only guessing because, so many Arabs live in this small area and most of them are there illegally. Think we're the only ones with this immigration problem?" he continues.

"I have seen tapes of her when she was brought to the prison. At least three other people have had contact with her here in Belarus. What did they tell you?"

"Fucking contractors like that jerk Tom. They know nothing about interrogating potentially high value prisoners.

They're a couple of former military types but not in intelligence, police or special ops, just assholes with some connections. No bid contracts to friend of friends in the White House or the Defense Department, but amateurs," he can hardly contain his disgust.

"What about the guys who flew me here on some CIA plane?"

"Those are genuinely scary guys. Word is that they oversee all those extraordinary rendition prisons. Torture experts. We don't need them anywhere near this prisoner. What kind of horrible press would the US government receive if any word got out that we tortured some woman."

"I agree. You may know my history?" I ask.

"Oh, yes. I have your file about your mother being a torture victim. Torture is unreliable," his voice unwavering.

"I am glad that we agree. We couldn't work together if we disagreed on this point," my voice adamant.

"No, we are in lock-step together on this," he smiles.

"Have you seen those tapes?" I sip the orange juice, taking it out of the waiter's hand as he quickly brings us napkins, silverware and the rest of the liquid refreshments. "No, is there anything of interest on them?" he pours sugar into his coffee and then drinks without blowing off the steam.

"No, the people asking the questions spoke in English and there was a translator present., but since I don't speak

Arabic, I don't know exactly what the translator said to her." I answer with the jaded skepticism of someone who has worked with cagey translators. There are those who don't properly translate but editorialize or worse, the incompetents, the American college types who don't understand slang or colloquialisms and fail to relay the proper message.

He turns to me. "That's a big problem. We've got fools who don't speak Arabic questioning important suspects. We don't know if she's a terrorist or just an illegal immigrant. You are my best hope. I trust you. I am surrounded with incompetents. I can't sleep at night worrying about what's going on and how little we know. I depend upon foreign governments to provide the best intel—the Germans, Spanish, Israelis, English. It's awful," he picks at his eggs once the waiter places them before him.

"I'm going to try my best," I feel the weight of the whole American intelligence community on my lean shoulders.

"I swore my allegiance to this country. I am ready to die for this country. I work with people whose allegiance is to the almighty buck, contractors who only work for the money. We have a few ex-CIA working for the contractors for money – money, what the fuck is that all about! Money and they leave and make two, three times their CIA salaries. Wash-outs, reckless idiots, dangerous, really. You would not want to put your life in their hands." He pokes at the food and then decides to try it. "Good," he digs into the potatoes.

"Do you think anyone beat or tortured her? Those guys from the plane?" I warily ask.

"McNulty and Wright have not been near her, no torture experts. Does she look like she's been beaten? The Belarus guards wouldn't touch her unless an American authorized it. I don't think anyone in Washington authorized her to be roughed up. There's still some regard against hurting women." He continues to eat. "Good."

My meal arrives. I test the stiffness of one yolk, gingerly picking at the surface. With one stroke it bursts, the yellowish yolk spilling out on the plate. I mop up a little with a slice of bread.

Smith notices the package and points to it.

"I got this Koran," showing him my precious packet. "This is my carrot. She is already living with the stick, a windowless cell, harsh lights 24/7. The book is to demonstrate my good intentions. I have also ordered the guards to dim the lights at night, but she's not leaving that cell. I have to play the roles of both good cop and bad cop – kinda schizophrenic really – I offer the carrot and then take it away if I don't get some answers." I clutch the small book close to my chest.

"Right, try and find out who she is, then we can get German intelligence and perhaps Israeli or Egyptian intelligence to confirm it. Once we know who she is, then it's what the fuck was she doing in New York with a bunch of scum gangbangers from El Salvador – MS-13. Christ what is going on?" he mutters, tasting the buttery toast; it shines from the thick coat of butter.

We sit in silence, slowly sipping our coffee; an important culinary achievement – strong but not bitter coffee -- the restaurant fails to produce. They need to clean the urn with vinegar.

"Going with me to the prison? Want to talk with her?" I ask as I push the plate away from the edge as the waiter hovers and pours more coffee.

"What good am I to you? I don't speak German and I certainly don't speak Arabic, but I'm going to school, so I can learn at least what they're saying about me with my back turned, defensive measure." For the first time, he gives me a buoyant smile.

"Alright but come along and watch the cameras while I question her. I think your presence will be useful to me regarding the guards. They treat me with great respect, but you look like the guy in charge." Mr. Smith possesses that arrogant American way that low paid guards truly fear and admire.

"Sure."

"We'll take Tom along?"

"He's the chauffeur, that's all he's good for," he shakes his head in exasperation.

I don't agree. Tom listens and observes. He is valuable,

and I need to let him talk more often.

The meal finished, we walk out of the restaurant together. The waiters wave, delighted with the nice tip I leave every time. People are not friendly in this town, suspicious of all strangers; we look like foreigners, too well dressed, our leather shoes polished, a crisp manner in our strides; we live in a world of hope.

"There's Tom waiting for us," I point my head towards his direction.

"Mr. Smith," he says and bends his head in deference.

"Take us to the prison Tom and then wait. You got a magazine or some music to listen to? Because we may be there for several hours."

"I'm ready Mr. Smith. I've got some new CDs, Christian rock groups. I can lend them to you," he opens the door for our leader. The car is roomy, plenty of space in the back seat for both of us.

"No Tom," John Smith responds. "You keep those tapes," John winks at me.

We all remain quiet as our chauffeur drives us into the countryside towards the prison. There is stillness. Fear hangs in the air, even the birds stay away, afraid to perch on the wires.

The guards are glad to see us, never knowing when we will depart, and the money will end, their salaries and possible pensions lost. We are greeted with a big smile by my talkative guard.

"Welcome this morning, Herr Erdmann," he says in Russian with a slight tilt of the head.

"This is my colleague from America, John Smith," I make my introductions in Russian.

"I am interested in seeing the prisoner." John says in English and the guard looks at me for a translation. I do the necessary verbal regurgitation.

We follow in the guard's steps through the entrance where we meet the others. With his buzz haircut and ramrod straight posture, the guards are immediately deferential.

I speak for us both. "I will see the prisoner while Mr. Smith watches us on camera." We accompany my friendly guard to the observation room with the rows and rows of blank screens, only our prisoner visible. John takes his seat and stares at the screen. She is completely immobile, almost like a mannequin; once again I marvel at her discipline.

I whisper to my colleague. "I'm going now with the Koran," the small bundle tightly held in my hand.

The one guard and I walk together through the empty corridors. Our footsteps reverberate, the sounds bouncing from the hard floors to the low hanging ceiling, back and forth as we walk down silent hallways until we stand in front of her cell. He unlocks the massive door and I enter. She does not move or turn her attention to me. Before he shuts the door, I request,

"Bring me a chair and a small table." The guard nods his head.

I wait with the door open until he returns with the Spartan furniture. He places the table in one corner and I grab the chair, placing it near her bed.

Standing near her, but not too close, I announce in German, "I have something for you."

Immediately, her eyes look up at me. I hand her the book, which she tentatively takes from me. Her first reaction is a deep sigh, clutching the book to her chest. She closes her eyes and sighing again, deeper and more demonstrative. Some of her anguish is leaving, the heaviness of her isolation, her chest moving in and out, the breaths coming at longer intervals. I am present but invisible to her.

I allow her these moments of pleasure and then I attack. I grab the book from her hands, holding it over my head. She gulps for air, the oxygen departing her lungs. Her face collapses, her eyes wide open, her mouth ajar.

Then I give it back to her. "Who are you?"

She lovingly touches the book, caressing the cover, then kissing it.

"I can make your life worth living or a torment. Which is it going to be?" I stand right in front of her. She acknowledges my presence by lifting her head and staring into my eyes. These are beautiful eyes, deep-set, luminous, dark and almond shaped.

"Who are you?" Again, I go to grab the book, but this

time she is better prepared and pulls away, shielding the book from my outstretched arm.

"I'll let you keep it, this book you hold in such regard, but only in exchange for information. Who are you?" I repeat myself, but my tone of voice is harsher and louder.

I hold all the cards.

"Who are you? What's your name and where are you from?" my tone demanding, my arm ready to snatch away the prize.

She pulls away, but I don't see fear. She doesn't make any attempt to protect herself from my out-stretched arms.

Standing, I tower over her, my shadow falling across her sitting body. Bigger and stronger, I grab the book and pull it away from her.

Her face is despondent, but she remains calm, no audible cries of anguish can be heard.

She watches me and the book.

"Here," I offer it to her, but my hand remains securely on it. "Who are you?"

We both grip the book. "Tell me your name?" We play at a push and pull game, neither one of us letting go. "Tell me and it's yours."

"Lateefa al-Banna," she announces, then returns to silence.

"And?" I say looming above her.

"I have been living in Hamburg," she tells me in German.

"Where exactly? I know Hamburg so be specific. I will know if you're lying," I tell her truthfully. Last year, I did go there with my uncle who lives in Berlin, Germany.

My captured suspect fingers the edges of her precious Koran then gives me a precise location; an address and a description of her neighborhood.

"Is that near the green grocer?" I try and test her. Does she really live in Hamburg?

"No," she quickly replies, and describes a different scene.

Although I do not know the neighborhood she is describing, it feels right. It will be simple to confirm.

"What bus lines do you use?" I ask as my best locator.

"I don't travel the buses," she tells me without hesitation.

"Where is the mosque?" I bellow.

"Two blocks away," and explains in intricate detail her path.

"Where is your husband?" I am not even certain that she has a husband.

She says nothing but presses the book against her stomach and covers it with her body.

That doesn't stop me. My hand wiggles and manages to wrangle a piece of the book in my fingers. My grip is too strong.

"Your husband, where is he? Tell me and you can keep this. No lies," my hand retains control.

She tries to pull the book away but cannot. Her angry eyes meet mine. "He is dead," she loudly proclaims, but her fury seems centered on the book, not about her deceased spouse.

"Then who do you live with?" a foreign-born, Muslim woman cannot possibly be living alone in Hamburg.

"My brother," she says, and I release my control. She quickly gathers up her prized possession and covers it with both hands.

"Who is your brother? What is his name?" I recognize the family name as belonging to the founding family of the Muslim Brotherhood.

More silence follows. My long arm reaches across the bed and towards her folded hands.

"Rashid," she mumbles, eyes focused on the book, not my face.

Some big gaps still exist. "Your children?" I'm still guessing.

"I don't know," her voice shriller, the words edgy; there is deep sadness.

"I am going to check this out," I immediately tell her. "Your name and where you come from. If you are lying to me, the book is mine. If you're telling me the truth, then we will continue our nice chat. I want you to think about this. I must know what you were doing in the United States. Forget about the book – you will never see natural daylight if you're not forthcoming. Tell me more – only the truth -- and I'll get you a cell with a window. Lie to me and the harsh lights return, the book is taken away and you'll rot here till you die. I have an American intelligence agent watching us. You don't want to lie to him or make him unhappy. Right?"

She nods her head, still holding tightly to the little book, which once again she kisses.

"Are we clear?" I stand with my head close to hers.

Her neck lifts and she speaks. "Yes, I understand."

I study her. The stillness returns. Only our breathing can be heard. She knows that I am observing her and does not move or even blink. She is waiting for me to leave so she can read her precious book.

"I am leaving. But I will return," I exclaim in a loud voice but without budging. Still she does not look up or move her body; she is motionless, which I understand from my SWAT days. We are both immobile. Finally, I take one step and then another. She does not look. I get to the prison cell door and bang on the metal with my closed fist. I turn towards her and I think I see a slight turning of her head. My friendly guard arrives to release me.

For emphasis, I noisily slam the heavy door shut. The brittle, metallic sounds shatter the silence.

The guard and I chat amicably as we return to the security room. "Anything interesting happen at the prison in my absence?" I ask without expecting real news.

"You are the interesting news," he replies with a big smile. "Someday, I will go to Germany, what do you think?" he inquires in a boastful manner, waving his arms.

"Sure, and when you do, look me up," I reply, knowing that cannot happen.

"The American is your boss?" he asks in a more serious, flat tone.

"He's the man," I answer and nod my head to affirm my response as we approach the room filled with computer screens.

John is waiting for me, rocking in the most comfortable chair, the guards standing far from him as if he is suffering from a contagious disease.

"Okay fellows, thanks," John tells them, standing and pushing aside the chair. They do not understand a word. "Herr Erdmann, we need to go," he informs me.

I speak in Russian. "We will be back. By the way," I face the senior guard. "Can we borrow the tape from today?" I haven't returned the other tapes, but no one asks for them back.

Immediately, a lower ranked guard goes to retrieve the valuable property. The senior man points to the log book and I sign it.

Carrying my bundle, we leave. Once in the daylight, Smith is ready to talk but first he turns around to see if the guards are watching us. My friendly guard is still there, waving. I wave back.

"What do you think?" I ask.

"I don't speak any German and certainly not Russian, so you tell me what's going on," he responds heading towards the car and the waiting Tom. As we advance, our dutiful young man opens the back doors.

"Well guys where to? It's not a bad looking day, how about Minsk?" he smilingly asks.

"First, we review the tapes, then we can go to Minsk for dinner," John orders.

"I have other tapes in my room from her first days. I have reviewed them, but another set of eyes could be useful."

"Good," he slips in the back seat.

"Fine with me," Tom replies as he closes the doors. He slips the key into the ignition. "Buckle up because the locals drive like drunken sailors," then he starts whistling.

John closes his eyes for a moment and shakes his head.

I am thinking that we are underestimating Tom. He may know more about the torture guys.

CHAPTER 18

John and I spend several hours reviewing and revisiting the tapes, over and over. While I translate, Tom makes elaborate arrangements for our night out on the town.

"Do you know the men who first interviewed her?" I ask Smith.

"No, but they could be contractors," he reports. "We are sending the tapes to Virginia, where they will be more carefully examined for any tampering. Someone in Germany or Langley should be able to verify the identity of our prisoner or at least the locations in Hamburg."

"Do you think she was tortured?" I ask again, even though I don't see any evidence.

"The guards would know. Did they say anything?"

"I haven't asked them directly. They want to be helpful. They would say anything they think I would want to hear. But I'm getting friendly with one. He, I will ask." That's my plan.

We did learn a key fact, "al-Banna is an important name," John informs me. "The Egyptians were right. This confirms the accuracy of the results of her DNA test. It indicated that she was genetically related to the al-Banna family. Now we know she is an al-Banna. This woman could be a very important person."

As the early evening approaches, Tom calls up to my room. "Ready?" he asks. "Our tour guide is waiting for us."

"Give me time to shower and change, thirty minutes," I tell them both. I seem to be the only person concerned with appearances.

As I emerge from the elevators half an hour later, there is Tom, as usual smiling and whistling. John is standing at his side looking distracted, examining his nails.

"I've got great plans," Tom reports and we believe him.

During the drive, we all talk pleasantries. I notice that John does very little sharing with Tom, treating him like a dutiful servant. "You'll take care of my dry cleaning, Tom?"

"Of course, Mr. Smith," although I can't see his face in the front seat of the car, I am certain he is smiling.

The drive is uneventful. We are the recipients of first class treatment at the restaurant; doors are held open, chairs are pulled out, napkins are slipped onto our laps, menus appear, and drinks arrive without a word spoken.

"We're going to have a five-course dinner and then the best seats in the nightclub upstairs. They asked me if you are interested in some girls, even boys," he whispers in embarrassment. "I told them to ask you directly," a reddish blush covers his cheeks.

John laughs. "Tom, do you think I like little boys?" his superior is pushing all the buttons; Tom's face is so red it looks like he is ready to explode; a hot comet, gases erupting, cosmic collision.

He can hardly speak. "Oh, oh," he faces the floor. "Mr. Smith, I'm only repeating their suggestions. Please, I don't know," he mumbles something we cannot understand. "Please," he clutches the napkin on his lap. The perspiration is soaking his palms.

John roars with amusement at Tom's awkward reactions. "Relax Tom. I don't think Herr Erdmann and I need anything more than a good dinner, a couple of drinks and a night club act," he pokes me on the arm.

"Right Tom, just the ordinary for me," I cannot stop laughing. My tears don't stop despite my constant dabbing in the corner of my eyes.

An open bottle of red wine is presented to us, then a bottle of white wine. "Something else?" the waiter asks in Russian.

"What's your drink, John? Tom?" I ask.

"I'll take a scotch – do they have Johnny Walker?" John asks, and I translate. The waiter nods.

"I don't usually drink more than beer so I'm happy with the wine," Tom replies.

"Vodka," I reply. "Got the potato version, a good Polish

brand?" I ask. The waiter nods in approval.

Our evening proceeds amicably, although Tom is certainly knocking back a few. After his initial refusal of hard liquor, he tries and likes my vodka. We are forced to help our chauffeur to our seats in the nightclub.

In the cavernous club with old-fashioned strobe lights and glittering walls, I ask the barely upright Tom, "Coffee?"

"I don't want coffee so late, it will keep me up" he tells us, his slurring words almost inaudible.

We don't need a nightclub act, Tom is our entertainment for the evening. The costumes are the most professional aspect of the several singing and dancing acts. My colleagues cannot understand a word the comic says.

"I don't think he can drive," I find the whole episode quite amusing, hiccupping between laughs.

John is even more entertained. "Go figure, look at him," he pokes his arm and the man practically slips under the table. We both grab his arms and place him back on the seat.

"Do you want to drive?" I ask John.

"Hell no, I'm not too steady, nor are you. Forget it; we don't have any reason to get back. There's a hotel right here, a nice one. We'll check in and spend the night. What's our rush? I made the report. It will take German and American intelligence days, maybe even a week, to determine if she's giving us reliable information. The Germans will probably consult the

Brits, Egyptians, maybe the Israelis. It will take two weeks before we have anything worthwhile," he announces. "Enjoy the respite because if she's playing us you will have to get nasty, and if she's on the level then we need guidance about what questions to ask."

With the help of a brawny waiter, we get Tom to his feet, the staff more than happy to find us three rooms. John and I manage to get Tom undressed to his boxers and leave him to sleep it off.

"I'm beat, see you in the morning," John announces and heads to his room.

I check out my room; it was large enough, the drapes not too cheap, the carpeting plush but not expensive, and the wallpaper not too dizzy looking. Liberated from dull and drab Soviet tastes, there's often a tendency to be too gaudy, but the decorating was temperate.

I attempt to go to bed but am restless. That happens with booze and me. I feel exhausted after a couple of hours of vodka straight up, no water, no ice, and then two hours later I'm ready to party. I decide to see what else the hotel has to offer, the noisy nightclub not one of my options.

I ask the desk clerk, "What else have you got for entertainment?"

"There's a nice quiet bar around the corner favored by the locals. Try it out. You speak Russian, you don't need a touristy place," I give him a few euros for his trouble.

"Thanks, let me know if you need anything else," he has a big smile for me. The new worker class was happy to be rewarded; it was not yet an expectation but a true appreciation.

The bar is tucked into the end of a narrow alleyway. It is still early for the hard-partying set, the place populated but not overly crowded, everyone speaking Russian or Belarusian.

I immediately spot her at a table with a few other people. She is striking in that Slavic way; dark, wavy hair, high cheekbones, fair skin and angular face, the sure sign of a Jewish intellectual somewhere in her bloodlines. I am sure that I know her, but from where? When her two friends depart, I make my move.

"I know this sounds like the worst pick-up line, but I know that I know you." I stand nearby waiting for an invitation to join her.

She stares at me and the small lines at the edges of her mouth thicken as her smile brightens the room. It's a 'gotcha' moment.

"Vasily's wedding," her arm extends towards me. "Sit," she points to a chair across from her but not the one next to her.

Yes, my best friend's wedding in Israel. It just after Marina's death. Vasily felt my pain in a way my jaded mother could not, and my methodical father just accepted as another of life's cruel realities.

The original wedding plan was for a double ceremony in Israel – Vasily and his bride, me and mine, oh, my dear, dear Dr. Marina. She called me sweetie; I was her love and she was mine. A moment of dark despair overwhelms me but the sparkling eyes before me bring me back to this world, my beating heart, my damp perspiration, my rhythmic breath.

"Of course, Natasha," I laugh, and she joins me. Her laugh is as full and inviting as her smile – she is life in all its fullness.

"What are you doing in Minsk, Belarus?" she asks, the smile fading as her lips pucker into a grimace. She is eyeing me with new suspicion.

"I'm here on business," I nonchalantly answer.

"Business? Aren't you an American policeman?" the tension grows as her anti-official instincts lock into gear.

"Yes, but I'm working on something else," we are not friendly enough for me to share too much. "I also went to see a relative who lives in a village not too far away, a cousin of my grandmother's, an old woman, the only Jew in the village, remarkable really." Temporarily distracted by the face of cousin Nadia and her dog Boris, I laugh out loud, picturing how Nadia and Boris were almost the same height. "The old woman said that I didn't recognize her immediately because she was taller when I saw her last."

Natasha isn't as amused; she neither smiles nor laughs. Well, she wasn't in that village.

"You came from America to Belarus to see a cousin? What police business is here in this backwater of a country?" she is nervous, her long fingers repetitively tapping the table top.

"You're a pharmacologist, right?" I ask and continue grinning; the vodka is fading.

"Yes," her mouth is open as if she is going to say more but stops herself, watching me for a reaction.

I fling open my hands in the air, trying to be as casual as possible. She's suspicious of an American cop doing business in Belarus; makes no sense. "Listen," I reach across the table for her hand, which she allows me to touch. "My business is terrorism. Are you a terrorist?" I gently stroke the top of her hand.

She smiles; it is slow in forming and gradually grows, the tiny lines around her mouth deepening, the cute little dimples making an appearance. She is almost relaxed. "Terrorism, what kind of terrorism?" she asks.

"The bad stuff, but I really can't talk about it. Very hush, hush," I place my index finger on my lips to exaggerate my point.

"Ok," she is satisfied for the moment and signals for the

waiter.

He stands by my chair. "A round of vodka?" he asks.

"I had my limit. I'll take a Coke," I touch my growling stomach.

He interprets that to mean hunger. "A menu?" the server inquires.

"No, just the Coke, and the lady will take a vodka?" I turn to Natasha.

"No, I'll also take a Coke, but bring a menu," she assumes control of the situation.

"You work in a pharmaceutical company here in Minsk?" I am trying to recall what she did tell me at the wedding.

A former Soviet official – a Ph.D. in chemistry from a prestigious Russian university, she quickly informs me of her position. "I run the pharmaceutical company."

"For domestic use or international?" I'm just curious. I know that Vasily must be connected to the plant, a silent partner, probably an investor with his brother. In America, my best friend is tagged with the dubious reputation as a Russian gangster. It is an inadequate moniker; it fails to describe him or his business interests. As a cop, I keep away. However, my boyhood friend is smart, a well-educated engineer; ambitious, not a menacing hoodlum.

Natasha hesitates. "International, we manufacture for foreign distribution. It's cheap here – the workers, energy, general expenses. It's not China; we don't cut costs so severely that we distribute dangerous medicines. I am an ethical person, not on my watch. But I don't want to talk about it. Why should we discuss business -- yours or mine? Tell me about your cousin in the hinterlands," we get our cans of Coke and she selects a potpourri of appetizers.

We talk amicably for a couple of hours and I regale her with tales of my family history. She is genuinely entertained with my stories. I cause tears of laughter and moments of sadness as I share with her. This storytelling comes easily; in my family, we all retain a bit of the theatrical. The best opener was discussing my grandfather, followed with growing up with my mother, and then there was the family legend – Uncle Vanya the Cossack. Stories, I have weeks and weeks of stories to tell.

Her business and my business are not discussed. It's too bad that she lives in this place. I'm not good at distant romance; out of sight often leaves me with no consciousness of the relationship. I'm a student of the immediate, although lately I find myself haunted by my women – the dead and the living – Olga's image continues to slip into my brain, or is it another organ?

"We'll keep in touch," I tell her as we depart the bar.

"Of course," she responds although we don't really believe our own words.

When I wake in the late morning, I shower and dress, then head for the lobby, looking for my colleagues, hesitating to call them in their rooms. Tom is probably still wiped out and John also dragging. The desk clerk tries to be helpful.

"Herr Erdmann, I have not seen your associates," he tells me. I hand him a few euros.

"If you see them, tell them I went to get breakfast," I announce. Since the day looks decent, I decide to try a restaurant nearby, the one without the tourists. I don't need translators, although Minsk does not feel at all like home. Even during the worst of Soviet times with the long queues and the diminished offerings in the market, St. Petersburg always retains the feel of a cosmopolitan city. I could never live in some backwater place like this.

The sun is deceiving. I am cold. I miss Brighton Beach, Brooklyn where the sun always feels warm this time of the year. The streets are not crowded in Minsk; people are going here and there presumably in pursuit of business or education, but not happiness. That's uniquely American, this pursuit of happiness.

I am engrossed in my own thoughts. The hand catches me unexpectedly on the shoulder; I quickly turn on my heels ready for action, my fists closed for maximum impact.

I face the intruder. "Shit, what are you doing here?" My best friend in the whole wide world, Vasily, smiles at me.

"I'm visiting. I come to see you," we fall into the same stride as we walk down the street.

"What are you talking about? What are you doing here?" my tone is persistent; no evasive answers will do.

"Natasha called me. She was very confused about seeing my friend the police officer in Minsk," he tells me, his arm on my shoulder.

"I told her, I was on terrorist business here, hush, hush" I am truly surprised to find him here.

"This way," he directs me with his hip, pushing me towards the right and a small cafe.

The waiter seems to know him, displaying an unusually wide grin. Vasily points to a back table, and the waiter bends his wrist in agreement.

"Sit," he enthusiastically says with his usual peppy voice, full of energy and ideas, the consummate dreamer who realizes his most farfetched dreams.

"Did you just come from Brighton Beach?" I can't believe it.

"No, I was in Kiev on a different business matter when Natasha called. She was very insistent that I come immediately to see you," he pats my arm.

"Two teas, and whatever tastes best and has no meat in it for us," Vasily tells the waiter. Our waiter then vanishes to leave us alone.

I shake my head and a little frown appears, then disappears because I am so happy to see him. "Is she a nervous type?"

"She is a typical Russian Jew – she hates the police. You are very charming, she liked you at the wedding but this police business."

"Listen you know me, we're like brothers, right?"

He nods his head and squeezes harder on my arm. "Of course, but the lady was insistent. She doesn't know you. She is naturally very nervous about police. You can understand," he explains.

"You know me. I'm not from the DEA, FDA, SEC or any other federal agency looking into the foreign manufacturing of pharmaceuticals. I don't know what is going on in that plant and I don't care."

"I know, I know. You are here on some type of terrorism business but in Minsk, Belarus? Belarus? Really?"

There is no point in evading his questions. "OK, I'll tell the whole story," I reluctantly respond. He places a napkin on my lap, then one on his.

"I'm listening," he bends his head; our foreheads are practically touching.

"Back a few months, there was an immigration raid and a bunch of Latin gang members were picked up in Long Island," I start.

"New York? Drugs, a cocaine bust?" He is too eager, filling in blanks before I get a chance to tell my story; such impatience, always since he is a boy.

"Maybe, but the point, which you are not letting me get to, is that something else was most unusual," I pause to taste the fries. "Good," I eat them although I surmise that they make them with pork fat.

"Okay, okay," he sips his tea.

"They find in the raid a woman, certainly Islamic, perhaps Arab, maybe Persian, they don't know, clearly not European, too dark," I get closer to the importance of the story.

"Okay, and?" then he quiets.

"My job is to question her and find out who she is, what was she doing with those El Salvadorans and what the hell was she doing in America?" I am finished for the moment, my attention shifting to devouring my food, my hungry stomach demanding nourishment.

"And you are in Belarus because she is here?" He is very smart and deductive, the best puzzle solver in our class in St. Petersburg.

I just nod my head.

"Shit, you're talking about what the Washington Post reporter is writing; American government without the courts or judges secretively takes people away to foreign countries to interrogate them. Reminds you of those good bad days when the dissidents were sent to the Soviet gulag. I hope your mother doesn't know what you're doing," then he laughs, hearty and full, jabbing my arm with his finger, just like my mother.

"I am not torturing her, nor is the Belarusian government. I am just questioning her in German."

"German?"

"They thought she may have been living in Germany. And it turns out the original investigators were right. She lived in Hamburg," I add.

"So, you're like a spy," and he giggles.

"Not quite James Bond but yes, I am assuming a role, I'm playacting."

He looks sharply at my features. "But you don't look German," his finger moving my chin in one direction and then another.

I push his hand away. "You want some terrorist wandering the streets of New York, who knows what damage they can inflict?"

"Is she being held at that old prison, the Soviet built one outside of town? Yes?" he knows the area. He whistles, but not the chirpy kind that Tom performs; his is a more sinister kind.

"Yes, but no torture. I am really just talking with her," I repeat my sincere motives in getting to the truth without bodily harm.

"I should judge you?" he stretches the words out like a

preacher making an important point during a sermon. "You are my Biblical Yehudah, our leader who is flawed and falters, but makes a fresh start because of his sincere repentance."

"Don't joke. He is my role model," I bang my chest like Tarzan.

"The romantic fool," Vasily says, rocking my shoulders.

"Well that's why I'm here, to talk, but I'm working with so few good tools of the trade. My colleagues – one only knows how to listen not to talk and the other is resourceful but not a Middle Eastern expert. I would like someone who speaks Arabic with me, someone I trust. While she understands German, we both know as immigrants that you can understand a new language but still be reluctant to speak it, the slang and colloquialisms are much too difficult," I sigh.

"Yes, a problem. I can help you. I know a guy, an associate, a Chechen, a Muslim who speaks Arabic. I can send him to you here in Minsk," he folds his arms and sits very contented.

I slap his arm. "Really," I say in English. Returning to the mother tongue I say, "That's great. I can trust him?" I can't believe the turn of events. Hashem has a purpose for me.

"Absolutely. Terrorists, he hates. I will speak to him, it will take a few days," is his quick answer.

"I'm glad you're here," we embrace the way Russian men do, with a masculine but emotional bear hug.

"See? Natasha did the right thing. You like her?" he winks.

"She's very attractive. You know how I am attracted to that look. Like my dear Marina; smart, in control, darkly exotic," I sigh deeply, catching myself and attempting a smile.

"You and those women," Vasily smacks me on the edge of my chin with a closed fist. "It's the women that get you into trouble every time. You love them all, even the *treife* ones," we both laugh knowing that he is referring to Olga.

"You know I did see my grandmother's cousin Nadia in some village not far from Minsk. Do you remember her?" I ask.

We spend the rest of breakfast talking about the old days.

CHAPTER 19

The message is delivered by John. "You are wanted back in New York," he tells me. "Your people in New York want a face-to-face," his manner is brisk and economical.

The suddenness of a command performance is unsettling. I have only to wait a few more days, perhaps a week, to gauge progress on the case. What is the necessity of my recall at this point?

"Should I book a flight on a plane from Minsk?" my ignorance is a chasm wide.

"You're kidding. You are a kidder," he slams my arm.

The black and blue marks increase every day that I spend with the man. "Shit no. They'll send the CIA plane for you just like how you arrived. Probably the same CIA guys. You think we must endure the indignities of using commercial planes? Please," he smacks me again for good measure. "You're in the business," he smiles his biggest grin, eyes wide open.

"Should I be concerned about this sudden request?"

"Hell no, they have to look good to their bosses whomever they may be. Shit, they know you've got days, perhaps weeks to wait, so they call you back for a briefing. It makes them look conscientious. Otherwise, you're free floating on the taxpayer's dime. Although, if any of them had to spend time in this shithole of a place, they would understand that to be called back to New York is a holiday. Relax," he punches the other arm.

Later that day the plane arrives and takes me back to JFK airport. McNulty and Wright are onboard; they don't ask me questions just return my American clothing and documents. I return the German documents.

It is the very same dark terminal on the outskirts of the main cargo area. My driver asks me where I want to go. "Home to Brighton Beach."

It is late when I arrive at my parents, but the two four-legged guards hear the car's engine idling on the street as well as my footsteps coming up the driveway. They alert the neighborhood someone is approaching in the hidden darkness of a cloudy night. My father comes to the back door in his underwear carrying a wooden rolling pin. For a small man, he is gutsy; never underestimate his willingness to protect those he loves. The dogs are howling at his heels.

When he turns on the back light, he sees me.

"Amos, Jackson, it's Sasha," he opens the door. We embrace. The dogs are jumping on my legs, so I bend down to pet them both.

Soon my mother in her coat of many colors appears in the kitchen. She hugs me, her thin frame pressed against my body; there are tears in her eyes.

"For God's sake, I was gone less than two weeks, why all the tears?" I realize that her soul lives in perpetual fear. The nightmare of prison and midnight raids by the secret police never leaves her.

"Sasha, Sasha my baby boy," she kisses my chin. "Hungry?" She is at the stove, the frying pan in one hand while my father hands her the rolling pin. He sits at the table anticipating a light meal.

"Don't you just love this macho man," she says, waving the kitchen weapon, then she bends over and kisses the top of my father's head, who smiles in satisfaction.

"What happened?" my father asks.

"Very hush, hush," I reply, my index finger pressed to my lips.

"Cut the crap," my mother answers. "I know you saw Nadia, she called. How does she look?" she asks as she prepares to make something in the heavy frying pan. I hear the swooshing of melting butter; it's diary.

"What are you cooking?" I turn my attention to her cooking activities while the dogs' heads point towards the ceiling, sniffing the air for a clue to what they will be receiving as a treat.

"Omelet? Onions and peppers? I've got red ones, green ones, even a yellow one from the grocer. Such a difference from our days in Soviet Russia. Such variety, it never ceases to amaze me, such choices, what a country," she philosophizes.

"An omelet sounds good."

"*Nu*, what's with Nadia and your assignment? You got what you needed? The mission is finished?" my father runs through the questions buzzing in his head.

"Nadia looks great for an old woman. She has this dog Boris. Picture it - the dog is part Russian wolfhound, so big," I dramatize with my arms spread wide apart. "And tall," I stretch my arm out. "And here's little Nadia. I tell you the dog and she are about the same height," I laugh, the sight of the two of them forever comical.

"And more important, her health?" my mother asks as she flips the eggs into the air. The dogs bark in appreciation.

"She appears to be in good health. She gets support from the *Rebbe* in Minsk. Her sons keep an eye on her through these surrogates and visit in the summer. She visits them for the Jewish holidays. It's a quiet life but she's contented. The only Jew left. She lives to make a statement, just like the rest of the family," I snicker. My father returns the gesture by smacking me on the arm.

"A crazy old woman, my mother's cousin. But it's good. She'll shock the whole village when she dies and leaves the place to the yeshiva boys," my mother lets off a brash and loud laugh.

"So, you know," I reply.

"My mother's only living relative," she sighs that dark, deep expression of lingering regrets.

"Anna, stop with the theatrics, you have several relatives alive in Israel from your mother's side. What about her two sons in Moscow?" and my father, the precise mathematician, sets the record straight, no inaccuracies permitted, even to make a dramatic point.

"Yeh, yeh, but of that generation," again she sighs, dragging the world's host of tragedies inside of her so that they can fester and open old wounds.

"Did you find the terrorist?" my father gets back to my mission and the subject of interest to him.

"Well, I don't know if she's a terrorist or an illegal immigrant. I just don't know at this point, but they will be checking out her information. That's why I'm home. It takes time to investigate," that's all I'm willing to say.

"Is she from the Middle East? A Muslim?" my father isn't satisfied.

"Was she tortured?" now my mother gets to the issue of her concern.

"Listen, I can't really say too much more. She was not tortured; she is Muslim, an Egyptian living in Germany. I can't say more," as usual I allow them to draw more and more information from me. I am the man of discretion except when it comes to my mother and father. Perhaps Vasily is another one.

But these are people I trust with my life.

"No more questions, right Anna?" my father quickly adds. "You're home in time for Jimmy's bout in Atlantic City tomorrow," he informs me.

"Shit, I almost forgot. It is Hashem that guides me. He brings me home so that I may rejoice in Jimmy's victory," I respond with relief that I will not miss the main event.

"I just hope he's not banged up too much," a mother expresses her reservations. "I know his mother does not go to these things because she doesn't want to see him get hurt, even if he wins. Such a profession, but I guess it's better than being a police officer." She never lets an opportunity to sound her displeasure at my occupation go unspoken.

"Enough, enough," the peacemaker answers. "Enough, finish and go to bed," my father orders. "You sleep late tomorrow. I'll take out the dogs and get them fed," he drops some egg on the floor and watches the two canines peacefully share.

"Good night," I kiss them both. Tomorrow, I must call Jimmy first thing and make arrangements to see the fight. And of course, there's Howie Stein. Does he have footage connecting my mystery woman to Oscar? And the cop protestor – who is she?

The time difference is still wreaking havoc on my poor body

because I'm up with the creeping dawn.

I make my way down to the breakfast table where I find my parents sitting and talking, probably about me because they quickly turn silent when I appear through the doorway.

"Sasha my boy, up so early," my father smacks me gently on the forearm.

"You look tired," my mother adds. "Let me make you something to eat, nutritious, a good healthy meal will get those gray cells up and running," she enthusiastically heads for the fry pan.

"I'll call Jimmy this morning, hopefully he's around and we can get together before the fight," I say as my mother hands me a large, cold glass of freshly made orange juice, her specialty.

"Funny you should say that because he just called. Apologized for the early call but he said he had so much to do. He'll be by in an hour before he heads to Atlantic City," my mother reports.

"Why didn't you say something sooner."

"All in good time. Eat," my mother orders.

"After I see Jimmy, I've got to get back to the house, see if everything is OK," I announce.

"I check every day, no rush to get back. You don't have any important mail –no bills. You and Jimmy should go to the Boardwalk, it's a nice day. I'll take the dogs for a long walk later," my father announces. He has his routine, everything in order.

The dogs know before the humans of Jimmy's presence. They start barking and my mother puts her prepared masterpiece on the plate, waiting for Jimmy.

I answer the back door with the canines yelping, hopping on his leg as he enters.

There is the demonstrative 'ohs' and 'ahs' as he kisses my parents and we hug, the dancing dogs gliding the way into the kitchen.

"Jimmy, Jimmy," my mother is almost in tears. She is so short compared to his big, muscular frame. I think immediately of Nadia and Boris.

"Sit. *Ess*," she points to the full plate, the piping hot coffee is poured in the mug with his name on it.

"Pretty exciting, right?" my father asks.

"Yeh, yeh," he tastes the vegetable and egg mishmash. Never a particularly articulate man, Jimmy displays his pleasure with that beautiful, wide smile and expressive blue eyes. You just know when he's happy, the bright face, without a wrinkle says it all.

"I made a bet on you," my father adds, "illegally, of course, with a guy who works for Vasily." He smacks Jimmy on his hard, tight upper arm. "Strong," my father lifts Jimmy's arm into the air. "A champion for sure," to make his point, my father smacks Jimmy again on the very top of his arm, close to the shoulder blade. Jimmy doesn't even wince or look like he feels any discomfort.

"A sure winning bet." Jimmy's charm oozes from his lips, the velvety voice so reassuring, the confidence of a man on the rise, but smart enough to be prepared for the bout of his young boxing career.

"I bought the event from the cable company. I can watch as if I were in the hotel," my father explains, calculating that his choice is an excellent use of his time and money.

My mother nudges my father with her pointy elbow. "We'll leave you boys to talk," my father gets the hint and rises.

"I'll take the dogs for a nice stroll," he announces and gets the leashes, the dogs barking in approval.

My mother in her robe of many colors whispers to Jimmy, "Good luck. Hashem smiles on you." She kisses him on the top of his head.

Jimmy leans towards me as if to tell me a secret, although we are now alone in the room. "I need a favor," he tells me.

"Anything, anything at all," I gesture by shrugging my shoulders.

"I want you to pick up Yana and Zipora and take them to the fight this afternoon. I'm so glad you were able to be home. I know with this hush, hush business you weren't certain if you would be able to make it. It's a good omen," he smiles, radiantly, with every line disappearing, youthfulness and energy emanating from every pore as he approaches his destiny.

His request seems absurd. "Yana, Yana, did I hear you correctly?" I strike my temple with a closed fist. "I just want to be certain. Did you say Yana? The same one I know, widow of the dead Hasid, the one we investigated? This is the woman who lives in Midwood? Am I right?" I repeat hitting my head.

"I know you think I'm nuts," he says sheepishly.

"Nuts. You're out of your fucking mind," I emphatically say, now beating the top of the table.

"You think it's not possible. A religious Jewish woman and Polish Catholic, but I love her." He seems so genuine, those blue eyes staring directly into my dark eyes.

"I don't think it's possible. I think it's ludicrous, impossible, implausible, insane," my mouth is ajar as I finish, my head shaking back and forth.

"She loves me," he categorically defines their relationship.

"How do you know? She hardly speaks English. What can you possibly have in common?" I am dismissive, my hand hanging in midair.

"We love each other. And her English is improving daily, we speak English all the time." He is ardent in his belief, the tone of voice strong and commanding.

"Please," the last syllable hangs for emphasis. "How can this be possible?"

"You will do this for me, right?" he pleads.

Against all reason I agree. "Of course, and Zipora is the chaperone?" this could be interesting.

"Of course, Yana can't come alone. I know how you feel about Zipora, and Yana tells me she is very attracted to you," he announces.

"But at least I'm a Jew who knows about their Hasidic ways. You are a Polish Catholic, probably your relatives back in Poland helped load her family into the cattle cars to the gas ovens." I realize that's a hard and callous statement, but still almost certainly true.

"You will do this for me," he waits for my approval. I nod my head.

"I am willing to convert. I could be a Hasidic boxer, there's nothing in the Talmud that opposes my new occupation. I am working with the *Rebbe* who you know, the one who helped your family with relocating the dead bodies to the Jewish cemetery in St. Petersburg," he says.

"You forget that he misled us before. You remember the case about the slashed tires," I add; a religious person is not without flaws.

"He used us to frighten his brother-in-law, who needed a

good scare. It was because of us chasing down the fingerprints on those tires that we got to be part of the Terrorist Task Force. It turned out to be a good thing," he goes to the *Rebbe's* defense. He was not wrong about the long-term outcome.

"Okay, so I pick up the ladies this afternoon and take them to Atlantic City. They will watch you box?" I can't believe that two very religious, sheltered women will observe a potentially barbaric display of manliness.

"Yes, they are both very excited about going. I think Zipora is happy to be with you," he adds. "We're set? It's good you're back," he taps my hand. "It's great. As you say, Hashem smiles on me," he winks.

I just sigh, the weight of my world on my slender shoulders, a family trait. I'm so like my mother, it's frightening.

CHAPTER 20

I am on my way to a boxing match in Atlantic City, New Jersey with too very happy, boisterous Hasidic ladies. Mostly they chat to themselves in Yiddish. I understand them but have no intention of interfering in the conversation. I am the chauffeur; they sit in the back of the car. I can see from my rear-view mirror that they are animated, arms in all directions, silly girlish laughter emanates from their lips. It's colored lips, bright, neon pink. Their normally pale cheeks are a luminous shade of pink. I think I see longish eyelashes. I know they're false because Yana takes them from a small case.

And the clothes. Yana was never one to wear black. Shortly after her husband's murder, she started wearing clothes of beige and tan. Zipora wore similar neutral colors. Tonight, at the moment of their liberation, they are wearing bright burgundy. A matching set, the two of them. The dresses are not long-sleeved but three quarters, and their flesh is showing. Not only are their arms exposed to sunlight but their necklines.

Their lives will never be the same. They have crossed a line from being part of a hidden, secretive society into the big, wide world. I doubt they understand what is happening. I don't think Jimmy quite understands. It must be love. The divine, inexplicable power of love. Yana and Jimmy are a couple. And

Zipora? Am I under some great obligation for taking them into this forbidden world?

My original plans were to go to the fight with my fellow cops. First, Jimmy's fight and then the party for our new Captain. Well, I had to excuse myself from those festivities and attend to my new responsibility. I creatively told them at the station house that I was taking care of family for Jimmy. A stretch, not a lie. I hoped to join them later, maybe. A promise to Jimmy is sacred.

I roll up in my modest sedan as the valet from the Borgata Hotel takes my keys and a bellhop roughly throws our luggage on a big dolly. The ladies cling to each other. I lead the way and feel Zipora's hand on my back. We are heading through the doors to Sodom and Gomorrah.

Each one separately and then together "ahs" and then "ohs" as we enter the ornately decorated main registration area. Nothing could be more garish and more appropriate for these two adventurers. Artificial gold on the molding, bright, sparkling chandeliers across the massive ceiling. Decorative tiles point to the check-in desk as if the architects stole the idea from the Wizard of Oz's yellow brick road.

Our rooms are two flights apart and the boxing arena within footsteps. Everything is done to make this journey as effortless as possible. Jimmy is considering everything to please his love.

"Is it time?" Yana asks in Russian as we approach their hotel room.

"We can put down the bags and go?" Zipora equally enthusiastic.

"No, no, we have a couple of hours," what will I do with them.

"We can walk on the Boardwalk," Yana offers a suggestion.

"Of course," I wait outside their hotel room. Through the open door, I can see them as they take out a huge make-up bag and continue applying brightly colored stuff from small plastic and glass bottles. Smilingly and approvingly, they study their images in the mirror.

"I'll go up to my room and put down my bags and you can meet me in the lobby."

"No, no, no," Zipora pulls on my jacket. "We go with you. We don't want to be alone."

We do everything together. I don't leave them for a moment. It's easy to find the Boardwalk. We saunter down the wooden planks. No cares, no one watching us; we are free. The weather is wonderful, warm with a slight breeze. My ladies are comfortable in their new clothes. The only thread of the past is their shoes, very sensible much like my Sears' specials.

Since we have already crossed the threshold of

accepted modesty, I take each woman's arm in mine as we stroll. Despite our best efforts at sophistication, we must look like country bumpkins because the valet tells me not to take the women off the broad Boardwalk, "Atlantic City is a dangerous place," he says.

It's time, I check my watch twice. "I'm not certain there's kosher food available at the arena so I hope you're not too hungry."

They giggle. Food is not going to be an issue.

Hordes of people are forming a crowd in front of the arena. I notice my three tickets are a different color than the others as we join a mass of people piling up near the turnstile.

"Wait there," the man directs me. "VIP folks will get you."

Seconds later, a nicely dressed young man approaches and we are on our way to the VIP lounge. The doors open, and I smell the lox and whitefish. I must herd them like a border collie to get them to move towards the food tables. I promised that I wouldn't leave them alone for a moment. But those smells got my stomach churning, screaming out: 'Feed me, Feed me.'

"Is Jimmy here? Will I see him before the fight," a smiling, blushing Yana asks. I dutifully get them both plates, which they have no use for, letting the china dangle from their hands. But I pile my plate up until there's not an inch uncovered.

Jimmy's trainer overhears her question. "No, Miss Yana,"

he wants to move closer but is reluctant since she doesn't really know him. Despite everything, she is still a Hasidic widow.

The smiling Russian trainer looks harmless. They stop clinging to me allowing Jimmy's trainer to stand next to them as he discusses the fight. Meanwhile, I eat. The ultra-orthodox kashrut symbols are in broad display. The women refuse all food placing their plates back in the rack.

"Are you hungry?" I look at both.

"No, no," Yana shakes her head and Zipora nods. "It's too exciting to eat," their eyes watch the crowd laughing and talking. They are observers, studying all these strange new people.

The lights flicker and it's the signal to take our seats. Jimmy's bout is first. The Russian heavyweight is the title match.

The same young man ushers us to our seats. Just as Jimmy said, 'not too close in case there's blood.'

The strobe lights pulsate, the noise level rises so you can't hear yourself. It sounds like constant, ear piercing drumbeats. The audience is on its feet. We follow the lead. My Hasidic women are holding tightly to each other and staring at the dark stage.

A man with a golden tongue speaks, "Ladies and gentlemen, please welcome to the ring, Charlie Coleman and one of the newest faces on the scene, Jimmy 'Smiley' Sutton, the Polish Shaygetz."

The room erupts in applause; feet are stomping, hands clapping, voices growing hoarse from screaming. I can see the cop section. They don't need to wear uniforms to be identifiable. I think I see the Captain, but not his wife. They have good seats but ours are the best in the house. Then I see Vasily hidden in a corner with his brother. He sees me; I smile and gesture at my two traveling companions.

The two fighters move to the center of the ring, touching gloves and the action begins. Jimmy is faster than his opponent; his legs dance. Only his arms are not as long, so he is careful to avoid this opponent landing a punch. They move left and then right like children playing a game of tag. A few quick jabs by both men and the bell rings and its back to the corners.

Coleman manages to land a punch, Jimmy rolls backwards. Yana screams and Zipora hides her head behind Yana. It is only a momentary loss of balance. Zipora places her hand against her heart and sighs.

His opponent leaves his chest exposed for a mere moment, and Jimmy begins his assault on the man's stomach area. We can hear the crunching sound from our seats as the gloves make impact on the naked skin.

Yana is yelling at the top of her lungs, "Kill him Jimmy, kill him."

Then Zipora mimics her friend, "Get him Jimmy, smack

him good," she shrieks with clenched fists.

I have entered a new world with my Hasidic women. The bell sounds and its back to the corners. There is a cut near Jimmy's eye, but the other guy looks a lot worse.

The women shout until they are hoarse and it's only the fourth round. They mouth their insults without too much noise from their lips.

The fifth round starts slowly. Jimmy has lots of energy while his opponent seems more sluggish. The voices return. The shrill sounds re-emerge from the ladies. And if you blinked you may have missed the punch. Jimmy catches him as he is turning away and down he falls; the mat shaking as the 160-pound body collapses.

The referee moves in to make space between Jimmy and the fallen fighter. There is the customary count. The man doesn't rise from the mat.

It's victory. Jimmy's arm is raised. The voice pronounces him the winner. My ladies are jumping up and down, holding tightly to each other. And their sensible shoes hurt as they land on my toes.

Where to next? I hesitate to take my ladies to the cop party, but from the corner I see him gesture. He is pointing to another door.

"Vasily, you know Vasily," I ask the ladies.

"Yes, yes, the gangster," Yana tells me with absolute

innocence, parroting the common knowledge.

It's difficult to escape one's reputation. "OK," I stammer.

"Vasily has a nice party for us to attend."

Vasily meets us outside the arena itself. There's still another fight, the heavyweights go at it.

"Just follow me ladies it's nearby," Vasily offers Yana his arm.

"Yes," Yana takes his arm and lets him lead us to another room.

So off we go to the party through the doors painted VIP lounge. This time there's even more food and vodka. I am careful to keep my ladies together and not lose them in this bellowing crowd.

There's the champ, center stage. She moves effortlessly through the milling folks gently pushing people aside. As they meet in the middle of the floor, he kisses her hands. She giggles like an innocent schoolgirl. Then he presses her hands against his beating heart. And they say I am a romantic.

Zipora, looks approvingly at the spellbound lovers. I am certain Jimmy hasn't even French kissed her.

Vasily shakes his head and holds up his arms. "*Nu*, is there anything stronger than love."

"Hate," I reply.

Both Vasily and Zipora give me dirty looks. The waiter hands us all the champagne glasses filled with the expensive

French brand.

Everyone raises a glass. "To the champ. *L'chayim.*"

CHAPTER 21

The fight is history and I have one gigantic hangover still managing to drive us all back to Brooklyn the next afternoon. I still have time to visit to Howie Stein, my NYPD civilian video guy. I have a little present for Howie.

"Hey, thanks," he eagerly takes the nicely wrapped package out of my hands and tears it apart, the pretty paper falling to the floor.

"Cool," he examines the Russian language tee-shirt of the Russian national hockey team.

"Howie what did you learn in my absence?" I sit next to him.

"Well," he puts the shirt in one of the drawers away from inquisitive eyes. "I've got news for you on both fronts – the gang guys and kid protestor, aka police officer Jacquelyn Rogers, a cop in Williamsburg who lives in Bay Ridge."

"Very good," I pat him on the back. "You have great contacts. This is unbelievable,"

"Moving along, what's with the illegals?" I know this is most important, but the other find is equally essential to my pursuit of happiness.

"I have looked at all the tapes. Most are crap, piss poor quality because who expected anything important to come out of the surveillance. I zeroed in on the first ones. Not much, they seem to always travel to and fro in hooded sweatshirts. Then I looked at the tape from the actual raid. I stopped every frame looking for clues, something," he pauses. "Want something sweet?" he reaches for two candy bars.

"Thanks," I unwrap the foil paper. "Nice paper," I announce, clearly belonging to expensive chocolate. I notice the Belgian label.

"Okay," he slips a tape into the machine. "This is from the day of the raid. I was able to capture the faces of seven guys. Never your Oscar, no matter how I tried, moving the angles, increasing and decreasing the magnification, nothing."

"What did you do with the seven?"

"In your name, I put out an alert to Mexican and Salvadoran police officers. We know some of them escaped arrest maybe they're heading south. Then I requested from the feds, again using your name and badge number, for them to check and see if the camera shots match any of those in custody."

I'm practically smacking him around in joyous appreciation. "Howie, Howie, you smart fuck, good thinking, such proactive work."

"I thought you would approve," and he smiles, taking a big bite out of the candy bar.

"Such a smart guy, a fellow Jew I can trust. Do you want

to be a cop?"

"Hell no, but usually the most I ever do is check ATM camera footage for a robbery. Once I worked a series of muggings at a public housing project from their surveillance cameras. But this is intriguing. Hey, I'm in on the chase for potential terrorists," he answers with a huge grin.

"Nice work. Did we hear anything?" this might take some time.

"You will hear directly. The requests are in your name," he reports.

"And the bitch in the police van?" my menacing tone finds life.

"Yes, ah yes, I do have information on her," he pulls out a folder in a slender drawer. "This is hush, hush, so when I discovered the intel, I just kept it under the radar. For your eyes only. I thought it too imprudent to send along any e-mail," he hands me the file.

"You've got her home address?"

He opens the file and points to the page. "That's what she looks like on her driver's license. The other photo is from her police file."

"Very good, she does look different in these photos, much older, probably closer to her real age. At that demonstration, she looked like a kid, a teenager with acne."

Howie stops chewing. "They went to a lot of trouble to

change her appearance."

"It shows how much planning was involved." I feel my mother's indignation boiling up to the surface.

"The guys in the van, I couldn't really get a name. Someone said Billy, but there's an awful lot of Williams, Bills and men who just use the initial B in the police file to locate a face and name. Perhaps if you confront Rogers, she will be more forthcoming," he astutely responds. "Get me a name and I can find them," he readily asserts.

"Nice work Howie, I owe you."

"Hey this is fun," he shrugs his shoulders. Jimmy has that kind of shrug, the "aw shucks" type of look.

"Howie, my man, the best tickets, you and me, just name the night. I owe you."

"That's great. Sasha Perlov you are a credit to our people, the chosen ones," he winks.

I'm angry; I'm excited. I've got to think. To the Boardwalk I go, find my favorite bench and just stare out at the gulls watching me.

"I thought I'd find you here," he gently touches my shoulder. I recognize the voice and don't even turn around to face the visitor.

"You come to the sea for solace and to relieve all your troubles." Vasily gently eases his slender body next to mine on the Boardwalk bench. No one bothers us; two men among dozens of others, mostly Russians, the old and the young. This is Little Odessa, Brighton Beach, Brooklyn. We dominate the Boardwalk; it belongs to us.

"You know me so well," I laugh.

"Too much vodka and celebrating," he admonishes me, handing me a slice of fresh lime.

"And this is my cure?" I ask.

"Suck on it," he directs. Then he places a perfectly round, reddish apple in my lap. "For later."

"What a fight. I mean it was so cool. He jabs him, smacks him around and pounds him out in Round 5. The poor bastard goes down with a thud. Very smart. Otherwise, the jerks in the media would have called it a lucky punch. Smart, probably owing more to his manager Igor's management."

"Where're the *Shabbes* ladies?" Vasily tries to suppress a laugh.

I look at him and we both burst into hearty laughter. I can feel the tears running down my face. It hurts my head, all this fun, but I can't help myself.

"Is it nuts or what?" I continue laughing, my head pounding as if Jimmy's fists were attacking my poor brain.

"You're too old for this," his strong hands knead the muscles of my shoulders.

"I make a stupid drunk, and my headache needs more

than a slice of lime."

"You always get into trouble when you drink," he adds, then winks. We are both thinking about Olga and my drunken wanderings.

"Oh, oh," I mutter, my head dropping between my legs, so he can work my entire back.

"Good?" he asks.

"Keep it up," I order in a friendly tone.

"The ladies looked good last night. Even the ultra-orthodox can look like they belong in the modern world. That Yana, with those beautiful blue eyes. Wow. Doesn't look too Russian; she must have some Cossack blood," he begins to laugh again.

I just shake my head while he continues his massaging magic. My shoulder muscles starting to relax, the thundering, pulsating veins in my temple slowly fading.

"The Polish Shaygetz and the Hasid widow. What could be stranger?" I add as my body weight sinks to the ground. He doesn't stop.

"How about the cop and 9/11 Hasid widow," Vasily jabs me in the ribs.

"I don't know, but she is lovely. Look how nice they looked last night. The wigs were beautiful. These religious women can buy ones with real hair. They were wearing make-up, very attractive looking. Right?" I suggest and feel the aches starting to leave as his powerful fingers pressed against my temple.

"Insane, but love is crazy. I heard them screaming and egging on Jimmy. They were jumping up and down, very unladylike," he laughs, tightly closing his eyes as the tears start up again. The chuckling gets louder and it's contagious. I'm laughing but I need to stop because it hurts my head.

"I know, I know," I can barely get out the words between the laughter.

"What happened to the women? Leave them in Atlantic City? Jimmy running off with Yana?" he cackles like an animal being punished.

"Hell no, this afternoon I took them back to Midwood," I inform him.

"Is he serious about converting?" Vasily shakes his head and we're both at it again.

I have trouble speaking between the tears, now with added hiccupping. "I don't know. Will it matter to his career as a boxer?"

"No, not really. I can't imagine an arena filled with Hasids, but he's white and that's all that matters."

"But you won't have the two Slavs to promote, your Russian heavyweight and Jimmy, the Polish Shaygetz, as middleweight."

"Wait and see. By the time he gets through all the

machinations of those loony Hasids, his boxing career will be over. I mean he's in his early 30's; at best we've got five years left. Maybe he can sing as his next career move. I know there's that Hasid hip-hop singer."

"My head is still pounding," I let his fingers squeeze and massage the skin around my temple.

"The sea is the best medicine. You could dunk your head in the ocean, but that might be a bit cold. But you're a Russian accustomed to the bitter cold. Just sit here, breathe in the ocean breezes. If you're adventuresome, go to the edge of the beach and splash the salt water on your face," he stops, slapping me on the back.

"Okay," my unhappiness about his departure evident. I need those magic hands.

Then he leans over my shoulder and whispers in my ear. "I've got my Chechen all set. He should be available to you in a few days. Let me know when you are returning to Minsk," he disappears.

I sit breathing in deeply, considering dunking my head into the surf.

Sensing that my window of opportunity in New York was limited, I had one more rendezvous before it got to be too late. With Howie's assistance, I have the intel on my cop informer.

I find her address and park the car, no small feat in a

congested neighborhood. What's my plan? I don't have one. I sit in the car considering my options. Should I ring her bell and identify myself? Or should I just sit here all night and catch her on her way out?

As I fumble for a decision, fate deals me another plan. She emerges from the house and starts down the limestone steps. She glances my way but doesn't see me.

From behind a row of metal garbage pails he appears. A big guy, broad with thick shoulder muscles, but not height.

Suddenly, he grabs her and as she starts to scream he cups his hand around her mouth. She continues to struggle but he is firmly in control. She cannot escape him.

I don't hesitate to run from my car with my hand sliding into my holster going for my gun. I am quick and silent. She is wiggling, trying to evade his hand now gripping her throat. He is much taller with massive hands. She is wiggling like a big rag doll.

I stealthily sneak behind him, and with great force whack him on the back of his head with the butt of my pistol. He stumbles down the steps, his legs losing their footing. His hand partially supports his plummeting body while his elbow scraps against the rigid stone.

I have surprised him and his body folds into a large ball with his hands and feet sticking outward. I grab him by the hair. My fingers holding tightly. He cries out in pain while I pull harder. His arms forcibly swing at me, but the gestures are aimless. I can get my arm under his chin and I start to choke him. I need him to be more immobile, so I can completely control the situation.

I am about to strike him again with my gun. One hand holds my gun and the other my cuffs. He is still squirming, and we go tumbling onto the concrete sidewalk. I still have him in a head lock, pressing with all my strength. But she grabs my arm and my gun falls to the sidewalk. In those precious moments, he escapes.

I get ready to give chase, rising to my knees, but she pulls me back.

"Jackie." And I am about to spew a long list of curse words. I never got a good look at his face.

"Let him go," she hoarsely whispers. Her neck is red, and she rubs it barely able to speak. Then she clasps my arm leading me up the stairs into the building.

She slams the heavy front door shut and turns three locks to secure our safety. Her ordinary rhythmic breathing returns.

We stare at each other. Her eyes focusing on me. "Who are you?"

"Jackie," my voice is soft. "You don't recognize me?" I smile.

"No, who the hell are you?" she asks, her body

remaining alert for further potential danger.

"Sasha Perlov," I very slowly open my jacket to reveal my police badge on my belt.

"Do I know you? What are doing here?" she glares at me.

And I can understand her tentativeness. Am I another threat? Was her attacker a boyfriend, didn't seem like a mugger.

"Detective Perlov of the 60th Precinct. I was the one who arrested you at the demonstration. You remember?" I wait a moment. "Who was that guy? Nasty bastard."

She backs away, then changes her mind, moving towards me. "Why are you here?"

"Actually, I wanted to speak to you about that day."

"You should go. And thanks," she half-smiles pushing me closer to the door.

"No, no, no," I protest waving my arms in front of me. "I can't go. Was that an ex-boyfriend? That was some scary minute. Let me help you. You don't have to be afraid of me. Tell me what's going on?" The demonstration may have to wait for another meeting.

"Shit I'm such a fool. Fucking fool. I got involved with these people."

"Let's go inside your apartment, sit down. You can tell me what's wrong. I'm a helpful guy. Looks like you need some help."

She hesitates; but then guides me from the building foyer through her apartment door. Again, she triple locks the door.

We enter a large, airy room. During the day, the sunshine must fill every corner and nook of this room with lightness. The ceiling is high, oak floors; there's a fireplace, pretty nice on a cop's salary.

We sit apart. She on a love seat across from me on the couch. "I got in with this crowd. I am an idiot. I saw money. Not illegal shit. I know vice and narcotics cops can get into real shit. That's not me. But when people start throwing money around. You should be suspicious. I was so blind to the money. I figured what the hell. It isn't like I was taking money from drug dealers or keeping pimps safe. It seemed at first so innocent. But money without strings doesn't exist. God damn it. I am such an idiot."

"Why don't you start at the beginning?" I fold my hands in my lap. This may be a long evening.

She stares at me. A white cat appears, and its presence immediately calms Jackie. She slowly strokes the cat with the furry beast rubbing up against her mistress' chest. All is peaceful. We listen to the cat's soft purring.

Her hand remains on the cat's back. "You won't believe me."

"Try me. I'm a Russian immigrant; we understand the

surreal, the insane, love gone mad. Test me."

"Perlov, yeah, Perlov. What's that moniker of yours. Yeah, I know about you. Perlov the Protector. And you saved those babies from the cop shooter. Yeah, yeah, Perlov."

"I can be trusted. A man of discretion."

She continues to stare at me still not trusting my words of assurance. "I don't know how it got started. It was that God damn demonstration. Jesus, Mary and Joseph. I was volunteering for undercover work as a protestor. I needed the overtime. You think this apartment is cheap," the tone is defensive.

"What about the demonstration?"

"It started so innocent. Like could you pretend to belong to one of those protest groups. I mean the Patriot Act. We can spy on our own citizens. 9/11. We could be hit again. Right? But I should have known better when they start dangling money. Real money not chump change, real money. But I am such an idiot," she strikes her fist at her chest.

"You volunteer to go undercover and join a protest group and spy on them?"

"Yeah, make sure they aren't going from planning a protest to planting bombs. We live in dangerous times. At first, it seemed so innocent. Sure, I want to save my city. I was born here, all my family lives here. I am New Yorker. We don't take shit from terrorists. We are tough."

"OK. You join this group of cops," my worst nightmares coming true about cops becoming enemies of the people.

"I did undercover work before posing as an under-age teenager, cigarette stings and drug busts in high schools. I was good at that."

"And what's with the guy who tried to strangle you?"

"Well here's the crazy part," she stops to take a deep breath. "What I didn't realize because I knew one of these guys. Not a boyfriend, but a friend of my brother. But my brother knows nothing about this," she rambles but keeps petting the cat, her security blanket.

"The guy who just tried to kill you is part of this cop group? He is also a cop?"

"Exactly right. I join this group with the purpose of spying on these protestors with a group of my fellow officers. Undercover work. It seemed so innocent. But when money is involved my better cop instincts should have warned me that something not kosher was going on. But the smell of money. How could I have been so naïve and stupid."

"Are you telling me there is some rouge group within the police department who is spying on protestors. Not an official NYPD sting operation. And you are one of these members? And they have money to throw around?"

"Right, we are our own group. Some guys are really into punishing these protestors. You could call this the ideologue bunch. Some like me were caught up with the money. I should know that nothing ever comes without strings. I should have known," the cat stops purring and jumps off her lap.

"Where's the money coming from?"

"I don't know. I should have asked more questions. But really, I didn't want to know. I preferred to be ignorant."

"What's with the threatening guy? Some kind of split within the group?"

"Yeah, it gets complicated." She calls beseechingly, and the cat returns to her lap. "We harassed some of these protestors. We knew their addresses. We slit their tires, burned their mail, nothing too serious, more like pranks."

"None of these protestors complained to the police?" citizens are always complaining to the police and about the police.

"Well there were complaints, but they went nowhere. Then it got notched up. That guy from earlier," she goes silent, simply stroking the cat.

"He does something crazy?"

"Yes, really stupid," her leg moves uncontrollably up and down; she can't keep it still. "He placed a bomb in a garbage can of one of the protestors. Not a cheap fireworks bomb but a real explosive one. One that could have put people in the hospital. Maybe got someone killed."

"The cops then take the pranks seriously? Now there's a

real problem."

"No, not until a different protest leader, a law professor, knows somebody on Police Row. He complains to one of the brass. Now, we have an investigation, pulling together these seemingly unrelated pranks."

"You're afraid of getting caught up in the investigation? The guy threatens you to keep your mouth shut," I try and fill in the blanks.

"It's more complicated," her leg can't be still, the cat is annoyed and jumps off her lap.

"More complicated?"

"That guy wants to kill the law professor and me, if I alert the police. I think he wants to kill me since I was there from the beginning. I could be dead meat. He's not the only crazy person in the group. They are off the charts. I'm in big trouble."

I look at her. "This is crazy."

"Can you help me?"

"Are you willing to be an informer? Tell what you know?"

"Will I get protection?"

"Depends. But I know a guy."

"I did a stupid thing, I know that now. But I don't want to die. Fucking money, it is a curse," she angrily swings her arm in the air punching at invisible ghosts. "I am such an idiot."

CHAPTER 22

It's late but I place a call to US Attorney Cohen. Jackie's story has so many juicy elements. This could be another bright achievement for Cohen. His bosses at US Department of Justice in Washington, D.C. should be thrilled. They hate the NYPD.

Cops gone rogue? Police over-reaching? Murder plots? Money, lots of payoffs. Always follow the money to find the real Mr. or Ms. Big.

This could be bigger than big; newspaper headlines across the country hailing the new conquering hero who battles dirty cops. It's better than any plain vanilla corruption case this is cop death squads. It's right out of a Central American dictator's playbook. Cops gone amuck, the press will love it, the politicians will be asking for stricter laws; the public may simply yawn.

Yet, she is worthy of police protection with something extremely valuable to share. And this requires witness protection and relocation. Is she willing to radically change this life for some unknown in the Dakotas or desert?

On the phone, I retell the tale I was told to Cohen.

"I don't know Perlov how do these people find you? You have this natural talent for drawing people to you. Lost souls who have gone astray. It's that face. You look honorable.

Someone they can trust with their lives, but practically strangers. Oscar, this Jackie, our terrorist suspect. It's a talent."

"You can help?" I enjoy the flattery but is he going to offer her witness protection.

"Shit, this is good. Rogue cops? Fucking money everywhere? This is too good. I will need this woman," he stops himself. He's too giddy.

"What should I do with her? Right now. I'm in her apartment in Brooklyn."

"Hang tight. I realize she's in danger. You got your gun. Lock the windows and doors. Make certain she is not calling anyone. Keep her calm and I will send my personal body guards. I will authorize them to immediately pick her up. It shouldn't be too long."

"What about informing NYPD?"

"No, you don't do a thing until or unless I tell you. For now, the NYPD is out of the picture. Who knows how high or how many are involved? Could be guys on Park Row. I will send my personal detail. No calling anyone at NYPD. You understand? Right now, it's just you and me. Got it?" his voice hard and determined.

"You don't like the NYPD?" I just know it.

"I like you," he laughingly responds.

"No respect," I try mimicking in my clumsy Russian fashion, Rodney Dangerfield.

"Except for you, my dealings with the NYPD are about police corruption; cops sampling the drugs they confiscate or slipping a few thousand in their pockets after a huge drug bust. Or cops beating on civilians, choking them to death or shooting them in the back. I'm never asked to present NYPD officers metals for bravery. Our relationship by its nature is always going to be tense."

"OK, I get it. I will just wait patiently for your guys. Then what?"

"Tell her to pack a bag, take any medicine with her because she may not be back in that apartment for awhile or maybe forever."

"Are you taking her to some safe house?"

"The less you know the better. My guys will be there shortly. Perlov, I should never be surprised by you. You've done good. We smart Jews got to stick together."

"And what about my NYPD career when this does get out?" I'm practically a cop informer as bad as Jackie, a pariah.

"Perlov, this just brings us together. I want you to head my investigations unit. Finish law school, pass the bar and you're one of my deputy prosecutors. You got a great future."

True to his word, the security detail arrives, and off Jackie goes with her cat in a carrier. She leaves me the key to the apartment. I am exhausted and involuntarily my eyes close.

The call wakens me from my dreams of frolicking on the beach with Vasily and Olga. No Jackie, no Cohen, no terrorists although watching us is my mother. I think she's smiling.

I stare at the number. It's late. I'm disoriented forgetting that I am still in Jackie's apartment. I just want to go home to Brighton Beach, curl up in my old bed and let Amos lick my face.

I recognize the voice.

"I've got something to show you," Lewis replies in his usual hard-ass fashion.

"Can't it wait till tomorrow? It's late," I wearily tell him.

"What happened? Go on some special assignment and become a pussy? Get your ass here," he announces in his demanding manner; no point in arguing.

"Where are you?"

"Belt Parkway," giving me more precise instructions.

I know that road from end to end. It doesn't take me long to locate him, and the massive police presence on an isolated and dreary section of the roadway. The overhead lighting is missing most of the bulbs. Driving on this road feels like being a passenger on a roller coaster ride -- up and down, the sinking roadway never gets its fill of asphalt, the bumps really jarring; but, if you're half-asleep it keeps you alert.

The uniforms allow me to enter the crime scene, yellow tape everywhere; quickly I find him; he's the primary. "What's so important?" I don't act perturbed because it's obvious this is a big deal. Yes, how I miss this routine, chasing bad guys that are recognizable, not some elusive terrorist.

"I have something to show you," he leads me to a car, the center of all the attention. "I know you will appreciate my call."

It's an ordinary sedan, foreign, newish but not brand new. The tires are still on it, the dashboard is one piece, no stolen airbags. I assume it's been recently abandoned.

"The uni's were patrolling the Beltway when they find this abandoned car. They check the fancy new computers we've got in the cars," we both nod in appreciation for the technology. "Naturally stolen, they do a little exploring, smart enough not to touch too much, not dirty the evidence. And viola," he sticks his finger in the air and one uniform pops the trunk.

I look in with my police issue flashlight. "Oh fuck," I move my head closer. "It's him, shit. It's Oscar," I take the gloves Lewis offers. I get real close, staring at his badly beaten face, looking for his gang tattoos. I touch at his sleeve and move his face, so I can get a better view of his tattoos. The bright light shows the bruises.

"It's our man Oscar."

"When do you think it happened?"

"Well, he doesn't smell, so recently. We need to find out where it happened. Obviously, they decided to hide the body, not simply visibly dump him in a public place. They didn't want to make it too easy for us to find him. Perhaps the killers thought we wouldn't know who he was," he explains. "The ME is on his way, and we've got those pesky CSI guys coming as well."

"I can't believe it," I stand by the car waiting for the evidence collectors. "I was depending upon him for some answers," my exasperation showing. I can't keep from shaking my head from side to side. "Shit," is all the imagination I can demonstrate at this moment.

"The life of a gang member is usually short with a violent end."

"The gang shit is not of interest to me. Now I don't have any collaborating witness. I still can't link him to my mystery woman, my terrorist. Maybe there's a connection. We're still guessing. Who did this?" I stammer.

"I know it's gang related whether he's involved with your woman. I don't know. You don't believe in coincidences, so he could have been her babysitter. He got killed because he fucked up and our government caught her. Or he's a fucking liar and he got killed by some gangbanger for some gang offense, stealing from them or something about a gang member's woman. Busting gang members is never easy or gentle but I will not give up. I owe you," he says.

"Wasn't he under our protection?"

"We'll ask his protector," Lewis says in his most sarcastic tone pointing to an approaching man.

"Agent Johnson," he introduces himself with the badge practically hiding his face.

Lewis knows him. "Look inside," Lewis pushes the FBI agent's head towards the dead body.

He looks, but not too long. "Yes, he's beaten, but I think I recognize him," the agent responds without compassion or understanding.

"Beaten, tortured," Lewis pokes the agent's arm. "Look at his feet and hands, bound with wire, the guy was tortured. You assholes were supposed to have him in protective custody, some protection. I won't be asking you guys for any protection if I want a suspect to remain alive." He speaks with a touch of revulsion in his voice, spitting as he talks, showering the agent with his disgust.

The agent is defensive but not intimidated. "He left, ran away. We couldn't physically hold him. He wasn't a prisoner."

"He was a material witness," I pipe up, adding my own sense of outrage. "You were supposed to keep him out of harm's way. Is this your idea of 'out of harm's way'? Please, why not just hand him over to the people who wanted him dead."

"He kept insisting he had to find some woman," he is not remorseful; the FBI is too arrogant and smug to readily accept mistakes or responsibility.

I grab his neck with one hand, holding tightly. "Asshole, that is why we wanted him -- to identify a woman, a very important woman on a very important terrorist case, asshole," I release him. He stumbles, his flat footedness keeping him off balance. He grabs the car's rear fender for support.

"We did our best," he impassively answers, standing several feet from my reach and a good distance from Lewis.

"I want everything you know about this woman. What did he say about the woman? Did he describe her? What kind of relationship did they have? Lovers perhaps," I try hard not to strangle the guy.

"I don't know for sure, but we have tape recordings and videotape of our conversations. But he insisted on being released so that he could track down a woman," he coldly replies.

"Why didn't you offer to track her down? Or better, why didn't you contact us at NYPD?" Lewis asks as he takes a menacing step closer to the FBI agent.

"That's not part of the assignment," he quickly responds.

"You should have called us. We would have taken responsibility and tracked her or spoken with him. This is totally unacceptable," I scream at him.

Poor Oscar, but really, poor Hector. It's Hector that I care about, not his cousin. I owed Hector so now I got to tell him this awful news. There's no way around it – we fucked up.

I can feel the heat rising in my neck, the anger ready to explode. Can this case be missing some vital link because of the FBI's laxity? I turn towards Lewis. "So now what?"

"You've got the job of telling Cousin Hector," he explains with a jab at my chest. "You know the family."

CHAPTER 23

They tell me I'm good at telling loved ones someone is dead. Hector cried but spared blaming me. It was his life that got him killed.

My mission continues. Although the missing link between my mystery woman and Oscar remains. It's them again – McNulty and Wright, taking me back to Belarus, stripped of my American identity. When the plane lands my favorite 'go to' man is waiting for me on the tarmac.

"Welcome back boss," he effortlessly grabs each bag. "Pleasant flight?" he opens the passenger door for me.

"Let's go to the prison."

"Will do boss."

The scenery is more colorful than last time; the weather is turning more moderate. In the distance the prison becomes visible, the tall towers hovering above all else in the countryside. It is the eerie center of prominence among the stalks of grain and cluster of trees. Once it did hold the population in fear and intimidation. Now it stands as a gray monument to a withering past, a relic except for the American's new use. World terrorism is an international commodity for sale. We live in strange times.

I wave to my favorite guard as I emerge from the car. As

usual, Tom does not approach, preferring to stay in the car. He doesn't want to bear witness to what goes on inside, preferring to stay on the margins.

"Any visitors since I left?" I asked my guard in his native tongue. It's possible some other secret agent has been here, someone unknown to Tom, perhaps unknown to Mr. Smith.

"No, only you and your guest have been here. We don't get visitors. It's good to see you again." The wrinkles of gloom and anomie are gone from his face.

It's quite bizarre to be the source of such happiness on the part of these strangers. It's a crazy mixed up world if this assignment, this ugly, Soviet-era construction, this half-alive village needs my presence for sustenance.

The hard-ass superior is waiting for me and gives me a smile. The weather must be improving everyone's disposition.

"Welcome. Good to see you again," he tells me in Russian.

"Do you want to see her?" the superior asks.

"No, just let me view her on camera," gently my friendly guard elbows me towards the lit screen.

There she is, reading her book in her cell, completely alone, the only semblance of normality the lights reflecting the daylight outside. She is lost in thought; perhaps a forgotten memory reasserting itself, fragments of that past reality. She knows that she is being watched but appears to live a totally content, solitary life. If she hungers for more, no one hears her complaints; if she thirsts for the soft, loving words of relatives and friends, she demonstrates no remorse. She is beyond stoic.

"Is that all she is doing, reading that book?" I inquire of her capturers.

"That's it," they all chime in unison.

"Does she talk out loud to herself? Do you notice her lips moving," I probe, as I stare at the screen and then at her guards.

They blankly look at me. Then one guard that I don't really know speaks. "She does at special times of the day make real sounds, words I guess, although I don't understand the words. I think it's Arabic," he smiles at his sleuthing achievement. The others approve with their nodding heads.

"Good. That makes sense. Muslims pray five times a day. Good, very good observation. I'll look for that."

I sit with the guards and spend the next two hours watching her. Her silence is contagious as we quietly observe, only the sounds of our breathing audible. Based on some mystical clue, because she has no clock or time keeper, her mouth moves. We all witnessed the event, actual words uttered, first quietly and then with some higher volume. She opens and closes her eyes at some appropriate point in her praying.

We are voyeurs. It is creepy to be watching her via a small camera tucked into a corner of her cell; still we are all mesmerized. Her actions physically constrained, she is not an athlete or an actor or dancer performing, but we are all glued to that screen. Her motions are not jarring or erratic in any way, although the fact that she is completely alone yet being observed is weird. This is different than a stakeout.

The prisoner is remote, a vision, an image before us but not really with us. Real but not really a person, or a living and breathing individual, yet someone connected to me. My job is to discover her secrets. I am convinced that she holds tightly to a treasure of unknowns. I must unlock facts, dates, names, locations from her. I am sworn to do so without physical coercion. I promised myself and, of course, my mother.

I am her protector? Because in the absence of controls, assurances, legal barriers, nothing prevents me from doing anything to this potential conspirator except for my moral compass. She was caught up in a system without any checks and balances. I am the balance, providing checks on the system.

The first hour moves with speed, then it becomes a static exercise watching her on the screen. After a while, there is nothing new to learn; it is enough for now.

When I emerge on the other side of the barbed wire, I am happy to see Tom. He is the vehicle of my escape.

"Say boss, where to now? Want to freshen up at the

usual hotel? I took your bags there while you were doing your business. That's OK? Right?' he needs assurances.

"Very thoughtful of you,"

"Doing my job."

"Later, I need a car to see someone in Minsk." I keep my own secrets.

"I can chauffeur," he cheerfully tells me, back to whistling.

"No, I prefer to drive myself. Can I get a car?" I am the boss.

"No problem, boss. You can use this beauty. Sweet," he flashes a wily smile.

Tom drives and then the whistling stops. "About that last time in Minsk. I don't know what got into me. You're not angry? Not trusting me to drive?" he sheepishly asks with a tinge of a whine.

"Hell, no Tom, you're human. We both got a great chuckle out of it – John and me. You don't know how to hold your liquor, but we were all drinking way too much. It's this place, nothing else to do, so drab and dreary even in the sunlight," I respond. My tone is calm and not judgmental. He is quite a loopy guy under the influence. "Tom, don't underestimate yourself. You can do better than this place."

"Oh boss, you are a great guy. I just don't want you to think less of me," he's relieved. I expect him to wipe the uncertainty from his brow.

"I'm going to rest for a short time and then take the car. I'll be back after dinner," I announce.

When the car stops in front of the hotel, he hands me the keys. "Have fun," he adds with a wink.

I am tired, but I don't want to rest. I make my call at the proscribed time as directed by Vasily and a gruff voice answers.

"Yes," he waits.

"Sasha, Vasily's friend. Is this a good time to meet?" I am asking in Russian and make a point to show no faltering in the tone of my voice. For most of Vasily's contacts, strength and force are the mediums of exchange, display not a whiff of uncertainty or trepidation.

"Yes," he waits.

My voice is showing my jet lag and my growing need to show results. "Are you available?" I ask in a curt tone.

He can hear my irritation, but hopefully not the fatigue.

"Of course, any friend of Vasily is a like a brother to me." I even hear something like friendliness creeping into his words.

The time and place are set. How effective can this man be? I am without too many options – he is my secret weapon. At this junction, he is my only weapon. With Oscar dead I have no links to this woman.

I am early and so is he, but only by a few minutes. We

don't wave; we know each other without introductions. I am told he is bald, of medium build but compact, a euphemism for a heavily muscular man who can beat your brains into mush with his bare hands. Surprisingly, he is an impeccable dresser, European cut suit that highlights his frame and bulging physique.

I point to a back table in the bar. His head faintly moves. The motion could be mistaken for a blowing sea breeze, but not in landlocked Belarus. It is an acknowledgment, he follows me to the rear.

Neither of us wait for formalities. We sit at the exact same moment.

"What should I call you?" I inquire since he is still nameless.

"The Chechen," he quickly responds with a big smile. His teeth are beautifully straight and white. This man regularly goes to a dentist. Money makes the man; he is the empirical evidence.

The waiter hovers nearby us but not too close. The Chechen is one of those guys you meet on the street and walk, no, stroll quickly, to the other side of the road. Don't look too obvious as you flee because you don't want to attract his attention. He is not wearing gang tags, no tattoos, no flashy jewelry; you just know to stand at a distance, giving this man significant personal space.

Strangely, I am not afraid; my pulse does not rise in anticipation, no drops of perspiration alight my shirt. I watch the waiter but that only gives me greater fearlessness. Like the dog that smells fright and attacks the weakling, I give him my best cool attitude.

"A drink? Vodka?" asks the waiter.

"I am a Muslim and supposedly we don't drink, but I love to drink. A bottle of the best vodka, the potato kind, none of that silly grain stuff. If you drink, it should only be the best." He slaps his palm onto the tabletop, the waiter jumping at the sound. The Chechen laughs, and I join him.

We stare into each other's eyes. His are dark as are mine, but small and beady like a bird of prey. His eyebrows are dark, suggesting so is the rest of the hair on his body. Despite his completely bald head, you can just about see the outline of his hairline if he were to let his hair grow.

"I understand you will act as my translator. I have a prisoner that is Muslim and speaks Arabic, a religious woman. I gave her a Koran, showed her I'm a good guy. I think she is hiding very important, secret, vital information. I don't want to beat the shit out of her, but I need that information. Can you help me?"

"I am at your service."

"I speak to her in German, which she understands having lived in Germany. She thinks that I'm a German intelligence officer. But you know that when you're afraid or just considering your options, you think in your native tongue. In her case Arabic. We'll work it like a tag team, you watch that silly American wrestling?"

He laughs but answers, "No. I get the picture. What do you know about her? Details help," the drinks arrive.

We sit and drink; the contents of the vodka bottle vanishing as I tell him what I know. I trust him because he comes to me from Vasily. He is my best chance of prying something valuable from her lips.

What's in it for him? I don't know and it's better that I don't learn. This is an arrangement, a deal, an agreement between Vasily and the Chechen. I am only a recipient of that largesse. I assume the connection is business, but it could be about Afghanistan or the Army. Ignorance is my best shield.

CHAPTER 24

At our predetermined time, I meet the Chechen at the gates of the prison. Tom is driving me, but he is not one to ask questions. He sees me talking to another man and stays in his car.

My companion makes an immediate impression on the prison staff. The guards don't dare stare at him as we enter. My friendly guard diverts his eyes, looking only towards me. I know that technique; never say that you got a good look at the suspect or a witness. The guard walks close to me and makes no motion or movement to attract the attention of my comrade. Since I don't introduce him, the guard makes no attempt to make a personal introduction.

The Chechen is wearing the garb of an imam. He looks good in his tightly fitted woven cap and flowing robes; a modern Mohammad, someone who looks like he converts the infidels through the power of the sword.

I sign in as usual.

The senior guard is the only one to look the Chechen in the eyes.

"Sign sir," he points to the page.

The response is not a shocker, "No," the senior guard locks eyes with him. Then, as a dog shows capitulation to the alpha canine, the senior guard lowers his eyes.

I feel the guard's finger on my elbow and he looks for my approval.

"Fine," I answer.

They divide into two so that we can walk through the line. I know the way, but I let my guard play the role of scout leader. Today, he does not chit chat with me, the Chechen's presence saps him of all his sociability and gaiety.

The heavy metal doors open, and we enter. We make enough noise that she knows without looking up that I am not alone. Reluctantly, she turns her head towards us, the intruders. Her eyes shine brightly, in this artificial world, in his presence.

He speaks to her in Arabic. I don't understand a word, but her face is aglow with piety and unexpected joy. Perhaps she knows without an introduction of his status as imam, or else he is telling her something about himself -- lies.

Saving innocent lives is my goal and she is the keeper of secrets. His role playing is the way to pry open her secrets.

I hear what I think is my name in Arabic, "Herr Erdmann," they both stare at me. I don't smile although this is like play-acting.

Then he faces me, and we speak Russian. "I told her, I am an imam from the Central Caucasus, that I know you and trust you. She must trust you or she will never leave this place."

"Good," I reply. We have a playbook. "Explain to her that we did check her information about Germany, and it was correct. Now we need more facts."

As he speaks to her, I take the only chair in the cell, moving the legs closer to her, scraping the wood against the hard concrete. I like to use grating sounds to get the suspect's full attention. Her eyes moving rapidly between him and me.

"You have kept your word," I touch the edge of her bed. "To tell the truth," I am speaking to her in German. "I have followed through to make your life easier. I have even found you an imam to provide spiritual support." I turn to glance at the Chechen and he smiles.

"Now, let's get to the serious matters. I brought him to you so that you would feel protected in what you say to me. I know that you don't trust me, but hopefully you will trust his judgment and be truthful. Christians have an expression of how the truth will set you free. That's my motto to you today." I bend closer towards her and she backs away, the end of her clothing accidentally touching my fingertip. The Chechen motions with his head and she sits still.

"What were you doing in New York? In America? Are you part of some group?" I demand, my voice rising in volume.

The Chechen stands with his arms folded against his chest, his head nodding although he does not understand German. He knows where I am going with my questioning. She looks at her imam and then back towards me; her eyes pleading for help, advice, assurances that she will not burn in some kind of hell. His bobbing head is what she sees.

"Tell me," I look back at the Chechen, returning to her face. "What were you doing in America? You are part of a bigger group? Do they have plans to do something in America? Blow up a building, set off a bomb somewhere? I understand that there was a man there, at that house where you were living. A Latin man, Spanish, short and solid, perhaps a man you loved." I lean into her face; my nose is practically touching hers. "A forbidden love, how are you connected to that man?" I pause, "the man is dead," I coldly announce.

She does not react. She appears to have no relationship with the dead Oscar.

The Chechen suddenly drops to his knees, inches from the woman; but, not making any direct contact with her or the bed. His face twists in strange contortions as if he is being tortured, the eyes bulging, the neck muscles tight and pulsating, his blood racing through his veins. His hands are held tightly against his chest as if he is pleading with her. His voice is soft but forceful, the tone strong but muted in volume. She looks shocked by what he is saying, her eyebrows rising, her eyes big and frightened.

I hear her cry out something in Arabic, shielding her face with her linked fingers. She shrieks in anguish. It is a cry of a mother's wail. I still do not understand a word, but this is as emotional as I remember seeing her. It appears as if she is saying something like 'no, no.'

The Chechen is on his knees; he moves his body so close that a loose thread touches the white scarf she wears to cover her hair. But that's as far as he goes. She violently shakes her head and peers at him through her closed hands. The volume of his voice increases; the words come out tumbling like an acrobat at a circus, consonants and vowels rolling from his tongue, around and around as if in a tight circle. She is pulling away and something like 'no, no, no,' repeats itself. She continues to push her body away, trying to hide from his words, but he is relentless; as she retreats he moves closer to the point where his body is inches from her. He is still not touching her, never actually violating her personal being.

I am a voyeur watching and observing. I try not to demonstrate any emotion, impassively sitting.

Then the Chechen slips back on his heels, and speaks to me in Russian, in a composed but arousing tone of voice. "I tell her that she is responsible for the deaths of children, children, their badly burned and mutilated bodies strewn across the road from the bombs of her terrorist friends. Perhaps she is directly responsible for those bombs that kill innocent children. Children, children, I hammer on the word. She denies it all," we both glance at the woman.

"I call her a terrorist repeatedly, baby killer, but she says she has done nothing wrong. She is a servant of Mohammad, it is his directions that she follows," he tells me.

I look at my suspect; her eyes are filled with hate. I am the infidel, godless and therefore not worthy. Her voice is shrilly and the words high-pitched. Her stare is hard but clear. It's OK to kill me and my kind.

"She hates me?" I ask the Chechen.

"It's not personal but you are the enemy. She has this soft spot for babies burning. It could be that her children were killed by Russian or American bombs."

"Go after her about the babies. And see if you can find any information about children. If this is her vulnerability, then we go for the jugular. Is her mission to bomb us in America?"

The Chechen on his knees is taller than the slumping woman. He talks to her; almost whispering, so low is his voice. Her reaction is to jump as if she wanted to vanish through the wall of her cell, to flee his words.

He turns towards me. "I tell her we have pictures of the babies, babies. I use that word babies, of their heads shot off, headless, the blood everywhere, their maimed limbs lifeless, incapable of even crying." We both stare at her rigid body as she covers her head with her hands.

"Nein, nein," she screams at me in German pointing a threatening finger.

"We have her weakness, let me continue," the play-acting imam tells me.

Again, the Chechen gets close, talking to her in a hushed tone, but her response is immediate. She tries to hide from his words, covering her face with her hands. She screams out at the top of her lungs, her head shaking ferociously like a captured, injured animal cornered with no hope of escape.

He barks at me. "Show her the pictures," he returns to Arabic. He gestures to me. "Get your attaché case, show her the pictures."

I reach for my case but of course I have no pictures. He forcefully grabs the case from out of my hands and lays it on her lap, repeatedly pounding it with his closed fists. Then he tries to shove it into her hands, but she refuses it, pushing further and further away, pressing her back against the hard wall of her cell. I hear what I interpret to mean 'no, no.'

He purposefully throws my case to the cement ground. It bounces from the impact. I'm glad my cell phone is in my pocket and not in the case.

He nods to me and I know it's my turn. The chair legs rub against the unbreakable floor, squealing in pain, as I move close to her side.

I talk to her in German, hoping that I will not need the Chechen to translate so I can get a flow of dialogue, without interruption, one long sure surge of words. "Are you part of a terrorist group? What were you doing in New York? Tell me and I can help you. Otherwise, the Americans will let you rot here until you die. Talk to me. Who is this Oscar, now dead? A comrade? A fellow conspirator? Talk to me." My voice goes from loud and indignant to softer and then almost a whisper. "Talk to me, you can trust me. I am your only hope. The Americans will let you burn like the babies. Speak. I can save you and your babies. I can save your children. Talk to me."

She inhales deeply, looking directly at me with her pointing finger directed at my head.

"Who is Oscar?" I ask. "He cannot save you. He is dead."

I rearrange myself on the chair, my head within inches of her face, hanging there waiting for the words that can unlock the mysteries. "Oscar? The little Spanish guy?"

She gathers her composure. "He is dead?"

"I can save you. He cannot. Talk to me about Oscar. How did he get you into America? Did he smuggle you into America in a van, on a plane, in a boat?"

She looks first at the actor imam and then at me. He is nodding his head, encouraging her to talk to me, moving his hands to form a prayer position.

I hear him mention the name Allah. He repeats the word several times and she closes her eyes as if praying. He is gentle with her. I want to slam her head against the wall, but I remain calm.

She speaks to him but not to me. The conversation is too difficult in German; only Arabic flows from her lips.

"She is a tortured individual. She is on a mission from Allah to burn your houses down in America but something about burning children frightens her about this plan. I think her children were burned to death."

"Oscar, this El Salvadoran what's his relationship with her?"

"She doesn't know him by name and he is not the person who brought her to America. That was some other short, little man who left her. A new person was supposed to take her to another place in New Jersey."

"New Jersey? What the hell. Oscar was going to take her to New Jersey where she was then going to burn down houses in America? New Jersey?" I am stunned and dumbfounded, but I keep my cool. "New Jersey, who is in New Jersey?"

She watches me and tells me in German. "Safe there. I must wait."

"How did you get from Germany to America?" I respond in German.

"Small brown-skinned men not Arabic speak different language. I am on a mission to America," she answers.

The Chechen watches us. "Did she tell you how she got to America from Germany?" I ask him in Russian. She now studies me.

"She thinks they spoke Spanish, but she is guessing from watching foreign language TV shows in Germany."

"What set her travels in motion? Ask her to start at the beginning."

They talk together, she is animated while he is quiet. The discussion is long and is broken up by her long sighs. At moments it appears she will cry but inhales deeply and continues in Arabic.

After more than fifteen minutes. "I think I have the story. It's about her dead husband who died in Syria, her terrorist brother who she is following to America and her dead children. I'm entirely sure her children are dead because I can't understand where her children died. It may have been Syria. Why they were all in Syria I don't know. She was last in Germany before this journey to America. It maybe that her husband and brother were freedom fighters in Syria, she and her children were forced to join the men. The husband is killed, possibly her children. She followed the evacuated migrants out of Syria to Germany. Burned children is a sore issue and I think her children were burned by bombs out of the sky. She believes it was American bombs, but if it's Syria, I think they were Russian."

"And coming to America? Not for freedom?"

"No, her intent and her brother are to hurt Americans. That is clear."

"What about her recent journey? How did she get to America? Where is her brother? Were there others? Her destination is a place called New Jersey? Crazy and scary if true," I stare at her and she returns my gesture.

"She was vague, but she knows some details. Ask her again," he suggests.

"How did you go from Germany to America? And who was with you? Your brother? Other people?"

She looks to the Chechen for advice. He nods her head gesturing with his hands for her speak.

"Train took us from Hamburg to Cairo. We boarded cargo ship in Alexandria, Egypt. My brother got me a room just for me. He slept somewhere else with other man who joined us in Alexandria."

"There were three of you – you, your brother and a third person?"

"Yes," she responds quickly.

"This other man – a friend, relative, stranger?"

"Cousin, I think from Egypt never met before."

"Did you stop anywhere else?"

The Chechen says something quietly to her. She looks at him and then speaks to me. "Stop where black people came on board."

"What was on board this cargo ship? Oil? Cars? What? Did you just walk aboard? No passport? No papers?" I am incredulous at the porous international borders.

"No, nothing. A Chinese looking man took my bag and we departed," she matter-of-factly replies.

"Did you notice the name of the ship?"

"No, no," she shakes her.

My attention returns to the Chechen. "What do you think?" I ask my companion his opinion.

"She got on board in Alexandria. That's right. Who knows what was on the ship? Possibly, they stopped in a West African port or Azores," he replies.

"Then where, next stop?" I ask her.

She glances at the Chechen and he nods his head. She responds, "We just stop. End of the ship ride, everyone speaks another language – Spanish my guess."

"Is it there that you met Oscar?" I repeat this question because it doesn't make sense that she first met him at the Long Island house.

Again, she looks to the Chechen for reassurance. "No Oscar, the rest of the trip is bad, very bad, bumpy, hot, never bathroom. Always hiding in vans with white cloth over our heads. Living with strangers."

"Who takes you to the first house?"

"Barely see his face. Then at house in America, a man this Oscar tells me he take me to safe place. I will see my brother again. He tell me I go to New Jersey," stumbling on the pronunciation. "But he never takes me. Liar," she loudly tells me. "Liar."

"When did you separate from your brother?"

She and the Chechen have a lively conversation with lots of gesturing.

He says, "she won't say. She's afraid you will kill her brother."

"I might not kill him, but I would arrest him,"

"It doesn't matter where or even when they went their different ways. You know he's no longer at that place. Look forward. This New Jersey," the fake imam suggests. "The future is New Jersey."

I let the travel plans of the brother go for the moment. "Did anyone come to visit you at the house in Long Island? Your bother? Other man on the ship? Strangers?"

"No, I waited for Oscar to take me. No one else came," she slaps her hand on the bed.

"Where is your brother and this other man?" I can't ignore the brother. Two very dangerous men are loose.

"I don't know and if I did I would never tell you. You kill them," she says.

I ask the Chechen. "Does she know the location of the New Jersey house?"

"No, she doesn't even know where New Jersey is. But I bet that's where you will find the brother."

"Do you think she knows more?"

"Probably nothing useful. The existence of a safe house, the Chinese cargo ship, the two guys on the run. These are important. You will need information from your intelligence sources to fill in the blanks. She is at best some foot soldier. Her brother may not be anything more. But you will want to find him."

"What else will she tell me?"

"I think you got a lot. Keep her away from gasoline or bombmaking materials," he laughs.

I'm glad someone is amused and while not satisfied the Chechen is right. There's not much more I'm going to get today.

The two Muslims speak words of good-bye and he appears to offer prayers. I retrieve my battered attaché case.

We bang the cell door and my friendly guard quickly appears. They are probably watching the camera, realizing that the interview is finished. He leads us to the exit and freedom. I stop at the camera room.

I ask. "Can I have the tape from today?"

The man sitting behind the screen answers. "Of course," he goes to eject the tape.

"There is only one copy?" I inquire.

"You have it in your hands," he answers.

"No other copy is made? Nothing automatically creates a second copy for the records?" they immediately understand the nature of my conversation. "No other copy will be made?"

We leave together. Outside I thank my fake imam. "Well. I owe you. What can I do to repay the favor?" I ask the Chechen.

"Just tell Vasily that he owes me. Someday, he will pay," the man laughs.

I smile and watch him go.

CHAPTER 25

Mission accomplished; she talks without torture. US Attorney Cohen is waiting for my call.

"Nice work Perlov. As we speak, I am contacting agencies across the globe. Come home."

"Happily."

They are at the tarmac my two traveling companions and I am their only passenger. The steel door shuts and I throw a kiss to Belarus. I cannot imagine what attracts Nadia to this land. Nationalism dies slowly or is it the family's trait of stubbornness. If they hate me then I must be a constant irritant.

My clothes are returned with all my identification. Once again, I am Sasha Perlov. Watching through the window as the plane lifts, my eyes begin to close.

Hours later when I awake, the plane makes its descent. I am back in New York City; my winged chariot brings me home where I park my still sleepy head at my parents' house. Amos is at my side.

The cell phone breaks my dreamy sleep screaming at me. Is day or is it night? Where am I? I turn over and Amos licks my hand, and then my nose. It tickles. The noise continues. "Perlov," I answer.

"We need to talk," I recognize his voice. "Got new intel

on Oscar. You need to hear this in person. And Murphy has just been sent to some Rehab Center because of his injuries. They need to strengthen his chest and arm muscles damaged by some bullet. Meet me there."

I understand despite my unfocused mind still thinking I'm in Belarus. "OK," I immediately answer Lewis; he gives me the address in Brooklyn.

The place looks like a nursing home certainly not a hospital. It's quiet when you walk inside, no beeping sounds, no irritating wails, screaming sirens, no blue lights flashing. Lewis is waiting for me at the entrance.

"Let's go say hello to Murphy and then there's a small cafeteria where we can talk," he tells me.

I follow him. Murphy is sitting in a wheelchair with his wife by his side. He looks human, no tubes or wires everywhere, no bandages, he almost looks like himself.

We all exchange hugs and slaps on the back. It's been a long rehabilitation and it's still not over.

"I will never forget," Murphy says to me while shaking my hand. "Whatever I can do for you. You got the bastard, thanks is not good enough."

I respond modestly, "Hell no, we were all in it. The whole squad not just me."

We chat amicably. The rehabilitation is the new stage of

his recovery and now poor Murphy is formally on disability. I don't dare raise the issue of whether he can ever return to the force.

Lewis excuses us, and we move from Murphy's room to the small but empty cafeteria. Our little table faces the exit door. No one is serving any food; the shelves are not bare but there is no staff. I can't get a cup of tea.

Lewis places his hand on my arm. "It was luck and solid, shoe leather detective work. I went back to that house in Riverhead with a buddy, Suffolk County detective. We went through that house, literally on our knees. We found a key to a bus station locker. Fucking key had the address of the bus station. Shit it was a treasure trove."

"Fabulous. What was inside the locker?" I'm a kid in a candy store.

"Unbelievable. There were three photos: the woman, and two other guys. And a Salvadoran passport in Oscar's name with his photo."

I share with Lewis about the two guys on the loose. "The woman can help us identify those guys. What else?" he's grinning so there's more.

"Those photos are now on an Interpol list circulating worldwide. But it gets better. An address in northern New Jersey."

"Holy shit," I am so excited it's hard for me to get the

words out of my mouth. I'm suddenly speaking Russian. "This is exactly the break we need. The woman was expecting to be delivered to some safe house in New Jersey. Can that address be the one?" I'm too giddy.

"It also explains Oscar. He was not a lying piece of shit. He actually did run away from that place in Riverhead. His job was taking this woman somewhere until he got permanently stopped."

"Any word on Oscar's murder?"

"There's good news and bad news. What do you want to hear first?"

I possess a dark Russian soul. "Bad news, of course."

He chuckles. "Yeah, yeah, that's what I figured."

"And?" my mouth hangs open.

"OK, we may never know for certain who pulled the trigger. That's the bad news but we got the guy who ordered the hit."

"One of the guys from the house in Riverhead?" I'm hoping.

"Yes, one of those who escaped. He and three others got into a shoot-out with cops in Washington Heights. He's dead so is one other but two we captured. The two we got under questioning, separately, pointed to one of the dead guys as the leader of the pack. This dead guy was carrying money and passports. The other dead guy wasn't mentioned."

"You believe them?"

"Yes, they're all habitual liars, but this feels real. And they both fingered the same guy. He was holding the goodies."

"OK am I allowed to tell the family Oscar's murderer is dead?"

"I would wait. We got all the living lowlifes in a federal prison in New York City. But the feds are behaving; Oscar's murder belongs to NYPD. And these scum like to boast. We are banking on them opening their mouths to impress other pieces of shit. Each of them is in a jail cell with an informer we planted there to hear those boasts. We expect that we will be able to get more useful information about MS-13 plus Oscar's murder."

"That's great," my voice not overly expressive.

"I know your interest is the woman. But getting inside MS-13 in America will be very valuable. Oscar was a good find."

He hands me a paper with the address in New Jersey.

I take it from his hand. "Have you told anyone about this address?"

He shakes his head. "No, I wasn't sure what to do with this intel. I was waiting for you, smart fuck," the familiar pounding on my shoulder blades begins again.

"This address may prove to be the most important piece of evidence. Thank you, thank you," he is not yet releasing me from a shoulder hold.

"Go get them Perlov the Protector," the grip is released.

"I got to get this intel to Cohen. You have saved the day. I will recommend you and your guy from Suffolk PD receive a police commendation.

He blushes.

As I am leaving the rehab center, I call Cohen and rely Lewis' treasure trove of information. He remains completely silent for what seems like minutes.

"Holy shit," he finally speaks. "Can it be that your guys found the missing link. Can it be? Address in Jersey just like she said. Really a Jersey address? Pinch me. Tell me it's real."

"It's fucking real. Lewis is a great investigator. Best there is. This is real. Address in Jersey."

"Text it to me right now. Then give me a few hours to make arrangements and then get your ass in here. We have to make plans. Holy shit the address in Jersey. Give me a few hours to contact the appropriate law enforcement," he sounds breathless.

"I'll be there in three hours, unless you call me," I'm so excited I don't know what to do with myself skipping like a school child to my car. I wish Jimmy was around.

I go back to Brighton Beach and the Boardwalk to fill up the three hours, stopping at every food stand. My preference for something either sweet or salty. I don't go back to my parents with their endless questioning, instead I stake out my favorite bench. The gulls gladly accept my scraps. The sun beats on my face as I wipe away the traces of mustard. Time can't move any faster. My patience fading, I jump in my car hoping the traffic will eat up the time.

A coveted parking space is waiting for me. I briefly surrender my gun as I enter the security gate, returned to me after I pass through all the metal detectors and explosive sniffing machines. The canine unit is patrolling. The place is on heightened alert. I don't need the guard's direction, I know my way.

He is standing as I enter his office, gazing out the big windows at the skyline of lower Manhattan, absent the presence of the World Trade Center buildings. He hears me enter but continues staring into the blue sky. He is good at multi-tasking – me, the panoramic views, the ghosts of the dead of 9/11, a future election campaign.

"I'm glad to see you, Sasha. Your work as always is commendable. I can't begin to tell you how important it is. The public outside New York is forgetting, but the terrorists are out there. Probably a sleeper cell in New Jersey." He shakes his head, not at me, but into empty space. Below us construction teams continue to find ashes and bone fragments of those killed at the World Trade Center.

"The woman is no longer such a mystery. And these

Oscar finds, true treasure trove," I say with the feeling of one dedicated to saving my adopted country.

His face is strained, tired, a few new wrinkles around the mouth, from what I can only imagine are conflicting calls of duty. His many masters at his heels, some want him to succeed while his political enemies hope for his dismal failure. "The address in Jersey. Holy shit, the mother lode."

"What next?"

"Key to everything is that address. I immediately ordered surveillance of the address. I've prepared court papers, so we can conduct surveillance unimpeded. We'll get wiretaps on any phone linked to the address. The mail will be screened."

"You want to raid the house and retrieve cell phones, laptops? Make sure no evidence is erased?"

"No, not at this time. Let's wait. Hopefully, those guys running free will show up at the house. Perhaps others will come visiting, new faces, unknowns who are dangerous. Don't want to scare off anyone. Our people must be invisible."

"Going for a wider net, entire neighborhood? Stores that sell phones? Pay phones on the street?"

"Lots depend on money. I have to prove to DOJ that this operation is a number one priority."

"It is. A link between MS-13 gangbangers and foreign terrorists. You should be able to persuade them. You're a greater talker. This is the most important story of the year," I sit in one of the comfy chairs.

"Coffee? Bagels?" he asks as he sits in his cushy chair.

"You know I can't refuse a good bagel," I tap my stomach.

"I envy your good genes," staring at his own expanding mid-section.

"What's next for me?" the Lewis find, and my interrogation has produced such colossal intelligence. When I left for Belarus, I thought I'll find useful information. Never could I ever dream of the extent of what would be found.

"I want you to head up the investigation in Jersey. You will oversee the surveillance. If there's a moment when you think a raid is necessary, I'll trust your judgment," he answers while pouring me a cup of coffee, the steam rising in looping circles. My attention is temporarily fixated on the curling waves of mist as it draws up towards the ceiling ducts.

Returning to my host, I ask. "What does that mean head up the investigation?" Is there a set of goals just for me? As a cop, we live by our statistics such as arrest records, homicides solved, gang members sent to prison in upstate New York for twenty years.

"You put the pieces together. You know this woman better than anyone. You don't know the brother or the other guy, but you know the back story." He pours himself a cup, eyeing the bagel, then pushing the platter towards me.

"Do you want me to visit the house as Karl Erdmann, German intelligence?" Will I continue to live a charade now that I'm back.

"I don't think the Germans will want you to continue impersonating one of their intelligence operatives in America," he shakes his head.

"As a NYPD detective what authority do I have in Jersey?" I ask.

"You will take a leave from the NYPD. I have the necessary paperwork for you to sign. I want you as my point man on this operation. How can you return as a NYPD detective? You're going to law school on the taxpayer's dime. You work out of this office. Before you get that law degree you will head up my whole investigations unit. I need you. Your adopted country needs you."

"Very flattering, really," I didn't feel as if I had many options. I look at the papers; an 'X' appears where to sign.

"We don't know how long the Jersey investigation will last. This is an open-ended assignment. You go wherever the evidence points. You have no boundaries," he hands me the gold pen from his desk.

"Do I get a new badge?" I am teasing.

"If you want one?" he's surprised by the request, scratches his chin. "If there's a problem we can get you some other form of identification."

"It's OK although if I'm canvassing the neighborhood someone may ask for my identification," a practical concern.

"You'll get formal identification," he writes something on a pad near his elbow.

"When do I start?"

"I want you to start tomorrow but the paperwork takes a few days to process. I'll have information sent to your encrypted laptop, whatever we have about the house, its owners. Then I'll introduce to you my FBI on-the-ground field agents. They will report to you."

He manages to sip his coffee and nibble on a small piece of bagel. He wipes his hands on a napkin. "Welcome to federal service Sasha Perlov."

We shake hands. Life is too strange to make sense of it all. Hashem must have a plan for me.

"There's a couple of other important facts you need to know. After I got the news from you yesterday, we moved her to an American Air Force base in Germany. Because of your newest intel about the Jersey house, her next stop is the federal prison right here under my watchful eye. Everyone wanted to claim her. But she's mine because of you and Lewis.

"And the real prize is the brother?" he and his pal are the real terrorists, my mystery lady a mere follower. Although she is certainly capable of creating mayhem even deaths.

"Yes, and he is on the loose. A major headache," Cohen

places his hand on his forehead.

"My first objective is to catch him when he comes to that house. I am certain he is looking for his sister," I reply.

"I hope you're right and somehow the brother doesn't know Oscar is dead or his sister was picked up my law enforcement." Cohen nervously cuts another piece of bagel.

I have been thinking about whether the sister and brother have made contact here. "It's contingent on how big their circle is. Was some other party watching the house in Riverhead?"

He pokes at my arm "You are going to sort all this out. And there's a further complication. When they got her to Germany, I insisted that a medical examination be conducted. I don't want anyone accusing us of mistreating her," he studies my face as I raise my arms in protest.

"Nothing bad happened during my time with her, and those Belarusian guards would never touch her," I adamantly state my case, pumping the air with my arms. It is important to include praise for those guards, reaffirm their value in this terrorist game, which only makes me a more worthwhile contact for them.

"I know you did nothing but there were weeks between her leaving Hamburg, the immigration raid including a cargo ship trip across the globe," he calmly asserts.

"She got a clean bill of health?" I know that she looked

fine at the time of my departure.

"What we found a total surprise. Nothing we would have expected. A female military doctor examined her and reported that she is several months pregnant," he repeatedly shakes his head.

"The father of the child who could he be?

"We are conducting DNA analysis to exclude at least Oscar," he replies.

"What else did the doctor say?" I see tension; he's back to slicing another piece of bagel.

"The military doctors think after examining her that she was raped. We are taking DNA samples from everyone from the house – the living in jail and the dead."

"I can guess that they don't want her on American soil when she delivers that child. Immigration rules—you know, anyone born here is automatically an American citizen." I laugh at all of life's absurdities and he joins me.

"She won't be coming to America until she delivers that baby. They're wrangling over the possibility of her giving birth in an American military hospital on the base in Germany. They don't want the possible public exposure if she delivers in a German hospital. Potentially too many questions. DOD and DOJ lawyers are deciding whether a child born on an American military base could be considered an American given these unusual circumstances. Wouldn't that be ironic if the child is an

American by birth," we laugh, a good tension-reliever, the absurdity of the situation.

"Do you want me to go to Germany to the military base to further my interrogation?"

"No, I don't want the German government to think we overplayed our hand using their intelligence service as a ploy. No, the baby will be born, and they will be moved here. The other fact you should know. I am going to release her once she gets here. She will get a new Oscar, one of my undercover FBI guys posing as the MS-13 guy, who will take her to that Jersey safe house."

"She knows Oscar is dead," I tell him. "I told her."

"That's good. The old Oscar is dead, now she gets another one. Someone paid to get her to New Jersey. A Latin guy from MS-13 is delivering her as promised."

"I like this plan. Do you give a reason for her release?"

"We don't lock up women nursing babies. It's humanitarian on our part. We don't think she's dangerous," he considers another piece of bagel but instead pours himself a cup of coffee and offers me some.

"This can work. She goes to the house. Hopefully, the brother and the other guy follow. Sounds good."

He stares me. "I'm happy you approve because you're going to oversee it."

He opens a desk draw and pulls out a bottle of Johnny

Walker's. He pours a good amount in both glasses. I can't tell him I don't like scotch.

"L'chayim," the glasses clank.

CHAPTER 26

My head is spinning. Cohen is certainly a golden boy and I can attach myself to his wings. Having no political ambitions, I am not a threat. Terrorism is the new avenue to success in law enforcement. If Teddy Roosevelt was alive as the NYC Police Commissioner, he would be out chasing terrorists.

Terrorism creates opportunities for professional growth, acquire new skills, get your face on the cover of Time magazine. Learning Arabic should be easy; I'm very good with languages. The TV loves my face with its earnest, immigrant look. I could emerge as a law enforcement spokesman.

But do I really want to leave the NYPD? Jimmy just decided to pursue his ambitions, walked away, shed no tears, fell in love with a Hasidic woman from the Ukraine.

Do I actually have ambitions? Law school was my mother's idea. Terrorism was thrust upon me. I will follow my instincts, go with my gut.

To clear my head with all this thinking, I will walk Amos on the Boardwalk. The sea is part of my redemption. We are undisturbed walking together.

"Look at the sky," I remark to my dog, who lovingly looks

up at me. It's a beautiful day to be alive.

The sun's radiance is shining down on us and we are far from alone. The old people are here in a huge mass of creaky metal and plastic beach chairs. The slats are frayed and in need of repair. The chairs are too worthless for any further expense, so these frugal people keep them until it's impossible to sit on them.

To my surprise Tatiana's is still open, a most famous Brighton Beach restaurant located right on the Boardwalk. Because of the glorious day, the owner has set up tables and chairs outside.

I check my watch; well, it's not quite time for lunch and too late for breakfast, but the restaurant is open. I can't resist the smells of freshly baking bread and meats roasting on a spit, besides I can sit outside, and Amos can join me.

A young waiter quickly finds me and hands me a menu. I don't recognize him, although I know most of the staff. My own Aunt Tatiana, a masterful cook and inventor of culinary delights of indescribable delicacy sometimes chats or compares notes on recipes with the restaurant owner.

"What do you want?" he asks in a sullen tone.

Before I can answer, Olga appears from the shadows of the overhanging awning. She sees me and instantly smiles.

I hesitate for a sheer second. "Olga, will you join me?" I ask in the mother tongue, rising from my chair.

She has a blushing type of smile, sweet and innocent although she is clearly a woman of sophisticated tastes and experiences.

"Sasha," she gently touches the top of my hand. "Of course," I pull the chair out, her curvaceous body easily gliding onto the plastic. Two other waiters come running to help. Her beautiful blue eyes glance at the three hanging jaws. The taller one pushes aside the younger one and hands her a menu, holding on to it, not quite ready to release it. Her gaze returns to me although she bends down to pet Amos. His tail wags in appreciation—clearly, he has good taste in women.

"Okay fellows," I say, the waiter letting go of the menu. "I'll call you when we decide," I announce in Russian with annoyance clearly in my voice. These are vultures, trying to win favor with my beauty.

She smiles at my confident and commanding posturing.

"How are you doing? Occasionally, I see you on TV on that soap opera in the afternoon," I try not to trip over my words, remain calm and cool. My heart is racing, the blood rushing from point to point, speeding along an interior highway, thundering inside my shirt; hopefully, she can't see my reaction to her presence. My mind and much more basic instincts are on full alert.

"I just returned from the Motherland," she informs me and her hand brushes against my fingertips.

I try hard not to appear too eager, not grab her and kiss her on the mouth, right here, in front of all these people. "Did you have a nice time?" I ask a stupid question that an indifferent, casual acquaintance might pose.

"Actually, I went because my grandmother was dying. While I was there, she passed," she tells me with a small sigh.

I press closer. "I'm so sorry to hear that," I feel my shoe touching hers.

"She has been sick for some time, so it was not unexpected," she blinks back a tear.

I gallantly hand her a paper napkin from off the table and smile. "It's tough to lose someone you love," I answer without any clue about her relationship to this grandmother. It's not a person she ever mentioned to me, but most people love their grandmothers.

"The extraordinary thing," she pauses to look into my eyes.

"Yes," I can't contain my eagerness, a bubbly child eyeing a delicious treat, forbidden but within arm's length. She is so close to me, the tiny hairs on my arm erect, the chills of passion running up and down my spine.

"She made this deathbed confession. Extraordinary," she stops and gazes into space, a gull shrieks overhead. I turn my apt attention from her perfectly symmetrical face to the squealing scavenger.

The moment's distraction fades. "Extraordinary," I repeat her word.

A dazzling smile returns to her face. "Listen," she looks first at Amos, his ears perk up; then back at me through my corneas into my soul.

"I am listening," I quickly reply, folding my hands as if in prayer.

The prying waiter steps into view, asking in Russian. "What can I get you?" he looks at her, just managing the slightest glance my way.

We order appetizers and coffee as I attempt to get him away from her.

She tucks her chin under her folded hands, resting her elbows on the tabletop. "She confesses as she is dying that she has lived a complete lie -- all her life," she tilts her head in such an appealing, little girl, watch me perform the best cartwheel fashion.

"And," I am interested in this story, she can drag it out all afternoon. I have nowhere to go more satisfying than sharing my time with her. Even Amos lays down in contentment; I give him a few scratches behind the ears and a dog biscuit to chomp on.

"This is the amazing part," she pauses, and I rest my elbows on the table staring into her unblinking baby blues.

I gesture with my hand, beckoning for more of her story.

"My mother was born a Jewess," she stops, placing her palms on the table's top. "A Jewess, and my grandmother is not really her biological mother," she suddenly jerks back her head as if she is being shocked by an errant electrical cord.

"Wow, a Jewess" is my first response, it is extraordinary.

"It seems my mother was the infant daughter of a neighbor, a Jewess from a local family, who were all caught up in Operation Barbarossa. Members of this family were paraded out of town and shot, the bodies buried in a huge pit in the woods. My grandmother confessed that she and many others knew what was happening but remained silent. They were afraid of the Nazis. This woman, who my grandmother knew, placed my mother in her care. She gave her to my grandmother, she said until the madness was over." She stops to catch her breath, her breathing labored, heavy, a burden to inhale and exhale.

I reach over and take her hands in mine. "Quite a story," my first response so silly, as I struggle for something more substantial to say. "I recently went to Belarus to see an elderly relative of my mother's, actually a cousin of my grandmother. She managed to live through Operation Barbarossa and told me stories about the killing of men, women and children in the open. The Nazis forcing these innocent Jews to dig their own graves, shooting them and pouring lime over the bodies, some while still alive. The Nazis knew they were committing heinous crimes. Your grandmother was a coward like so many others. Shameful—perhaps, but understandable," I stop, gently squeezing Olga's long fingertips. She is not responsible for her grandmother's actions.

"She never said a thing to my mother; hid this lie for so long. She raised her as a Catholic along with my aunt and uncle until the Communists made that impossible. When my mother asked her about her biological family, my grandmother claimed not to know what happened to them. All she would admit was that no one ever returned to the village to claim my mother. So, my grandmother just ignored the truth, made no efforts to locate my mother's real mother or any surviving relatives. She treated her as if she were her own blood. We were stunned, stunned," a small tear wells in the corner of her eye. It leaves a tiny trail down her arched cheeks to the edge of her well-shaped chin.

"What are you going to do now that you know that you are really a Jewess? A member of the tribe." I smile, placing my fingertip under her chin and after several moments she finally cracks a small grin.

"Well, after we recovered from the shock," the word 'shock' she says loudly and with indignation. "After the funeral, my mother and I went to the village hall of records. The Nazis kept meticulous records of the property they confiscated, the people they murdered, we were told, but the Communists destroyed much of it. My mother became possessed," she shakes her head, it bobs up and down, the blond strands falling around the contour of her face.

"Well, it was, as you said, a shocking revelation, a complete surprise. Right, a Jewess belonging to some unknown family. The family you thought was yours really a lie, all those relatives you thought were your cousins, aunts and uncles, someone else's," I sympathetically add.

"Yes, yes," she squeezes my hand. "Yes, exactly. It's not like my mother was adopted and my grandmother never said anything. That would be surprising, but this story is shocking because it reveals many ugly truths --the underlying anti-Semitism of the community and a guilt that the whole village shared. They let those people, their neighbors, some we would think were friends, be murdered. Okay, say nothing while the Nazis were present, but 50 years later, still say nothing. That's the shocking part," her sigh is soft and low, but digs deep into her heart.

"Did you make any progress in finding out who these real relatives were?" I inquire because the story is the unearthing of ugly truths. It's the other side of my cousin's Belarus story.

"We actually did by traveling to Kiev and visiting the Chabad group there. Those Hasids were fascinated and probably repulsed by our story, but it's hardly the first time they have heard something like it. They promised to help," she reported.

"And Israel, I bet there are records that were uncovered being kept in Israel," I know it is a national obsession to record and count every victim of the Holocaust.

"Yes, the rabbi gave us the names and e-mails for a number of organizations that might be helpful. He thought that at least someone had escaped. He didn't know for sure, but if they had, they were certainly not living in or near the village, probably not in the Ukraine at all but either in Israel or in America," she is positive of that fact.

"I will help you if I can," I answer with a big broad smile. Yes, any reason to keep her close.

"I knew that. I was going to call you because I know your mother has contacts everywhere – Israel, Brighton Beach, the rest of America, even in Europe," she seems more confident.

"I am a detective, I uncover secrets," my smile is tight, she is embarrassed, our secret rising to the surface. I tightly squeeze her hand and then nod my head. My wink secures our secret. No words need to be spoken. The blush fades and a wide grin frames her creamy skin.

"I hope your mother will remember me when I call." Her expression turns to a frown, a fear that the story of her birthright will remain clouded, too difficult to reveal.

"Oh, she will remember you. She watches you on the TV in that soap opera. Even if she didn't recall that last meeting at the theater, I could serve as your introduction. But don't worry, she knows you," my words are brimming with resolve, spoken by someone who has been given the choicest assignment in the entire world. My mother is aware of Olga, although not about our secret.

"She loved you in *Three Sisters.* Looks for your name in other announcements. Are you scheduled for another play?" I feel this overwhelming sense of joy in her presence. I hope to become her protector again.

"Yes, yes, I will be in something new but not there. No, at a theater in the very west side of Manhattan, off Broadway and in English," she answers with pride about her new achievement.

"We will certainly go," I hesitate. "The director and you," I point my finger at her chest. Is that man still in her life?

"Oh," those precious cheeks redden. "No, no, because he wanted me to go back to Europe and I like it here. I want to stay in America, especially New York. My mother wants to stay in Europe, if not Kiev then nearby, Berlin, even Russia but no, no. I like it in America," she ebulliently answers.

"Good," my hand strokes hers.

Then the pesky waiter interferes again. He makes his pushy presence known by noisily asking, "You didn't eat anything. Is the food bad? Not to worry we can immediately get you something else," he leans towards her.

"We're not hungry," I look for her concurrence and she

nods her head. "Take the plates away," I order, and he follows my instructions.

"I'm so glad I saw you today," her fingers return to the top of my hand. "It's the right karma," the huge grin envelops her face as the small lines around her eyes fade.

"Right, the karma. We were meant to be in touch," I squeeze her hand and her smile grows even broader, not a wrinkle of worry is visible.

"I'll call you. I still have your number. I must go; it's time for me to go to rehearsals. We'll stay in touch," she gently pulls away from my hold.

"Yes, yes, I can't wait," reluctantly releasing her from my grip. The waiters watch as she disappears down to the street level and out of view. Even Amos barks good-bye.

"Nice, very nice," the taller waiter says as he places the bill on the table. "Nice," he mutters to himself.

CHAPTER 27

A Jewess. Am I dreaming? Was that my Olga sitting with me sharing her family history. Part of a 1,000-year history – Ukraine, Russia, Jews, hatred, wars. The waiters want to get rid of me. My space on the Boardwalk is too valuable and she is gone. I am not worth looking at.

Amos and I move on. I can't sit still so we walk, aimlessly. No one on the Boardwalk cares, a man and his dog, quite ordinary. She is not ordinary. Hashem has a plan for me, so I am more than ordinary.

My mother needs to hear this story. She certainly has extraordinary tales to tell. Shouldn't I run home and discuss this story with my parents?

Oh, my mother will have her perspective. She will view it as a story of survival; as a survivor that's how she will see this play out. My methodical father will see this in its grander historical context. War produces unexpected consequences. A small story is part of a much bigger story. The year 1939 is related to 1917; layers and layers of meaning based on past conquerors and losers, a gigantic game of chess. The Russian Empire expires after hundreds of years, followed by the Russian revolution, only lasting 75 years, to present day mercurial times when an independent Ukraine hopes for international recognition.

"Amos it's time to go home," I bend down to scratch him behind the ear.

But my cell phone has another story to tell. "Yeah," I answer still caught between Olga and Operation Barbarossa.

"It's Howie," his voice is filled with excitement, peppier than usual.

"Hey, pal. Did you like the hockey tickets I sent you?" my present to a man that I owe, guardian of vital tapes.

"I've got big news," he practically whispers.

"I'm listening," I stop walking and press the phone to my ear.

"Someone called for those tapes. You know the ones in the box, the ones it seems were forgotten," he plays spy, talking in veiled expressions.

Cohen's men are starting the investigation of the rogue cops. I forgot to mention the tapes to him, but his interrogators probably got the news from Jackie.

"Where are you calling me from?" Cohen warned me that she will disappear, a new identity, new location, new occupation. I never expected that Howie would be so attached to the case.

"From a pay phone in Chinatown," he replies.

"Give me the number and I'll call you back." It no longer involves me, but Howie has to let go without learning the real facts of the case.

There are several phones off the Boardwalk and quickly I find one. Amos thinks we're hurrying home for food and is disappointed as I pull at his leash when I locate a street phone.

I dial. "Okay Howie give me the scoop," I am now excited.

"I got this call from the US Attorney's office. You know the feds. He said it was coming directly from US Attorney Cohen. Somehow, they knew about these tapes. They wanted them. He described the box that I found with all those tapes in it. Lots of questions about have I viewed them? Naturally I said no. Has anyone else seen them? I say no," he is wheezing, his eagerness and enthusiasm palpable.

"Okay," I pause to catch my thoughts. "More, is there more?"

"I made a copy of the tapes and sent it you. I went to the Post Office myself. I dropped them off in Midtown. You should be receiving them in two days," his breath is audible through the phone lines.

"You did good," I reply without sharing about Jackie's real case. If I am to be her protector, no one must know about the case. Not her involvement; years from now the rogue cops are jailed. There must be a graceful way to get Howie off the project

"I owe you probably a whole season of hockey tickets," keeping him ignorant about witness protection. No speaking about what the heart of the case was about: rogue cops, money and lots of it, assassinations of law professors and protestors. Mum must be my approach.

"I reviewed some of the tapes; I'm still looking for a few of those other cops playing as protesters," he breathlessly answers.

"Howie, Howie, my friend, exciting? Right?" how to dampen his enthusiasm without giving away too much information. "Computer nerd turned investigator," I'm making these false laughing noises.

"Cool, so cool. And a bit nuts. I mean double agent stuff. Shit, I don't support this fucking war," he answers. "Terrorists my ass," he insists.

"Appreciate it Howie, you can't know how much," where do I assuage his zealot impulses. Can't have him mucking up the case.

"I know you'll make good use of the stuff. I'll let you take it from here. You know best."

There's the graceful exit. "That's great Howie. I know exactly what to do. Just between us. Hush, hush, no spreading the word. Cooperate with the US Attorney's office."

"Perlov you're the man. I know you will do what's best. I probably shouldn't expect any articles in the New York Times."

"This case will unwind slowly; but I have a good feeling that it ultimately will have a good ending," I tell him. No lies, there are valuable lessons the case will reveal.

"US Attorney not NYPD?" he is still emotionally tied to the case.

"It's probably ending up in the right hands," reminding myself not to say more.

"OK Perlov, not another word," he says while hanging up the phone.

Can life get more complicated? Jackie and Howie. Olga and her grandmother. My poor brain is bursting from thinking. A new job perhaps?

Returning to my favorite Boardwalk bench, I hear a voice nearby but don't react. Then Amos' tail starts furiously wagging. It's the food I smell that gets me to react.

Turning around I see him approaching. "Hey," I say eyeing the tray that he is carrying.

"Kosher hotdogs, your favorite, plus knishes, fries and seltzer," he sits down. The tray rests between us.

Vasily reaches into his pocket and pulls out a dog biscuit. Amos greedily snatches it from his open palm.

"I've eaten maybe three times today and it's not close to sundown," I proclaim.

"Enjoy," he pulls out a flask and two plastic cups. I watch him pour out the clear liquid into the small shot glasses.

"*L'chayim*," we both say together, just touching our

glasses.

"Smooth. I like this vodka," I answer as he hands me a hotdog.

"*Ess*," taking a big bite, the mustard dripping from the corner of his mouth.

"The Chechen says you owe him," I answer between bites.

"It's OK, there will be many future opportunities to repay him. As long as he was helpful," he gingerly dabs the mustard away with a paper napkin.

"I owe you big time," I reply, stopping to gaze at his long, thin face, my face, a mirror looking back at me.

"You owe me nothing, we are like blood," he immediately answers, brushing his hand in the air like an abstract painter creating his masterpiece.

I put down the food and spontaneously hug him. He reacts by putting his arms around my shoulders.

"Like brothers," I reply.

"Yes," he pats my shoulder.

There are so many things to share. "I saw Olga," pointing towards Tatiana's which is a block away.

He slams my arm. "*Treife*, what's wrong with you. Women, always the women; it's what gets you in trouble," he smiles and then laughs, shaking his head.

"I've got a story for you about her grandmother. Not so

treife, she's actually a Jewess," I can't control my words, they spew out in my wondrous excitement.

He just shakes his head in disbelief. "Tell me," he continues to eat.

"Operation Barbarossa, the Nazi invasion of Soviet Union. A Jewess senses the danger, the barbarians are coming, the Nazis are nearby. Whether she thinks she's going to die or go to prison or whatever, it's certainly bad so she wants to save her infant daughter. She knows a gentile villager. She gives her the infant for safe keeping. Naturally, she never returns; burned in the ovens, probably. The woman never goes searching for relatives and just keeps the infant, raises it as her own, never says a word. If other relatives know anything they say nothing. On her deathbed, she tells her daughter, Olga's mother, that she was the offspring of Jews sent to their deaths by the Nazis. Some story, right?" I clap my hands together for emphasis.

"Shit, for real?" he is amazed, mouth hanging ajar. Eyes wide open.

"Yeh, can you believe it? My Olga, the granddaughter not of some village *goy* but dead Jews," I answer as I attack the knish, spreading packets of mustard on its crusty surface.

"When did she tell you this?" he replies taking a sip of seltzer.

"Just now, today, she's just returned from the Ukraine. She and her mother are now trying to locate these Jewish relatives. Went to see a Hasid *rebbe* in Kiev, he told her about contacting people in Israel. He agreed to search and uncover whatever facts he can with the records he knows about. Somewhere there are birth and marriage records, even if the Nazis burned down all the synagogues, some of those records may be around." I stop to watch his face, taking a big bite of the knish. Amos is sitting up waiting for another treat.

Vasily reaches down and hands the dog a French fry, looking first at me for permission. I nod my head. The dog devours the greasy food.

"She wants to talk to my mother because she knows that the dissident has lots of contacts all over the globe," I nod my head in joy.

He laughs and pokes me in the arm. "*Treife*, forget the Jewish angle. Didn't you investigate the death of her fat, dead husband? Yes?" he stares at me.

"Weren't you the one who told me she didn't deserve any punishment? It was you who advised me," I answer.

He stabs his finger into my chest. "Yes, I did. She didn't deserve any punishment. He was an evil man, took advantage of innocent immigrants. A bad man," he waves his finger in the air. "But," he lets the word hang in the air.

"It's karma, she told me, we can be together," I sheepishly say.

"Karma, my ass. A cop working a case lands up with the

lady under suspicion. Right," he vigorously shakes his head.

"Who is out there for me?" I feel dejected. Love never seems to come my way. "The *Shabbes* lady; she's a lovely woman, Zipora, but can I become so religious, a Hasid?" I shake my head.

He laughs. "No, but she is changing, going to the fight to see Jimmy. Look at Yana and Jimmy. A couple?" he closes his eyes, shaking his head. "Crazy."

"That's one outcome, why not Olga," I am more optimistic.

"Natasha," he suggests. "She's an educated Jewess, a Russian, you have much in common," he reports.

"She lives in Belarus, I live in New York. Do you think that makes sense?" I reply in frustration.

"She won't always live in Belarus and you don't have to live in New York," he calmly proposes.

"No, no, although she was nice looking. I liked her, but my obsession," I picture her blue eyes.

"You're just nuts," he slaps my leg.

"How could we be together?" I edge close to him,

"Not as a cop, but you could finish law school and," he places his strong hand on my shoulder, "join me and Mikhail. I've talked to my brother. You and I, we are like brothers. Become a partner with us. To hell with this cop shit. The son of one of Russia's most famous dissidents becomes a member of law enforcement. Stop messing around. Then I could see you and Olga, maybe." He stops and waits for my reaction.

I grab his shoulder and shake it; then we embrace. "I don't know," then a gull drops a gooey mess on my shirt. "See a good sign," I point to it.

"It's bird shit," he matter-of-factly responds.

"You're such a cynic."

"You're such a romantic. That's why we get along so well. You are you and I am me. We're a perfect partnership."

I smile "It's meant to be," pointing to the gooey spot "Hashem smiles."

"No, it means you have to wash your shirt," he laughs. "Think about it."

We stare at each other and then his mouth moves towards my ear, and in a whisper; he asks, "Is that woman a terrorist?"

"She could be, and her brother is certainly one and her dead husband. It's complicated but the Chechen made it all possible. I am still the NYPD's golden boy," I grin.

We finish our food, chatting amicably about the weather and Amos.

"Got to go," he informs me after thirty minutes.

"Thanks," I add, and we hug Russian style, Amos looks up approvingly.

I wave as he leaves. A partnership with the brothers? A

new career with US Attorney Cohen? Give it up, my cop career? Either way my NYPD days are over. But then I could be with Olga, my obsession. There's Zipora? I don't know? What next? What will happen to me? Amos barks and the gulls shriek. I stare out at the pounding surf, the waves rising; it's high tide. A nearby bird stares at me with its beady eyes, I search my dog's soft brown eyes for guidance. Hashem has a purpose for me, I just must figure it out.

OTHER OCEAN BREEZE PRESS TITLES

SASHA PERLOV MYSTERIES

Loose Ends by Anastasia Goodman

Death and Diamonds by Anastasia Goodman

WWW.OCEANBREEZEPRESS.NET

29200965R00209